"Begging your pardon, madam," the butler began, "but there is a gentle—that is, there is a man below who—he came to the service entrance—he seemed to be laboring under the impression—but under the circumstances, I felt you would wish to receive him, for you will see at once—"

Julia cast aside Mrs. Radcliffe's *Mysteries of Udolpho.* "If you say I should receive this man, I will do so, for I trust your judgment implicitly! Only give me fifteen minutes, and I shall see him in the drawing room."

Rogers seemed inclined to linger, but as Julia had by this time rung for her maid, he was obliged to make his exit and convey his mistress's message to the mysterious caller.

Fifteen minutes later, she gingerly made her way down the stairs and into the drawing room. The visitor stood with his back turned to her, seemingly making a survey of the well-proportioned room and its elegant furnishings.

"Good morning," she said. "I'm sorry to have—"

He turned at the sound of her voice, and his appearance was enough to make her blink. He was a tall, lean man of perhaps forty-five, whose tanned skin and sun-bleached brown hair testified to a life spent largely out of doors.

Julia had never seen him before in her life, and yet his features were so familiar that she knew him at once. She crossed the room with as much grace as she could manage and approached him with a smile of recognition, her hands held out in welcome.

" 'Gentleman Jack' Pickett, I presume."

THE JOHN PICKETT MYSTERIES:

PICKPOCKET'S APPRENTICE
(prequel novella)

IN MILADY'S CHAMBER

A DEAD BORE

FAMILY PLOT

DINNER MOST DEADLY

WAITING GAME
(Christmas novella)

TOO HOT TO HANDEL

FOR DEADER OR WORSE

MYSTERY LOVES COMPANY

PERIL BY POST

INTO THIN EIRE

BROTHER, CAN YOU SPARE A CRIME?

NOWHERE MAN
(Christmas novella)

DEATH CAN BE HABIT-FORMING

IN THE FAMILY WAY

In the Family Way

Another John Pickett Mystery

Sheri Cobb South

IN THE FAMILY WAY

1

*In Which John Pickett's Family Tree
Sprouts an Unexpected Branch*

He was being followed.

John Pickett couldn't say at exactly what point he had noticed the two tall young men keeping pace about a hundred feet behind him, but by the time he'd turned off Southampton Street into the Strand, he had been certain. In his defense, so many people crowded the bustling market at Covent Garden that one might conduct any number of surveillance missions there without attracting the least notice—as he had cause to know, having done so more than once over the course of a five-year career with Bow Street. He might have forgiven himself for his momentary lapse, had he not been well aware that his failure to take note of his pursuers was not due to the superfluity of shoppers, but the fact that his mind had been occupied elsewhere. In Curzon Street, in fact, where just the night before, he had endured a most unsatisfactory discussion with his wife of nine months.

"We're going to have to decide on a name sooner or later," Julia had reminded him. "Dr. Gillray says the baby might come any day now, and the midwife concurs."

"It might be a girl," he'd pointed out. "We might not need a name for a boy at all."

This much was true. Selecting a girl's name had been easy enough; since Julia's sister, Claudia, had named her own daughter after their mother, he and Julia had agreed that, if the coming Blessed Event should yield an infant girl, she should be called Lydia after his own mother, of whom he retained no memory. He had seen his mother's name, however, written in her own hand in the church registry at St. Giles-in-the-Fields: Ly Lydia Melrose Pickett. He'd smiled a little at the repeat of the first two letters, presumably an unsatisfactory first attempt she'd felt compelled to abandon. This, along with the rounded schoolgirl hand, had suggested she must have been very young at the time of her marriage. Which she must have been, he supposed, to be enticed into marrying anyone of so unsteady a character as his father. Pickett could only wonder that his father had married the poor girl at all; he had certainly never legitimized his connection with Moll, a union that, some six months after his transportation to Botany Bay, had produced a second son—his own ten-year-old half-brother, Kit.

"Then again, it might be a boy, and we'll have to call him something," Julia had insisted, with unassailable logic. "We need not call him John, you know, even if we do choose to name him after you. We could always call him Jack," she'd added coaxingly, laboring under the mistaken assumption that he might welcome this suggestion as a reasonable compromise.

"My father was called Jack. 'Gentleman Jack,' if you must know." He gave a bitter little laugh. "Believe me, two John Picketts are more than enough. It's hardly a name that deserves to be preserved for posterity."

Julia had been inclined to debate the matter, but she had been considerably hindered by the fact that this unsatisfying conversation had not taken place as it should have, in the middle of a warm bed with Julia lying within the circle of his arm. Instead, they had been obliged to call to one another across the width of the bedroom.

For the fact of the matter was that after nine months of marriage, Pickett had been unequivocally expelled from his wife's bed. Granted, this departure from the previous (and mutually satisfactory) arrangement had not been Julia's idea, but the midwife's, who had insisted that it would make matters simpler once the time of her confinement was at hand. The footman, Andrew, had unearthed an ancient camp bed left in the attic by some previous resident, presumably a relic of some long-ago military campaign—most likely against the Romans, if the condition of the mattress was anything to judge by. In any case, this had been set up in the dressing room, and it was here that Pickett was expected to sleep until sometime after the birth. Pickett found the implication behind this change galling in the extreme. He did not flatter himself that Julia currently had the slightest interest in the very activities that had led to her present condition, and it stung to think that he was deemed to have so little self-control that he must be bodily removed from his wife's bed to spare her any importunities on his part.

A few days later, as if to add insult to injury, Dr. Gilroy had prescribed bed rest for Julia until after the birth, calling it a precautionary measure. Pickett had wholeheartedly approved of this, well aware that Julia's fears for the baby's safety were every bit as acute as his own fears for hers. Still, there was something cruelly ironic in the fact that Julia should be confined to one bed while he was banished to another.

And so the question of what to name a boy had remained unresolved the following morning. Hoping to forestall any attempt on Julia's part to reopen a fruitless discussion, he had beaten a hasty retreat immediately after breakfast, offering as his excuse a visit to Fortnum and Mason in search of the pears which she had unaccountably begun to crave.

In fact, he'd gone to the market at Covent Garden instead, where he knew he could find them at a fraction of the price. In any case, the subject of the previous night's debate had been left.

Except that he had not been able to leave it, at least not entirely, and so had quite failed to notice the two tall young men who appeared to be dogging his steps from a discreet distance.

But he noticed them now, so in order to test a theory, he stopped before the window of a shop in Long Acre, pressing his face to the frosted glass to inspect this sampling of the wares offered for sale within. In fact, he scarcely noticed the bottles of wine attractively displayed in the window. Instead, he watched from the corner of his eye as his unwanted escort also paused before a shopfront he had passed a short time earlier. Seeking further confirmation, he stepped away from the window and continued his progress up the street for two or three steps before pausing to remove an entirely imaginary stone supposedly lodged in the sole of his shoe. When he bent down, he could see that his pursuers had halted before the window of yet another shop.

All doubts erased, he decided evasive action was in order. A few more steps took him to the mouth of Ryders Court, a narrow pedestrian passageway that jogged sharply to the west before opening onto Cranburn Street at the northern corner of Leicester Square. Once off the main road, he plunged down the dark passage until he could be certain the shadows covered him, then watched as the two men passed the entry to the passage at a fast trot, apparently fearful of having lost their quarry. Satisfied that his maneuver had been successful, Pickett continued down the passage until it opened onto Cranburn Street, then turned left to continue his journey on a more circuitous yet roughly parallel route.

Or such had been his intention.

Instead, he reached the end of the passage only to find it blocked by two young men who stepped forward, seized him by the arms, and informed him that "You're coming with us, sirrah."

"I—think—not," Pickett said breathlessly, and drove his elbow into the gut of the brute on his left.

Having grown up in the slums of nearby St. Giles, Pickett was no stranger to the necessary art of self-defense, and could give a reasonably good account of himself if ever the need arose. Alas, the fact that he was outnumbered two to one soon yielded its inevitable result. Having overwhelmed their victim, they dragged him, still struggling, toward a carriage approaching them from the eastern end of the street, a vehicle that bore on its side panel a coat of arms Pickett did not recognize. Not that he was given much leisure to study this emblem, for in spite of his attempts to wrest himself free of the viselike grips that held him fast, he was promptly bundled aboard this equipage. His captors entered the coach in his wake and closed the door, albeit not before giving the driver the order to "Go!" The horses were whipped into action, bearing Pickett away from the environs of Covent Garden toward an unknown destiny. He lunged for the door of the vehicle, only to be hauled none too gently back into his seat.

"Who are you?" he demanded with what dignity he could muster. "Where are you taking me?"

"You'll know soon enough," said the stouter of the two, the same fellow who had thwarted his attempt to leap from the vehicle.

"You're not hurt, are you?" asked the second in some concern.

"I'm afraid not," Pickett said with some asperity. "Better luck next time."

"Oh, we wasn't supposed to hurt you," Pickett was assured. "His nibs was very partic'lar about that."

"His nibs?" Pickett echoed sharply, recalling the coat of arms he'd glimpsed on the door panel. "Who?"

"Never you mind," the larger fellow said, giving his confederate a reproachful look. "You'll know soon enough."

"Do you mean his lordship?" He received no answer, but persevered nonetheless. "George Bertram, Lord Fieldhurst?" Julia's cousin by marriage was the only aristocrat he knew (not that his acquaintance amongst the aristocracy was all that extensive) who disliked him enough to arrange such a stunt, although what he might hope to gain by it, Pickett couldn't begin to guess. Then, too, such a course of action seemed out of character for him. "I shouldn't have thought he would have the cheek," Pickett said, expressing this last thought aloud.

"If he opens his mouth again before we reach Park Lane," the stouter of his captors addressed the other, "can I put my fist in it?"

"Not unless you want his lordship to be havin' your guts for garters," was his answer, to Pickett's profound relief.

Still, the man's threat had given him food for thought. *Park Lane*, he'd said. Not George Bertram, then, for the Fieldhurst town house was in Berkeley Square—as he had cause to know, having once paid a call on Julia there, forgetting that she would have surrendered the house and most of its furnishings to her late husband's cousin upon his assumption of the title. He recalled that Lord Dunnington, the husband of Julia's friend Emily, Lady Dunnington, owned a house in Park Lane, but if Lord Dunnington had required his presence, his lordship must surely know that he had only to ask and Pickett would call on him there. Pickett had always thought he and the earl got along surprisingly well, given that there was bound to be little common ground between a belted earl and a former pickpocket turned Bow Street Runner.

Who, then? And why?

Pickett watched out the window as the carriage trundled westward, his brain awhirl. The grassy expanse of Hyde Park on his left, sere and brown beneath the gray December sky, indicated that Park Lane was indeed their destination. Within the park itself, a few hardy souls rode or walked along the road that ran parallel to the street just inside the iron fencing intended to keep out the riffraff, and for a moment Pickett considered jerking the window down and shouting for help. It did not take long for him to dismiss this possibility without much regret. Aside from the fact that the more combative of his traveling companions would know exactly how to deal with such an attempt, "his nibs"'s orders notwithstanding, there was something demeaning about such a course of action. Any man worthy of the name, especially one with more than five years' experience at Bow Street, ought to be able to extricate himself from his present predicament without shrieking for help like a hysterical housemaid.

Perhaps more to the point, however, was the fact that his curiosity was fully roused. If he were to escape now, either by his own efforts or with the assistance of others, he would never know who had ordered his capture, or for what purpose—or if he might expect this unknown to make another attempt. Not until he was actually face-to-face with "his nibs" could he discover what the man wanted, or determine what course of action to take.

Even as he arrived at this conclusion, the vehicle began to slow until it finally halted before a tall narrow house with which Pickett was utterly unfamiliar. The front door of this residence opened, and a man in scarlet and gold livery exited the building, approached the equipage, and let down the vehicle's single step.

"I wouldn't be entertaining any notion of running, if I were you," the larger and more belligerent of his captors cautioned. A moment later the door was opened and the man preceded his fellows from the carriage, the better to clamp a strong hand about Pickett's arm as he followed suit. The more cautious of the two exited last, then took Pickett's free arm as the pair "escorted" him will he or nill he toward the door, putting him forcibly in mind of two jailers taking a prisoner to the dock.

"I'm perfectly capable of walking on my own," he grumbled, disconcerted by the image his thoughts had conjured.

He received no answer. Instead, the two men ushered him inside—an awkward business since the door, imposing as it was with its fanlight transom and long narrow sidelights of cut glass flanking it, was nevertheless far too narrow to accommodate three men walking abreast. Without relaxing their grip on his arms, they steered him down a long corridor carpeted so thickly that Pickett fully expected to sink to his ankles with every step. At the far end of the corridor, his captors decanted him into a room at the rear of the house that he judged to be a study, given the wide desk of gleaming mahogany and the bookshelves along two of its four walls, groaning beneath the weight of dozens of large calfbound volumes his benumbed brain identified at once as ledgers; if there was one thing he had learned during his three miserable weeks of employment as a counting-house clerk, it was how to recognize a ledger when he saw it. Above the desk, an array of knives, swords, sabers, and more exotic blades—a collection that did nothing to reassure him—were mounted on the wall, the smaller weapons artistically arranged on burgundy-colored velvet behind a protective glass barrier.

More impressive than the room or its furnishings, however, was its occupant. For seated behind the desk was a large man of about seventy, his girth contained within a fashionable yet far from dandified coat of olive green superfine, one sleeve of which was bound about with a black band indicative of mourning. His thick gray hair was combed straight back from his broad forehead, and his chins (for there must surely have been more than one of them, given the man's avoirdupois) disappeared into the stiff folds of his snowy cravat. Pickett, finding himself the object of a keen and disapproving scrutiny, had the fanciful and yet unamusing notion that he was being measured up by an aristocratic toad.

Weighed in the balance, he thought, *and found wanting.*

Even as his brain formed the thought, the man spoke, seemingly in confirmation.

"Well?" he demanded impatiently. "Stand up straight, boy, and let's have a look at you."

In retrospect, Pickett wished he'd thought to slouch, just to show this autocratic amphibian just how little he cared for the man's approval. But he instinctively stood taller, making the most of his six feet three inches and jutting out his chin in a manner that dared his inquisitor to disparage them.

To his surprise, the man gave a grunt of reluctant—no, not approval, exactly, but acknowledgement that there was less to criticize than he might have expected. Still, Pickett couldn't imagine why he was being subjected to such an appraisal, much less why the fellow should have any expectations regarding him at all.

He was not left wondering for long.

"I won't lie; you're not what I'd hoped for," was the unflattering conclusion drawn from this examination. "Still, I suppose it could be a good deal worse, and as they say, beggars can't be choosers."

"Your lordship," Pickett began impatiently, using the title by which his captors had referred to their employer. He could not bring himself to call the man "sir," let alone "my lord"; the latter, especially, conveyed a hint of subservience which could not be further from his sentiments at the moment. "Who are you, and why have you brought me"—he glanced toward his escort, the pair of them hovering somewhat sheepishly near the door—"rather, why have you had me brought here?"

The stern gaze swiveled toward his captors. "You've told him nothing, then?"

"I thought you—those were your orders, my lord." It was the more timorous of the two who spoke, albeit with obvious reluctance, while his counterpart was apparently at a loss for words in spite of his earlier braggadocio.

"Very well," their employer conceded grudgingly, almost as if he'd hoped for some reason to deliver a scathing condemnation. Pickett could only suppose that any such criticisms would now be heaped upon his own head. "You may leave us now, both of you."

The pair obeyed as if they could not quit the premises quickly enough, and Pickett was left alone with his host.

" 'Who are you?' " the latter echoed mockingly. "Impertinent whelp, aren't you? I'll have you know I'm the Marquess of Melrose!"

Clearly, he expected this pronouncement to mean something. In this, at least, the marquess was doomed to disappointment, for Pickett was at a loss; he had never heard the name before in his life. Or had he? No, Pickett thought with growing conviction, he'd never *heard* the name, but he had *seen* it once, seen it written in a church registry, the letters carefully inscribed in a rounded schoolgirl hand...

"Good God," he breathed as realization dawned.

" 'Good God'?" returned his lordship with a contemptuous sneer. "Is that all you can think to say to your grandfather?"

* * *

Meanwhile, in Curzon Street, Julia sat up in bed, propped against the pillows with a book in her hands and a second pillow, the one upon which her husband had formerly rested his head, positioned beneath her swollen feet. Whatever the trials of the beautiful and virtuous Emily St. Aubert, Julia thought, turning the page with a sigh, at the moment they must surely compare favorably to those endured by a lady restricted to her bed in hourly expectation of her confinement. She had hardly begun to lose herself in Mrs. Radcliffe's thrilling tale when Rogers peered into the room with an air of confused distraction entirely out of character for a butler who was usually equal to any situation.

"Begging your pardon, madam," he began, "but there is a gentle—that is, there is a man below who—he came to the service entrance—he seemed to be laboring under the impression—but under the circumstances, I felt you would wish to receive him, for you will see at once—"

"Say no more!" cried Julia, casting aside Mrs. Radcliffe's *Mysteries of Udolpho*. "If you say I should receive this man, I will do so, for I trust your judgment implicitly! Only give me ten minutes—no, best make that fifteen—and I shall see him in the drawing room."

Rogers seemed inclined to linger, but as Julia had by this time rung for her maid and thrown back the counterpane, he was obliged to make his exit and convey his mistress's message to the mysterious caller.

Fifteen minutes later, she gingerly made her way down the stairs and into the drawing room. The visitor stood with his back turned to her, seemingly making a survey of the well-proportioned room and its elegant furnishings.

"Good morning," she said. "I'm sorry to have—"

He turned at the sound of her voice, and his appearance was enough to make her blink. He was a tall, lean man of perhaps forty-five, whose tanned skin and sun-bleached brown hair testified to a life spent largely out of doors.

Julia had never seen him before in her life, and yet his features were so familiar that she knew him at once. She crossed the room with as much grace as she could manage and approached him with a smile of recognition, her hands held out in welcome.

" 'Gentleman Jack' Pickett, I presume."

2

In Which John Pickett's Chickens Quite Literally Come Home to Roost

M y—my grandfather," Pickett echoed dumbly, painfully aware of the fact that he was hardly appearing to advantage, and yet unable to form any more intelligent response. He remembered his mother's signature in the church registry at St. Giles's. *Ly Lydia Melrose*, she'd written, and he'd imagined her as a very nervous young bride, wanting to make a good job of this, her first act as a married woman, but so unsatisfied with her first attempt that she'd been compelled to start over after only two letters. But it had been no mistake of penmanship, and the fact that her given name began with those same two letters was nothing more than a coincidence. No, not an error, but an abbreviation for a courtesy title: Lady Lydia Melrose, daughter of a marquess.

While Pickett's wits had gone wandering, the older man gave a jerk of his head that Pickett supposed indicated confirmation of the relationship. "Useless to deny the obvious," he said grudgingly. "You've the look of your mother about you."

Pickett stiffened. "I'm said to look like my father."

And he had taken no pleasure in the resemblance, for more often than not, his father's dubious reputation was assumed to come with it. Still, if this repellent man imagined he would rejoice in so exalted a connection, he would very soon learn his mistake.

"Oh, I'll not be such a fool as to deny that, although there's something about your eyes that's Lydia to the life. Something in that stubborn chin, too. Aye, and speaking of eyes, you'd like nothing better than to scratch mine out, wouldn't you? I'll wager you'll be singing a different tune before you're much older."

"I very much doubt that—" Pickett put in, but the older man continued as if he had not spoken.

"This is the matter in a nutshell: my son, the Earl of Huxton, died last month while out with the Quorn. Rushed his fences and came a cropper."

Pickett understood very little of this speech beyond the fact that Lord Melrose's son—his own uncle, Pickett supposed—was dead.

"I'm sorry to hear it," he said, feeling some response was expected of him.

"Why the devil should you be?" demanded the marquess. "If you ever set eyes on the fellow, it's news to me."

"No," Pickett conceded. "But it's a common expression of sympathy—"

"I haven't the slightest need for your sympathy! The fact of the matter is, he was my only surviving offspring, and as he had no issue, I'm left with two choices: I can do nothing, and allow a six-hundred-year-old title to fall into abeyance, or I can make the best of the one descendant left to me."

If Pickett had any doubts about what constituted "making the best of" him, he was not left to wonder for long.

"Granted, the original patent makes no provisions for descent through a female line," the marquess continued, leaning back in his chair with something akin to smug satisfaction, "but I've petitioned the Crown for a special dispensation that would allow it to pass through my only other child."

"Your only—your other—"

Lord Melrose inclined his head in acknowledgment. "My daughter, Lydia. Your mother."

Pickett had the sudden sensation that the thickly carpeted floor was giving way beneath his feet. "But that—that would mean—"

Lord Melrose gave Pickett a nod that, while not quite approval, seemed to indicate satisfaction that his unworthy descendant was not quite so stupid as he had thus far given his noble grandsire reason to suppose. "Just so. Mind you, I've no idea whether or not the king will agree to the request, or if he'll even retain sufficient possession of his senses to make a decision one way or the other. I'd prefer not to be put in the position of applying to the Prince of Wales, should a regency be necessary, for I hold no truck with his Whiggish leanings, nor with his spendthrift ways."

With something akin to relief, Pickett recalled his own meeting with the Prince of Wales some five months earlier, at which time he had respectfully declined an invitation to become the prince's personal bodyguard. He seriously doubted that His Royal Highness, who had taken offense upon having had this generous offer spurned, would be inclined to bestow a marquessate on the spurner instead. He thought it wisest not to mention this unintentional breach of civility to his grandfather. In any case, he was given no opportunity to do so, for the mention of the prince's legendary spending habits had apparently reminded his lordship of another matter that must be addressed.

"I'll make you an allowance, of course, although you'll answer to me as to how you spend it, at least until I know I can trust you not to be taken for a flat. I know young men must have their independence, and so I'll not require you to reside beneath my roof, but make no doubt that my eye will be upon you, and I'll not tolerate being made a laughingstock by an upstart as near to being a bastard as makes no odds."

Pickett, having only recently discovered that his parents had been legally wed, would have taken exception to this slur upon his mother's honor (and by her own father, at that), had not his lordship bared his teeth at him in a smile that was no doubt intended to be reassuring, but that put Pickett forcibly in mind of a stuffed and mounted tiger he'd once seen on display at Bartholomew Fair.

"You are no doubt wondering what I may be expecting of you in return," his lordship continued smoothly, in a reassuring tone that nevertheless made Pickett's hackles rise even more than his confrontational air had done. "Your first responsibility, of course, will be to provide an heir to succeed you in his turn—best make it two, for accidents do happen, you know. I'll drop a word into a few ears at White's, let 'em know that I'm looking about for a suitable wife for my grandson. I'm thinking a well-born female who's been out for two or three Seasons might be your best bet—one old enough to fear being left on the shelf, or else one holding out for a title and eager enough for a marchioness's strawberry leaves that she won't be too fastidious as to the bridegroom who comes with them. I'll do you the justice to own that you're a good-looking lad—as you say, much like your father; in fact, one might say that's the root of the whole sorry business—which should make you a bit easier for any young woman to swallow."

"I'm obliged to you," Pickett said, although nothing his tone conveyed any noticeable degree of gratitude, "but I have no interest in your money or your title. As for the wife, I'm afraid you're a bit late to the fair. I've already chosen one for myself."

Lord Melrose's smile, such as it was, froze on his face, and his countenance assumed a greenish hue that rendered him even more toadlike. Clearly, his grandson's being already married was a complication he had not foreseen. "Any children?" he asked sharply.

"No," conceded Pickett, "but—"

"Thank God for that!" pronounced his lordship. "I know your kind rarely bothers to solemnize such unions, so there's likely no danger of your already having sired a legitimate heir

22

off some St. Giles doxy. Still, the fact that there are no children will undoubtedly simplify matters. As for the wench herself, she need not concern you. I'll buy her off."

Pickett's eyebrows rose. "And if I've no mind to give her up?"

"You won't find me unreasonable in these matters," his grandfather assured him. "I've no objection to your keeping her as a mistress, if you insist. But mind you take care of the heir first, to avoid any possibility of a rival claim."

Pickett could think of so many objections to this plan for his future that he hardly knew where to start. On second thought, he decided, addressing the insult to his wife's honor must be his first priority. "I can't speak to the tendencies of 'my kind'—whatever that may mean—but I can assure you that my wife and I are legally wed. In fact, we've been married twice over: once in an irregular marriage in Scotland, and again here in London, by special license. Oh, and by the bye, I doubt the former Lady Fieldhurst would appreciate your describing her as a 'St. Giles doxy,' married or not."

"Lady Fieldhurst? The one accused of murdering her husband a couple of years ago?" Without waiting for confirmation, the marquess gave a grunt that seemed to indicate grudging approval. "You've done better for yourself than I'd hoped, although I don't mind saying I'd liefer not have such a scandal attached to my name. Has she any money, or do you support her on your wages? I can't imagine you earning enough to support a viscountess in style. Well, boy, which is it: your money or hers?"

"First of all," Pickett said stiffly, "my name is not 'Boy.'

Second, my finances are no concern of yours."

Lord Melrose slapped the surface of his desk in triumph. "Ha! Hit a sore spot, have I?"

In fact, he had hit a very sore spot indeed, but Pickett refused to give his lordship the satisfaction of hearing him admit it. Instead, he said, "If you followed the trial in the newspapers at all, you must have seen my name."

"Aye, I saw it, and wondered if it was Lydia's brat giving evidence. Thought it unlikely, given your father's habits, but—"

"Do you mean to tell me," Pickett interrupted, "that you've known of my existence for almost *two years*, and never said a word?"

"Two years?" scoffed his lordship. "I've known of your existence for a hell of a lot longer than that!"

"And yet you never lifted a finger to contact me—not until your only surviving child died without issue, and suddenly you needed me." Except that even then, his lordship hadn't lifted a finger; he'd had his henchmen do it for him.

"Why the devil should I?" asked Lord Melrose, bristling. "Lydia made her choice when she eloped with the thatch-gallows who sired you. She'd made her bed, so she could damned well lie in it. Whatever became of her spawn was no concern of mine."

"On that, at least, we can agree," Pickett put in. "I'm obliged to you, sir, but I have no need of your money or your title or anything else you can offer. I'm perfectly satisfied with my life just the way it is, with my wife and the child we expect to have before the year is ended. So you may take your petition to the Crown and—"

"Oho, so there is to be a child, is there?" His lordship's eyes gleamed with a rather malicious amusement. "You'll be singing a different tune once there's a boy to educate or a girl to dower. You'll come begging for my assistance—and you'll be well-served if I've changed my mind in the interim and cut you off with a shilling."

"I'll take my chances," Pickett said. "I'll be leaving now. I won't say I'm pleased to make your acquaintance, your lordship, for I was doing jolly well without it."

He turned and left the room, albeit not before hearing his lordship's parting shot.

"Fine words, boy! You'll come crawling back, just wait and see if you don't!"

Pickett reached the pavement outside, and was furious to discover that he was shaking, although he could not have said whether his anger was directed at Lord Bloody Melrose—his grandfather, damn his eyes—or himself. For it was disturbing to realize that he was more tempted by his lordship's proposal than he cared to admit; he would be lying if he said he never lay awake long into the night after Julia had fallen asleep, worrying about where the money would come from to establish his child in a manner worthy of its mother.

The thought of Julia raised another possibility that he found entirely too appealing for his peace of mind. If Lord Melrose's petition should be successful, then he himself—a former pickpocket and the son of a convicted felon—would someday be Marquess of Melrose—meaning that Julia, as his wife, would be a marchioness—a title even more exalted than the one she'd had as Lady Fieldhurst, the wife of a mere viscount.

A *mere* viscount? He pulled himself up short at the thought. What a snob he had become! He hadn't inherited his grandfather's honors yet; in fact, he'd never even known of the man's existence an hour ago. Even if Lord Melrose's petition was successful, he had every intention of refusing the honors it conferred upon him. And yet here he was, ready to look down his nose at the same man whose memory was a constant irritant to him, an incessant reminder of his dependence on the jointure left to Julia by her first husband.

The distance between Park Lane and Curzon Street was not far, but the walk home gave him sufficient time to work off his spleen, and when he opened the front door and heard a merry peal of feminine laughter, his heart lifted. Julia, bless her, had never expressed a desire that he should be anything more than what he was. Ironically, it was that very acceptance that made him want to be worthy of her. In any case, Julia would know just what to say to restore his equilibrium.

Alas, this state of pleasant anticipation was destined to be short-lived. Following the sound of her laughter (wasn't she supposed to be in bed?), he crossed the foyer to the drawing room and froze in the doorway, regarding in stunned disbelief the man seated next to Julia on the straw-colored satin sofa. In an instant, the respectable life for which he'd labored for more than a decade came crashing down.

Some small noise must have betrayed his presence, for the man looked up at him and offered a cheery greeting.

"Hallo, son!"

Pickett, standing amidst the wreckage of his hard-won respectability, put a hand to his forehead as if shielding his eyes from a sight too painful to behold.

"Da," he said.

3

In Which Father and Son
Renew Their Acquaintance, with Mixed Results

Is that any way to greet your old man after ten long years?"
chided Pickett, Sr., rising from the sofa to meet him.
Suddenly it was all too much. First Lord Melrose—his
grandfather, impossible as it seemed—and now this: his
father, returned from Botany Bay just in time to throw his life
into chaos.

"If that isn't just like you," Pickett fumed. "Yes, ten long
years! Ten years since you went off and left me with Moll,
who chucked me out of the house before your ship had
reached Gravesend! Ten years since I was put out on the
streets to fend for myself. And now you come back and think
to pick up right where you left off? Well, think again!"

Gentleman Jack made no reply, but then, he didn't have
to; the pointed look he cast about the room, encompassing the
Axminster carpet, the Adam fireplace, and the elegant

Hepplewhite furnishings, said it all.

"Yes, I know," Pickett said with a sigh. "First of all, you have to understand that the house isn't really mine. Oh, it is according to the law, but only because it came to me when I married. It really belongs to Julia." Belatedly recalling that some form of introduction was in order, he added, "Julia, in case you haven't already guessed, this is my father. Da, make your bow to my wife, Julia."

"Aye, it's a hard fate that shackles a man to such a woman," Jack said sympathetically, shaking his head in mock sorrow even as he winked broadly at his daughter-in-law.

"It's a hard fate that leaves a fourteen-year-old boy sleeping under bridges and stealing food to keep from starving to death," retorted Pickett, unmoved. "Julia, where is Kit? Have you—? Does he—?"

"Kit is in the garden. He has taken it into his head to tame a squirrel that has taken up residence there," she added as an aside to her father-in-law before turning back to her glowering husband. "No, I thought you would want to perform that introduction yourself."

In fact, there were fewer things Pickett wanted less. Still, his father was Kit's father too, and he could think of no valid reason for keeping the two apart, much as he might like to do so. "Yes, I suppose—I'll ring for Rogers to—"

"Never mind ringing; I'll go and fetch him myself, shall I?" She gave him a reassuring smile before quitting the room.

Left alone together for the first time in more than a decade, father and son eyed each other warily before Gentleman Jack broke the silence.

"So you stole food to survive, did you? I must have taught you well, then, for it's clear you've not been going hungry. Pity you weren't arrested, too; you could've joined your old man in Botany Bay."

"I was. Arrested in Covent Garden for stealing an apple, by a Bow Street Runner who thought to teach me the error of my ways by blacking my eye and breaking my nose."

"Oh?" Jack's carefree air vanished. "Only point me in his direction, and he'll rue the day he messed with any son of Gentleman Jack Pickett!"

"Stubble it, Da," said Pickett, unimpressed. "He's dead. Shot by the Bow Street magistrate, Patrick Colquhoun. I don't know if you remember him, but—"

"Oh, don't I just?" Gentleman Jack broke in bitterly. "I remember him, all right. I thought of him every day, the bastard, on that hellish trip around Cape Horn."

"That's enough." Pickett never raised his voice, but if his father had harbored any doubts that the scrawny fourteen-year-old boy he'd left behind was now a man grown, they would have been instantly dispelled by tone in which this simple comment was delivered. "You'll not say one word against Mr. Colquhoun, not in this house. I owe him too much."

"The man who sent your da halfway 'round the world? Aye, you owe him, all right. I owe him, too."

"He might have ordered you hanged, you know," Pickett reminded him. "As for my own arrest, he—I guess you could say he took an interest in me, although I've never understood exactly why. He didn't make me stand trial—never handed down any form of punishment at all, in fact. He took me to a pub and bought me something to eat, and then arranged for me to be apprenticed to a coal merchant. Five years later, he brought me to Bow Street."

The elder Pickett scowled. "He did, did he? What'd he have you up for this time?"

"Nothing!" said Pickett, bristling. "I don't mean he arrested me! He only thought I—well, he thought I had brains, and that I was capable of something more than hauling coal. He bought out the last two years of my apprenticeship from his own pocket, and gave me a place on the Foot Patrol. Five years later, I became a principal officer. That's how I met Julia; her first husband had been stabbed to death, and—"

Gentleman Jack, listening to this speech in growing indignation, could no longer keep silent. "That bloody beak turned my son into a damned *prig-napper?*"

"That 'bloody beak' has been ten times the father to me than ever *you* were, even before you were transported!"

Fortunately for the harmony of the household, Julia returned to the drawing room at that moment with Kit at her heels, his cheeks flushed and his clothes rather the worse for his most recent encounter with the recalcitrant squirrel.

"John?" he said breathlessly. "Julia says you want to—" He broke off abruptly, staring wide-eyed at the visitor.

Even the eldest Pickett appeared to be somewhat taken aback, eyeing the boy in surprise before glancing uncertainly at his elder son. "Yours?"

"No," Pickett said. "Yours. It seems you left Moll with a pudding in the oven. This is Kit—short for Christopher. Kit, this is your—our—father, back from Botany Bay."

"H-how do you do, sir?" asked Kit, sketching a rudimentary bow.

"Well, and aren't you the little gentleman!" exclaimed his father, chucking the boy under the chin. "How d'you do—Kit, is it?"

Apparently bereft of speech, Kit merely nodded emphatically.

"Well now, let's see," said Gentleman Jack, reaching a hand into the inside pocket of his coat. "A gentleman needs a good watch, doesn't he? D'you think maybe this one'll do?" He drew out a gold watch by its chain, and dropped it into the hands Kit held out eagerly.

"When Kit is old enough to need a watch, I'll buy him one." Pickett snatched the timepiece out of the boy's hands and gave it back to his father, noting the engraved initials on its case that read *H. B.* "I wouldn't want him to be taken up for thievery. One Pickett might as well have a clean record," he added dryly.

"Hey!" cried Kit. "He gave it to *me!*"

"*Thievery?*" echoed the elder Pickett in tones of outraged dignity. "No such thing! Won it fair and square, I did, in a friendly little game of penny-up-the-wall on the voyage home."

Julia laid a hand on her husband's arm, forestalling, at least for the moment, what was bidding fair to becoming a quarrel of no small magnitude, all the more so for having been delayed for more than a decade. "I'll just ring for tea, shall I?"

"Don't bother," Pickett said, glowering at his father. "Da

isn't staying."

"Why not?" wailed Kit.

"Well, if that don't beat the Dutch!" exclaimed Jack, adding, "But then, it's no more than I would expect from a turncoat who'd go to work for the very man who ordered his da sent to Botany Bay…"

The rest of this speech was lost, as it was delivered in a low and no doubt profane grumble that Pickett thought a good thing neither Julia nor Kit was able to discern.

But however unintelligible the words, Julia had at least taken in enough to form a very fair assumption of their meaning, for she slipped her hand through Pickett's arm, saying, "And I, for one, am very glad he did, for it was John who saved me from the gallows when it appeared I would hang for my first husband's murder."

"And then he saved me," Kit piped up, determined not to be left out. "He broke into the Bank of England for Roger and Jud, so I wouldn't have to do it."

This claim had the happy effect of seizing Jack's full attention. "The Bank of England?" he breathed reverently, all his anger evaporated. "I take it all back, every word! What did you get away with?"

"One ten-year-old boy," Pickett said, ruffling his brother's curls affectionately even as he recognized with an unexpected pang of jealousy that their father had replaced him as Kit's idol.

"That's all?" demanded his father, rendered tactless through incredulity.

"That was all I wanted," Pickett said impatiently. "I'm

respectable now, Da. I want to stay that way."

"You call it respectable, casting off your poor old father and taking up with the man who sent him away? John, I'm ashamed of you!"

"But not so ashamed that you'll give back all the money I've sent you over the last ten years, I'll wager," Pickett predicted with grim certainty.

"Well, and I couldn't do that in any case, could I?" observed the "poor old father," unabashed. "Seeing as how I've spent it."

"Now, what does that not surprise me?" Pickett asked of no one in particular. "What did you spend it on? Those togs you're wearing, I suppose. What else? I didn't know they made Blue Ruin in the Antipodes. Or did you take up with another prime article like Moll?"

"In fact, Mister High-and-Mighty—" retorted his father, "I spent it on land. Aye, your old da's a man of property now. What do you think of that?"

Pickett, unimpressed, chose to ignore this claim. "I suppose we'll have to put you up for the night, but you're *not* living here! It's bad enough that Julia's jointure has to support me, and Kit, and soon the baby. I won't let you sponge off her, too. And if you're thinking to move back in with Moll, I'll tell you to your face that Kit stays with me."

"John," Julia began, her hand tightening on his sleeve, "may I have a word with you? Kit, why don't you tell your father about the school you'll be attending next year? We'll be back directly, and then I shall ring for tea."

Kit launched eagerly into a spate of words in which

cricket, riding, and marksmanship all strove for prominence, and Julia practically dragged Pickett into the dining room.

Once she could be certain of relative privacy, she turned on him. "John, how can you speak to your father so?"

"Very easily," he replied, then added, "And I thought you were supposed to be in bed."

"Well, yes, but I could hardly receive your father in my bedchamber!"

"Believe me, he would prefer it that way," Pickett said dryly.

She gave him a reproachful look, but refused to take the bait. "I know his treatment of you left a great deal to be desired, but do him the justice to own that his life over the last decade will not have been an easy one, either. You've changed since then; why should not he? Although," she confessed in a lighter tone, "I hope he won't change too much. I rather like him."

"Everyone does," Pickett said in a flat voice. "Everyone who doesn't have to live with him, anyway. I had fourteen years of him, and that was more than enough. He can go back to the Antipodes, or to St. Giles, or to perdition, for all I care, but he's not staying here."

"In case you have forgotten"—Julia's voice was gentle, although a hint of steel lay beneath the soft words—"you are not the only one of his sons who lives in this house."

"Oh, I don't doubt Kit thinks he hung the moon," Pickett readily conceded the point, albeit it not without bitterness. "He never knew him the way I did."

"Exactly." She took a deep breath. "If you were the only

one of Jack's sons who lived here, I would honor your wishes, whatever my own views on the subject. But you're not. This is Kit's home too, and he deserves the chance to know his father."

"Oh, of course!" exclaimed Pickett, flinging up his hands in surrender. "In fact, why don't we invite Lord Melrose, and make it a family party?"

"Lord Melrose?" echoed Julia, utterly bewildered by the introduction into the conversation of an elderly aristocrat with whom she was barely acquainted. "What does he have to do with anything?" Receiving no response, she changed tactics. "When you left here earlier, you were going to Fortnum and Mason to buy pears. John, did something happen there to upset you? What was it?"

The pears. So much had happened since he'd left the house this morning that he'd forgot all about them. He'd gone to the market at Covent Garden instead of the more expensive Piccadilly establishment of Fortnum and Mason, and he seemed to have a vague recollection of something rolling beneath his feet as he struggled against his captors.

"I—I think I must have dropped them," he confessed, deflated. "I'm sorry."

She waited in silence for some explanation beyond bruised fruit, but none was forthcoming.

"I'll—I'll tell you all about it later," he said evasively. "In fact, I'd hoped—but then *he* was here, and—but that's neither here nor there." Looking back, he wondered how much of his ill temper was not due to his father's unexpected return at all—at least, not entirely—but rather to the fact that his presence in the house must of necessity postpone the tête-à-tête with Julia which he desperately needed—even if he could only call to her from the accursed camp bed in the dressing room.

"Later, then." Steadying herself with her hands on his shoulders, she stood on tiptoe and gave him a quick kiss. "But in the meantime"—her hands slid down his chest until her right hand rested over his heart—"it seems to me that perhaps you and your father are long overdue for a conversation of your own. Now that he sees you're no longer a boy, he may be willing to tell you things he felt he could not, when you were younger. We shall have tea, and then I shall take Kit upstairs so the two of you may speak privately."

"Oh, Julia." Breathing her name with a sigh, he drew her close and put his arms around her, burying his face in a nest of golden curls. "I love you. You know that, don't you?"

"I had my suspicions." She lingered in his embrace for a long moment before extricating herself with great tenderness and not a little reluctance. "I suppose we'd best return to your father and Kit."

"Before Da corrupts him," Pickett agreed, but his voice held none of the bitterness with which he'd spoken of his father before.

True to her word, Julia requested Rogers to bring tea and cakes, and once these had been consumed, she spoke to Kit.

"Why don't we go upstairs and leave your father and John alone to talk about grown-up things? I'll give you another drawing lesson if you like, and you can choose one of your drawings to give your father as a present."

Whatever else might be said of him, no one had ever accused Gentleman Jack Pickett of being stupid. He was quick to take his cue, and when Kit seemed disinclined to forsake his newly-discovered parent in favor of the schoolroom, Jack expressed his approval of this project with all the enthusiasm Julia could have wished. In the end, Kit followed his sister-in-law upstairs with obedience, if not eagerness.

Some twenty minutes later, as Kit applied the finishing touches to a pencil sketch of the squirrel whose taming was his particular project, he asked in an offhand manner, "D'you think John might give Da's watch back to me if you asked him?"

However carelessly the words were spoken, Julia had the distinct impression that the answer mattered very, very much. But Kit's confidences, much like his brother's, could not be rushed—which made it all the more remarkable that the elder of the two Pickett sons was impatient to pour his troubles into her sympathetic ear.

But that was a conversation for later, and in the meantime, Kit awaited her answer with bated breath.

"He might," she said, being careful to match the boy's tone of feigned indifference.

Abandoning his attempt at apathy, Kit looked up from his drawing with flushed cheeks and shining eyes. "Would you, then? Ask him, I mean," he added hastily, clearly wishing to avoid any possible misunderstanding on her part.

"I will," she assured him with a smile. "But if I know anything about your brother at all, I won't have to."

4

In Which a Truce Is Declared

Julia had not exaggerated when she'd said father and son were long overdue for a conversation. For Pickett, however, finding some way to put this suggestion into practice proved to be more than a little awkward. Pickett dispatched Rogers to fetch a bottle of something a bit stronger than the tea they had just finished, then sank down onto the sofa facing his father and tried to think of something reasonably amicable to say.

The butler returned a few minutes later with a particularly fine brandy, and Pickett noted that, although Da must surely have betrayed himself with every word he uttered, Rogers had made no attempt to fob him off with the cheap stuff, but supplied them with the best the cellar had to offer. Pickett knew not quite what to make of this gesture, and could only suppose it was further evidence of his father's ability to charm his way through any situation; he would have been stunned (and very likely embarrassed) to know that it was in fact a token of the high esteem in which he himself was held below stairs, and the determination of the butler to see that the young master made a good impression on a caller who could only be his father.

It was perhaps for the best, then, that Rogers said nothing beyond "Will there be anything else, sir?" before decanting the brandy into two pot-bellied glasses, placing the bottle on a small table at Pickett's elbow, and, having received an answer in the negative, retiring to his pantry.

Left alone with his wayward sire, Pickett asked, with an attempt at civility if not warmth, "So, did your ship reach London only today?"

"We docked yesterday, but it was this morning before anyone was allowed to disembark. I sailed on a merchant vessel, and apparently there's a lot of paperwork involving the ship's cargo."

Pickett nodded in understanding, having learned more than he'd ever wanted to know about international commerce during his mercifully brief career as clerk to a firm of importers. "What was she hauling?" he asked, more for something to say than any real interest.

"Timber, mostly, and flax. And half a dozen passengers."

The two men lapsed once more into uncomfortable silence, and after a long, awkward moment, Pickett refilled both glasses in spite of the fact that they were still almost full; in fact, he had ordered the drink mostly to have something to do with his hands, as neither he nor, presumably, his father could possibly be in need of further sustenance after having put away substantial quantities of tea and cakes.

Finally, he took a deep breath and grasped the bull by the horns. "Today I discovered I have a grandfather."

"Oh?" It was a curious thing, but although his father's voice held a trace of wariness, it contained nothing at all of surprise. "How did you find that out?"

Pickett gave a careless shrug, quite as if it didn't matter. "He had me abducted off the street near Covent Garden and brought to his house in Park Lane."

If Pickett had hoped to break through the awkward silence, he had all the satisfaction of knowing he'd succeeded with a vengeance.

"You don't say!" exclaimed Gentleman Jack, with a convulsive start that sent the brandy sloshing in his glass. "The old buzzard's still alive, then? Well, well! They say the devil looks after his own."

Pickett leaned forward intently, all traces of indifference banished. "Then it's true, what he was saying? Lord Melrose really is my grandfather?"

Jack nodded. "The father of your mother, God rest her soul."

"You married the daughter of a marquess." It was a statement, not a question, but it was intended as one nevertheless, and Pickett Senior understood it as such.

"You married a viscountess," Jack pointed out defensively.

"Yes, and don't think I didn't try to make her see reason, for I did! But you—! I can see how the wife of a marquess might have taken you as a lover, if you'd happened to cross her path"—in fact, that was precisely the arrangement Julia had proposed on that rainy day in Scotland, neither one of them dreaming they'd already contracted a legal marriage according to Scottish law, but Pickett wasn't about to make his father a gift of this information—"but the daughter of a marquess willingly accepting you as a husband? I'm sorry, Da, but no. Even your legendary skill with women would fail at that endeavor. So, how did it happen? What hold did you have over the poor girl?"

"Son, you wound me to the quick!" In demonstration of this claim, Jack pressed a hand to his heart in a gesture that would have brought down the house at Covent Garden Theatre or the Haymarket. "I was one of her father's servants. First footman, to be exact."

"Oh?" Pickett's tone was skeptical, although he recalled seeing his parents' marriage lines, and his father's name recorded as *John Pickett, servant.* "I don't see how that exonerates you. In fact, I should have thought it would put you in a better position for gaining some hold over the daughter of the house: passing letters between her and some undesirable suitor, providing cover for clandestine meetings—"

"The only 'clandestine meetings' Lydia kept were with me! That was her name, you know. Lady Lydia Melrose. She was betrothed to Sir Godfrey Graham—her father's doing, you understand, not hers."

"Lord Melrose seems to have a predilection for arranging other people's marriages," Pickett observed cryptically.

"Lord Melrose has a predilection, as you call it, for running other people's lives." He grinned mischievously at his son with the same smile Pickett occasionally glimpsed in the mirror. The sight was more than a little unnerving. "Now that I'm back in London, maybe I ought to pay a call on my dear father-in-law."

"Now that you're a man of property," Pickett put in dryly.

"Go ahead and laugh, son. Mark my words, you'll soon be laughing out of the other side of your mouth."

It was the second time in less than three hours that one of his progenitors had predicted that he would someday approach them with hat in hand, and Pickett liked hearing it from his father no better than he had from his grandfather.

"Never mind that," he said impatiently. "Go on; you were a footman in Lord Melrose's household, carrying on a clandestine liaison with his daughter."

"It wasn't at all like you make it sound! Lydia was being pressured to accept Sir Godfrey's suit, and there was no one to take her part. Well, I couldn't take her part, either—I'll wager you've seen enough of his lordship to reckon how much a servant's opinion would weigh with him—but she needed a shoulder to cry on, and I had one. Two, in fact."

"That was convenient," Pickett remarked.

"Make no mistake; I knew my place, and I knew it wasn't with Lady Lydia Melrose." The words stirred a chord of memory, and Pickett realized he had once said the very same thing about himself and his growing love for the recently widowed Julia, Lady Fieldhurst. Since he had been speaking to his magistrate, Patrick Colquhoun, at the time, however, he thought it best to keep this recollection to himself.

"And then one night," his father continued, "there was to be a grand ball announcing her betrothal. I'd been sent on some errand—I don't remember now what it was—but anyway, I stumbled across her in the conservatory, hiding behind a potted palm and crying as if her poor heart would break."

"I think I see where this is going," remarked Pickett with a little smile, leaning forward to catch every word, nevertheless.

"Aye, well you might! We ran off together that very night, me and Lydia, and wasn't Lord Melrose beside himself when he found out! I don't know which was worse in his eyes: the insult she'd dealt Sir Godfrey, or the fact that she'd defied his order that she marry Sir Godfrey, and had run off with me instead. No, I take that back. I *do* know what was worse, at least in his eyes. Lydia could've wed the Prince of Wales in Westminster Abbey and he wouldn't have liked it any better, not unless he'd arranged the match himself. Anyway, that's how it happened, and if you've any idea that you were born on the wrong side of the blanket, you can put that thought right out of your head. We were married as soon as the bans were posted—that's three weeks, mind you, and me half expecting his lordship to show up in church and object to the marriage— and don't be thinking I laid a hand on her before the knot was tied, neither!"

"I always assumed I was illegitimate," Pickett confessed. "At least until quite recently, when I found your marriage recorded in the register of St. Giles-in-the-Fields."

"Now that you mention it, I might just go and have

another look at it myself," his father said, with a reminiscent gleam in his eye. "They were happy times, in spite of everything. Maybe the happiest days of my life."

"What happened to her?" Pickett asked softly, not wanting to interrupt his father's expansive mood.

"She died when you were four years old. You got sick— typhus was going around—and she nursed you all day and night. I couldn't be much help to her, I'm afraid. I'd managed to get a position with the Duke of Weybridge in spite of not having any references, Lydia's da having given me the sack at the same time he cut her off. There was no love lost between the duke and Lord Melrose, and I think it amused him to have his lordship's son-in-law at his beck and call.

"Anyway, you pulled through, but by the time you were out of danger, Lydia'd come down with it herself. There was no money for a doctor— she'd spent what little money we'd had on a doctor for you—so I swallowed my pride and went to Lord Melrose. It was the first time we'd spoken in five years. Lydia wrote to him after you were born, telling him he had a grandson, but if he read the letter, he never acknowledged it. I told him his daughter was going to die if she didn't have a doctor." Jack had been staring blindly down at the glass in his hands, but suddenly he looked up at his son, and his grip on the glass tightened until his knuckles turned white. "Do you know what he said, the bastard? He said she'd made her bed when she ran off with me, and if it turned out to be her death bed, it was no more than she deserved. I didn't know what else to do. When I went to the duke's house the next day, I pocketed one of the silver snuffboxes he kept in a marquetry cabinet, thinking to sell it. He had so many, I reckoned he'd never miss just one. I was wrong; he did."

"What did he do?" asked Pickett, enthralled.

"He said he wouldn't prefer charges against me, but nor would he keep me on. Me no longer having a position to go to, I nursed Lydia the best I could, but it was no use. She was gone within a se'nnight, leaving me with a boy scarcely out of leading strings. Well"—his voice became brisk—"I'd had two employers, and I'd eloped with the daughter of one and stolen from the other. I couldn't find honest work after that, so I reckoned if I had to settle for *dis*honest work, I'd be the best damned thief in London. Truth to tell, nothing much mattered to me anymore, not with Lydia gone. Dead and buried in a pauper's grave without so much as a stone to mark the place where she lay, and she not yet twenty-five years old."

Jack shook his head at the memory, then tossed back the brandy remaining in his glass and reached for the bottle.

Pickett, resolutely swallowing the lump that had formed in his throat, took the bottle from his father's grasp and refilled first his father's glass and then his own. "In fact," he said, hardening his heart, "you were so devastated that you took up with Moll before Mum was cold in her grave."

"And what would you have had me do? I had a motherless boy to care for, and not so much as a roof to cover his head, for I'd spent the rent money on nostrums the apothecary swore would cure your mum—not that any of them were worth a farthing in the end," he added bitterly before resuming his tale. "And then there was Moll. She was a pretty piece in those days, and she'd always fancied me, even when your mum was still alive. More to the point, she had a house—Moll's grandmum had been a whore early last century, and her cully had bought it for her. The street was never as smart as he'd thought it would be, but by that time he'd moved on to some other doxy. Moll's grandmum kept the house, it being her only security against old age, and hired out the rooms she wasn't using, just like Moll and her mum did themselves, each in their turn. So I took up with Moll, and moved with you into her house, she having put out her tenants to make room for us. I was that grateful to her, but I didn't marry her, and I made it plain from the start that I never would. I wouldn't disrespect your mother's memory by setting any other woman in her place."

Pickett could all too easily imagine his father's dilemma; he was all too keenly aware of what his own position would be if, heaven forbid, Julia should die in childbirth or afterwards of childbed fever. The jointure left to her by her first husband would cease, leaving him with an infant to care for and no money on which to support it beyond the sporadic income from his fledgling investigation service.

Still, he was not quite ready to completely absolve his father, not just yet. "Do you have any idea how Moll treated me when you weren't around?"

"Not at first; I only found out later. I didn't know she was so jealous of your mother, even after poor Lydia was dead. The two had never been what you'd call friends, but that was hardly surprising, seeing as how they had nothing in common."

"Nothing but you, anyway," Pickett observed dryly.

Jack stiffened in indignation. "No, not me, either. After Lydia died, I took up with Moll—needs must, you know—but while she was alive, I never so much as looked at another woman. Why should I? I was the luckiest man in the world!"

This sentiment was so familiar that Pickett could not quite suppress a grin. "I'm sorry to disillusion you, Da, but you were only the second-luckiest."

Jack acknowledged this hit with a wink, but made no attempt to dispute it. "But Moll wanted more from me than I could give. Mind you, I never claimed to love her—I thought she understood what I needed from her, and what I could offer in return—but she knew things had been different between me and Lydia, and not only the fact that we'd been legally wed. Oh, I tried; I owed her a debt of gratitude, and thought maybe I could make myself love her if I put my mind to it, but it was no use." He sighed. "That part of me was buried with Lydia, and Moll could never forget that another woman had been first in my heart. Well, and to be fair, how could she, with you there as living proof? Everyone said you looked just like me, but there was something about you—a certain expression in your eyes—still is, for that matter," he added, studying the features in question with a keen gaze. "Every now and then I could look at you and catch a glimpse of Lydia looking back at me."

"According to my loving grandfather, I also have her stubborn chin," put in Pickett.

Jack's eyes narrowed in silent appraisal. "I'm not sure but what he isn't right, though I'll admit I never noticed it before. Ha! Fancy me and his nibs actually agreeing on something!" His smile faded, and his voice grew serious. "If he intends to do something handsome for you, son, you let him—for your mother's sake, if not your own. God knows she earned it."

As this comment reminded Pickett all too clearly of the interview he'd endured in Park Lane, he quickly turned the subject. "Never mind him; you were saying Moll saw too much of my mother in me."

"Aye, and heard too much of her, too, what with you crying for your mum more often than not, and with the same plummy speech as hers, since it'd been her voice in your ear day and night. I had to shut you up for your own good, so I started boxing your ears every time you mentioned her. God knows it took you long enough—stubborn chin, as you say— but eventually you took the hint and stopped talking about her."

"We could have talked about her when Moll was absent, just the two of us," Pickett said, aggrieved on behalf of his younger self. "Instead, you let me forget all about her!"

His father gave him a knowing look. "Haven't spent much time around the nursery set, have you? Never mind, you'll learn soon enough. Anyway, I thought maybe that would serve the purpose, until one day I came home just in time to catch Moll in the act of selling you to a chimney sweep. Do you have any idea what a climbing-boy's life is like?"

"I've seen the results often enough to make a pretty good guess." Pickett suppressed a shudder at the thought of the thousands of little boys sold into virtual slavery to sweeps who forced them naked into the narrow chimneys of London—boys with filthy faces, bent backs, misshapen limbs, and, for those fortunate enough to survive to manhood, the cancerous "sooty warts" that would eventually kill them. Such a fate had nearly been his—and would have been, if Moll had been allowed to have her way.

"That's why I started taking you with me, teaching you how to pick pockets, setting you to mudlarking—" He shook his head at the memory of that long-ago decision. "If you'd been caught—well, magistrates don't like sentencing children to hang, but even if you'd ended up swinging from the end of a rope, it would have been an easier fate than what Moll had planned for you. It didn't take long for you to lose your mum's plummy vowels, which I hated to see for Lydia's sake, but there's no denying you attracted less attention that way when we were out and about, to say nothing of setting up Moll's back when we were at home."

"Moll's maternal instincts haven't improved, even where her own spawn is concerned," Pickett said, his voice hardening. "She sold Kit to a criminal gang, and I should warn you that I meant what I said: If you intend to go back to her, you'll go alone. I won't let you take Kit with you."

"And just how you'd stop me when it's plain as a pikestaff that I'm the boy's father, I'd like to know," his father retorted without rancor, then added somewhat sheepishly, "although, truth to tell, I'd not thought of picking up where I left off with Moll, seeing as how it's not likely she'd be wearing the willow for me for these ten years and more.

Besides," he added, still more sheepishly, "there's a woman I met on the ship that I wouldn't mind seeing a bit more of."

Pickett rolled his eyes. "Of course there is. You never change, do you?"

Jack understood the question to be purely rhetorical, for he made no attempt to answer it, only offering in his own defense, "We were on board ship for three months! *Three months*, mind you! A bit of flirtation to pass the time never hurt no one."

"The woman's husband might disagree," was Pickett's dry observation. "I'm assuming she's married."

"Of course she is! D'you think I'd seduce an innocent fresh from the schoolroom? That's a thing I've never done, and if any man says otherwise, I'll call him a liar to his face!"

"No one's accusing you of anything," Pickett said with perhaps less than perfect truth, reasoning that if ten years in the Antipodes had failed to change his father's nature, a lecture from his son was even less likely to do so. "Do you have a valise? Surely you must have brought something with you!"

"I left my things at a boardinghouse in Limehouse where me and Sully hired a room."

"Sully?"

"A friend of mine," Jack said, then added by way of explanation, "He just finished serving out his sentence, same as me."

And that settles it, thought Pickett, yielding to the inevitable. He supposed there must be men who were capable of enjoying luxurious living in Mayfair while their fathers lodged in cheap boardinghouses along the waterfront; unfortunately, it appeared that he was not one of them. He tossed back the last of his brandy and set the empty glass on the tray, then rose to his feet.

"Are you finished? If you'll tell me how to get to this boardinghouse of yours, I'll go collect your things before it gets any later. Darkness falls early in December—but you'll remember that—and it's not a part of Town where I'd care to linger at night. In any case, I'll be happy"—he had expected to choke on the word, but found it came more easily than he'd anticipated—"to put you up here, at least for the nonce."

"I'm obliged to you, son, but there's no need for you to go," Jack protested. "I can be there and back in a trice, since I know exactly where I'm going. Besides, you'd stand out like a mustard pot in a coal cellar. Where are you buying your clothes these days? I didn't spend all those years working in a gentleman's house without learning to recognize bespoke togs when I see them. Did Weston make that coat?"

"Oh, no," Pickett hastily corrected this erroneous but undoubtedly flattering assumption. "I'm not so modish as all that. I go to Meyer in Conduit Street. He was recommended to me by—he was recommended to me," he finished lamely, realizing too late that Gentleman Jack Pickett would not welcome the revelation that his son regularly sought advice from the very same magistrate who had ordered his own transportation.

Jack, however, did not appear to notice this slip—Pickett could only assume that his father's thoughts were already racing ahead to the prospect of a tryst with his comely shipmate—but announced his intention of setting out on this errand immediately after dinner, adding that there was no need at all for his son to accompany him.

His determination to carry out this mission on his own certainly added weight to Pickett's suspicions regarding his father's plans for the evening, but he made no effort to drag the reprobate's feet onto the straight and narrow. In fact, he wanted nothing more than a few minutes' private conversation with Julia during which to make sense of a family tree that in only six hours had sprouted an alarming number of branches.

5

Which Confirms the Old Adage
That a Trouble Shared Is a Trouble Halved

His father's immediate future having been settled, Pickett released Julia and Kit from exile and they returned to the drawing room, Kit bearing a sheaf of papers torn from his sketchbook, from which he presented several of his more successful efforts for his father's inspection. Gentleman Jack was suitably impressed—or at least made a show of it convincing enough to satisfy any budding artist—and to Pickett's surprise, the hours remaining until dinner passed quite pleasantly. His father was certainly putting himself out to charm his daughter-in-law and the young son of whose existence he had not previously been aware, and since even his worst enemy could not deny the fact that Gentleman Jack Pickett could charm the birds from the trees when he set his mind to it, it was hardly surprising that an audience already inclined in his favor should find much in him of which to approve.

Meanwhile, Kit's temporary banishment to his room had served to remind him of several favorite toys which he must needs bring to his father's notice, and with this end in view, he all but dragged this interesting personage up to the schoolroom so that he might behold these riches for himself.

Left alone with her husband for a brief tête-à-tête, Julia slipped her hand through Pickett's arm. "Well?" she prompted, casting an appraising look about the room. "Nothing seems to be broken, and I didn't hear any shouting, so I take it things went well?"

Pickett darted a wary glance toward the stairs, whence Kit's enthusiastic commentary could be heard. "It—it's given me a lot to think about. In fact, this whole day has given me a lot to think about. I'll tell you later, after Kit has gone to bed, shall I? In the meantime," he added, somewhat self-consciously, "I've told Da he can stay, at least for the nonce, so you can speak to Mrs. Applegate about preparing a room for him."

Smiling at him in approval, Julia promised to do so, seeing no reason to tell him that she had been so confident of his eventual capitulation that she had already consulted with the housekeeper on the matter, and a suitable chamber had been prepared and was even now awaiting his father's occupancy, with clean linens on the bed, fresh candles in the sconces, a fire laid, and a plate of biscuits on a small table beside the bed.

Alas, had Pickett but known it, his father's presence at the board had almost led to an uprising in the kitchen when

Cook was informed that the dinner over which she had labored for most of the day must, on very short notice, be stretched to feed an additional mouth, and the mouth of an adult male at that—the very same adult male who had earlier in the day called at the servant's entrance, apparently laboring under the misapprehension that young Mr. Pickett occupied some position on the household staff, rather than having been the master of the establishment for almost a year. Fortunately for the sake of domestic harmony, Rogers conceived the happy notion of suggesting that Master Kit's portion might be diminished so that his father might be fed—a proposal that so offended Cook (with whom Kit was a great favorite) that she resolved to demonstrate to the butler her ability to feed any number of unexpected guests without resorting, as she claimed, to snatching the food from the mouths of babes.

Upstairs, of course, none of the Picketts had the slightest inkling of trouble below stairs, so they repaired to the dining room in blissful ignorance—at least until Jack threw Rogers into confusion by insisting upon lending the butler his aid in serving the meal, just as he had done many years ago in the household of his lordship the Marquess of Melrose.

Julia, recognizing the same name her husband had mentioned earlier, darted an inquiring glance at him, but received only the slightest shake of his head in reply. "Later," he mouthed, under the cover provided by Rogers's shocked remonstrances.

Unquestioned master of the servants' domain he might be, but the butler was no match for Gentleman Jack Pickett. In the end, it had not been Rogers's persuasions that had prevailed upon him to take his proper place at Mrs. Pickett's right hand, but that lady's *sotto voce* protest that, kindly as his offer of assistance was, she would not want Rogers to think he—or, indeed, any of the family—found the butler's service unsatisfactory.

Balked in his purpose, Jack settled for entertaining the company with lively (and, Pickett suspected, highly expurgated) tales of his adventures in the Antipodes. Kit, not to be outdone, recounted for his father's edification a thrilling description of his own rescue from Roger and Jud (whose occupations he altered from "thieves" to the less specific but more ominous "Bad Men," lest his father, a thief himself, should take offense) by the elder brother he had once heard of, but had never actually met. As his heroics certainly lost nothing in the telling, Pickett was obliged to interrupt this very flattering narrative more than once in order to set the record straight regarding some of Kit's more lurid descriptions.

The end of dinner was signaled by a remove of fruits, cheeses, and nuts, and after sampling a few of these, Julia rose from the table, observing with some regret that she had defied her doctor's orders quite enough for one day. The three males at the table rose with her, as courtesy demanded, but Julia was surprised and dismayed to discover that her father-in-law did not intend to return to the board after she withdrew, but had the fixed intention of taking his leave.

"I told John I'd fetch my kit right after dinner," he said when she objected to his departure. "It's a goodly walk, and I've not been gone from London so long that I've forgot there's places it's not so healthy to venture late at night."

"But you need not walk at all," Julia protested, "not when a carriage can have you there and back in a fraction of the time."

"I'm that obliged to you, but after eating such a meal, the walk'll do me good." He patted his perfectly flat belly as if in demonstration. "John can see me off, so you needn't come to the door at all. You go upstairs and lie down, and I'll see you in the morning."

Pickett seconded this plan, adding only that she should wait for him to assist her in climbing the stairs, and Julia, recognizing the futility of argument, yielded with a good grace. For his part, Pickett watched as his father took leave (with considerable charm, he was forced to admit) of his newly-discovered son and daughter-in-law, then walked with him as far as the door.

His father stepped out onto the portico, then turned back to regard Pickett with a quizzical look. "The Bank of England, eh?"

Pickett could not quite suppress a grin. "Old Lady Threadneedle herself," he said, for the first time feeling a sense of pride in what had indeed been quite a remarkable accomplishment, however morally questionable.

"You were always a good lad," his father said with a chuckle, then set off down the street.

* * *

Having seen first Julia and then Kit off to bed—no easy task in the case of the latter, who seemed to be laboring under the delusion that his brother was going to permit him to stay up awaiting their prodigal parent's return—Pickett lingered in the drawing room for some time. While he would have vehemently denied any suggestion that he himself was awaiting his father's return, there was no denying the fact that Gentleman Jack held a prominent place in his thoughts. Pickett had been in deadly earnest when he'd said he would not allow his father to take Kit back to live with Moll. And yet he'd also meant it when he'd said he would not burden Julia with his father's support in addition to his own and Kit's and, any day now, the baby's. He could not lawfully prevent his father from seeing Kit; he wasn't sure he would have done so in any case, for Julia had been right when she'd said the boy deserved to know his father. Perhaps more to the point, the sooner Kit became fully acquainted with the man who had sired him, the sooner their father would tumble off the pedestal on which Kit had so eagerly placed him. Even as this pleasing prospect rose to his mind, he acknowledged the jealousy that had inspired it. It was disturbing to realize that, less than twenty-four hours after his father's arrival, he was already bringing out all Pickett's own worst instincts.

He had no idea how long he sat there, but suddenly Rogers was hovering solicitously over him.

"Would you care for something to drink, sir?" The butler cast a discreet glance at the small table at Pickett's elbow, on which stood a brass candlestick bearing what had once been a tall wax taper, but was now well on the way to becoming a misshapen lump. "Or another candle, perhaps?"

"Wha—?" Startled out of his reveries, Pickett gave a spasmodic jerk. "Oh—no, thank you. I didn't realize it was so—but—my father hasn't come back yet?"

Even as he asked the question, he recognized how foolish it sounded. It would be a very poor Bow Street Runner indeed who could remain oblivious while his father had knocked at the door, been admitted by the butler and, finally, been ushered upstairs to the bedroom that had been prepared for him.

But although Rogers must surely have noted the stupidity of this inquiry, he gave no sign. "I'm afraid not, sir."

"Oh. Well"—Pickett glanced at the long-case clock as he rose to his feet, but found it impossible to read, lost as it was in shadows—"he might have run into any number of old cronies. He may not return until morning. In any case, you need not wait up for him, but if he should knock—" He broke off, yawning.

The butler nodded in understanding. "I shall sleep with one ear cocked, sir, and if I should hear him return, I shall admit him myself."

"Thank you, Rogers," Pickett said, giving him a rather sleepy smile. "I'm very much obliged to you."

Rogers inclined his head. "My pleasure, sir."

Pickett rather doubted this, but accepted it in the spirit in which it was intended, then picked up the candlestick and started for the stairs. Upon reaching the bedroom he shared with Julia, he opened the door very carefully so as to avoid making any noise that might awaken her—and was taken aback to discover her sitting up in bed, propped up against her pillow and reading by the light of her own bedside candle. Or she had been, until his not-so-stealthy entrance caused her to look up from her book with a smile.

"Well?" she prompted, scooting to one side of the bed. "Aren't you going to tell me about it? I'll admit, I was beginning to wonder."

"Surely you haven't been waiting for me all this time!"

"Well, not entirely," she confessed. "I've been finding it very difficult to sleep lately, so your prolonged absence gave me a good excuse for delaying the inevitable. Darling, I am all agog! What, pray, does Lord Melrose have to say to the matter? You could have knocked me over with a feather when your father mentioned him, when you yourself had done so only a few hours earlier."

Picked did not answer right away. He shrugged off his coat and waistcoat, untied his cravat, and pulled his shirt over his head, then draped these discarded garments over the back of the nearest chair before lowering himself onto the despised camp bed and setting to work on his shoes and stockings.

"John!" cried Julia in some chagrin. Lest he miss the point of her complaint, she patted the vacant side of the bed with a mischievous smile.

"Are you sure?" Pickett was almost afraid to ask, so fearful was he of getting an answer he did not want. Suddenly there was nothing in the world he wanted—no, *needed*—so badly as her embrace. "After all, the midwife—"

"The midwife isn't here," she pointed out, lowering her voice to a conspiratorial whisper. "Tomorrow I shall obey orders as meekly as she or Dr. Gilroy might wish, but for tonight, what they doesn't know won't hurt them."

He needed no more persuasion. He slid between the sheets, but instead of sitting back against the pillows in the place where she'd made room for him, he stretched out beside her, resting his head on her shoulder with the contented sigh of one who has come home.

But where was he to start? Even as he asked, he knew the answer; she had provided it herself. "What do you know about Lord Melrose?"

"Not much," she confessed. "Why? Is he important?"

"I think perhaps he might be," said Pickett, displaying a previously unsuspected talent for understatement.

"Very well, then." She ticked off the facts on her fingers. "I know he is a marquess. I know he has been a widower for many years, for his wife died long ago. I know he doesn't seem to be a very pleasant person, but perhaps this must be forgiven him, for he has known his share of tragedy. In addition to his wife, I believe he also lost a daughter many years ago."

"He did," Pickett said tersely.

"And then," Julia continued, "only last month, his son and heir was killed in a hunting accident—"

"So *that's* what it meant!"

"That's what *what* meant?" Julia asked, interrupting her recitation.

He shook his head. "Never mind. Go on."

"All right, then. His son and heir, Lord Huxton, was childless—he had never married, according to Emily Dunnington. She says that rather than let the title fall into abeyance when he dies, he intends to petition the Crown to allow it to pass through his daughter instead. In that case, the heir presumptive would be his grandson, who is apparently a very unsuitable person, and not at all the sort one would hope to carry on one's legacy. Still, he seems to be the only blood relation Lord Melrose has left, so one can't really blame him for—"

"Sweetheart—" Pickett sat up and turned to face her, finding her shoulder not nearly so comforting as it had been a moment earlier. "Lord Melrose's daughter was my mother. *I'm* the 'unsuitable person.' "

"I beg your pardon?" Julia regarded him with a bemused smile, as if she could not quite understand the joke.

"It's true," he insisted. "Lord Melrose is my grand-father."

She shook her head. "I'm sorry, John, but it won't do. I don't know what you've been told, or by whom, but no one seeing the two of you together could deny that you are your father's son."

"Oh, I'll not deny that. But Lady Lydia Melrose was my mother. She eloped with my father while he was his lordship's footman. Ran off the very night her betrothal was to be announced, the pair of them."

He had the dubious satisfaction of seeing the smile wiped from her face. "You cannot be serious!"

"You heard what Da said about serving at Lord Melrose's table," he reminded her.

"Yes, but serving at one's table is a far cry from eloping with one's daughter!"

"Be that as it may, his lordship was apparently certain enough that he had two of his henchmen snatch me off the street, bundle me into a carriage, and take me to Park Lane so he could look me over. I'm afraid your pears were innocent victims in the struggle that ensued. I'm sorry; I'll go back and buy you some more tomorrow."

"Never mind the pears," she said impatiently. "Did you meet Lord Melrose, then? What did he say?"

"He said pretty much what you just told me: that his only son had died recently, and that he intended to make the best of his one remaining descendant. Sweetheart, can he really do what he said—petition the Crown to make me his heir?"

She considered the matter for a long moment. "He can certainly *try*," she said at last. "Although whether his petition is granted is another matter entirely."

"He might as well save himself the trouble," Pickett said, setting his jaw. "Even if he manages to persuade the king, he can't make me agree to it. If I do inherit the title, I intend to turn it down."

"Yes, but darling, I don't think you *can*," protested Julia. "That is, you can certainly refuse to tend to his lordship's estates, or take up his seat in Parliament, or see to any of the other responsibilities that come with the title. But it seems a shabby thing to do to your own heir, who would eventually inherit lands suffering from decades of neglect."

Pickett, usually not given to profanity, make a creative but physically impossible suggestion as to what Lord Melrose might do with his title and his estates.

"Would you mind it so very much?" she asked coaxingly, lacing her fingers through his. "Can you not consider such a thing—if it happens at all, which is far from certain—for the advantages it would give your children?"

You'll be singing a different tune one there is a son to educate or a daughter to dower... Yes, that was exactly what Lord Melrose was counting on—and it was frightening how accurately his lordship had got his measure, even on so little acquaintance. Still, that was not the greatest of the temptations offered by the marquess's petition.

"If I'm tempted at all," he confessed, "it's by the prospect of laying those honors at your feet."

"Oh, John"—she tugged her fingers free of his, but only so that she might slip her arms around his neck—"I couldn't possibly love you as Marquess of Melrose any more than I did plain John Pickett of Bow Street. As long as I can be 'Mrs. Pickett,' I need no other title."

"Oh, but you can't," he exclaimed, laughing. "I almost forgot: Lord Melrose intends to buy off my 'St. Giles wench' and find me a wife of his own choosing. He thinks I might be acceptable to some well-born female who's desperate enough to take me rather than end up on the shelf."

"He *what?*" Julia's tone was indignant, but secretly she would have endured any number of slights to her honor in exchange for seeing the distress banished from her husband's eyes.

"You have to hand it to his lordship, really," Pickett conceded with grudging admiration. "He managed to insult three people in one breath: You, me, and the poor woman he thinks to marry me off to."

"He might have saved himself the trouble," Julia retorted, relaxing into his embrace. "There isn't enough money in the world to buy off this wench."

6

In Which a Midnight Caller
Leads to an Unpleasant Duty

Pickett wasn't sure what woke him. But suddenly he was wide awake, realizing somewhat guiltily that he'd fallen asleep in bed with his wife, rather than on the camp bed to which he'd been banished until her confinement. In his defense, he'd had the best of intentions. Julia had not slept well of late, as it was becoming increasingly difficult for her to find a comfortable position, so when he'd realized at some point in their conversation that she was falling asleep in his arms, he hadn't dared to move for fear of waking her. Eventually he had fallen asleep as well, and now he couldn't abandon her bed for his own even if he'd wanted to: His right arm was pinned beneath her. He tried to move it, and realized he'd lost all feeling from the elbow down.

Was that what had awakened him?

No, it had been a noise—his father returning from his

errand, most likely. It was too dark for him to read the clock on the mantel, but he had the impression that it was very late—late enough, surely, for his father to have fetched any number of valises. The tryst with the beautiful shipmate, then, Pickett acknowledged with a sigh. Well, he hoped his father had found the rendezvous satisfying, for it was proving deuced inconvenient for the rest of the household.

At least, Pickett reasoned, he could go downstairs himself and let his father in, and spare Rogers the necessity. Slowly, so as not to wake her, he slid his arm out from under Julia's sleeping form.

"Don't forget the pears," she mumbled, rolling onto her other side.

"I won't," he assured her, his voice scarcely more than a whisper. "Go back to sleep, love."

He dropped a light kiss onto her temple, then pulled on his breeches, tugged his shirt over his head, and made his way down corridor and stairs in his bare feet, reaching the front door at the same time as Rogers, emerging from the servants' stair with his dark breeches and coat thrown on over his nightshirt.

"It's Da," he told the butler. "I'll let him in. You go on back to bed."

For a moment it looked as though Rogers intended to argue the point, but after a brief hesitation, he said, "Very good, sir," and returned to the servants' stair whence he had come.

In fact, Pickett was considerably annoyed with his father, but had no desire to take him to task before even so sympathetic an audience as Rogers. To say "don't wait up for me" was one thing; to roust someone out of bed in the middle of the night to let him into the house was quite another. He shot back the bolt and opened the door, drawing in his breath preparatory to reminding his scapegrace sire that he was no longer a resident felon at a penal colony, but a guest in his son's house, and was expected to act accordingly.

To his surprise, however, it was not Gentleman Jack Pickett on the other side of the door, but his own former magistrate, Patrick Colquhoun, who stood on the portico with his hat in his hands and a look of unaccustomed solicitude on his face.

Oh, Lord, Pickett thought, stifling a groan, *it needed only this. What has he done now?*

He let out his breath in a rush. "Sir?"

"Good evening, John, or perhaps I should say 'good morning,'" the magistrate said, and the familiar Scots burr contained a note of gentleness that he had never heard in it before. "I'm sorry to call on you at such an ungodly hour, but I must ask you to come with me. I need you to—to identify a body."

Pickett's hackles rose. "A—who—?" He tried to form a coherent question, but words failed him. In any case, he didn't have to ask; he knew the answer without being told.

"It's your father," Mr. Colquhoun said, confirming Pickett's worst fears. "I'm sorry to say he's dead, John. His body was discovered in Limehouse."

"What—how—?"

The knowledge that his suspicions were correct didn't

seem to have any effect on Pickett's befuddled brain. Mr. Colquhoun, however, deciphered this disjointed query without difficulty.

"His was not a peaceful passing, I'm afraid, but it must have been a mercifully swift one," the magistrate assured him. "He was knifed in the back."

* * *

Knifed in the back...knifed in the back...

The words seemed to repeated themselves in rhythm with the revolution of the wheels of the hired hackney on the cobbled streets as it bore them eastward into the City, past the silent bulk of St. Paul's cathedral, its great dome reared up against the night sky, blotting out the stars.

"How long had he been in London?" asked the magistrate, breaking the silence at last.

Pickett had no need to ask who "he" was. "I only saw him for the first time today—yesterday, that is—so the day before that at the earliest, I should think." Recalling something his father had said, Pickett added with more conviction, "Yes, I'm certain of it. That is, the ship arrived two days ago, but it was yesterday before the captain received clearance for his cargo to be unloaded and his passengers to disembark."

"Did he give any indication that he might have made an enemy among his fellow passengers?"

"No, not unless you count a flirtation with a married woman whose husband was also on board. Oh, and he had someone's watch off him on a bet. He says—said—he won it fair and square, but knowing him as you do, you may make of that what you will. Aside from that, he seemed to be in prime twig, boasting that he'd become a man of property." Pickett forced a wry smile. "Other people's, most likely, but property nonetheless."

They lapsed into silence while the carriage made its plodding way through the East End, until Pickett said abruptly, "Sir, I know I'm no longer connected with Bow Street in any official capacity, but I would be obliged to you if you would allow me to take part in the investigation to bring Da's killer to justice."

"I'm sure your sentiments do you credit, John, but I can't think it a good idea." Mr. Colquhoun's voice was kind, but underneath it lay a hint of steel. "I was obliged to fetch you for the purpose of identifying the body—aside from the very likely unreliable word of a drunken doxy who hasn't seen him in ten years, you're the only one who would be able to identify him with any certainty after so long an absence—but as for any more active role"—he shook his head—"no, I can't think it wise. Aside from the fact that you are much too closely connected to the crime to remain objective, there are ethical questions to be considered. If we succeed in bringing a man—or woman—to trial, it would be folly to give the defense counsel any ammunition to use against us."

Pickett made no attempt to argue the point, but he had no intention of meekly accepting this dictum without making the slightest push to change the magistrate's mind. A few minutes later, the hackney slowed and finally lurched to a stop before the Grapes, an ancient pub whose close proximity to the river ensured a great deal of custom from the men who made their living on the water. Mr. Colquhoun disembarked first and waited for Pickett to follow, then the two men entered the premises which, though it would normally be closed at so inauspicious an hour, had apparently been pressed into service as a temporary mortuary.

At their entrance, the proprietor (a man who bore all the appearance of one summoned from his bed on very short notice) gave a start of surprise. "God bless my soul!"

"The man's son," Mr. Colquhoun explained curtly, recognizing at once the reason for this outburst.

The proprietor nodded, saying with considerable relief, "Aye, I can see now that he's not old enough to—but he gave me a rare turn when I first seen him, and no mistake!"

"A strong resemblance, to be sure," and was all the magistrate said before turning to the business at hand. "Has he been brought in, then?"

"Aye, he's"—his tone was businesslike, but he darted a sympathetic glance at Pickett—"he's in the back room." He made a vague gesture in the direction of a closed door behind the bar, inviting both mourner and magistrate to follow him.

The room figured ever after in Pickett's memory as a small, cramped space, but this was quite possibly due to the number of men crowded about the heavy deal table that occupied most of the floor space not taken up with barrels, kegs, and crates. In addition to Mr. Colquhoun and himself, there was the man who admitted them, no doubt the proprietor of the pub; an elderly man with a croupy cough who, Pickett deduced, must be the constable who had been summoned when the crime had been discovered; another man Pickett thought must be the coroner; and a pair of wide-eyed youths who must have been the ones who discovered the body, judging by their not entirely successful attempts to convey a bored air, as if they stumbled across dead bodies every day of their lives.

And then there was the table, the focal point upon which all these persons' attention was fixed. Something had been placed upon it and covered with a white tablecloth whose folds fell in contours suggestive of a human form underneath. Pickett took a deep, steadying breath, and then, finding that the coroner seemed to be awaiting his signal, gave him a nod. With an air of dignity, almost reverence, the coroner took the two top corners of the cloth and folded it back.

At first glance, it appeared to be someone's idea—his father's, most likely—of a joke. Gentleman Jack Pickett lay stretched out at full length upon the table, his eyes closed as if he were sleeping—an impression heightened by the cloth which the coroner had folded back as if it were a counterpane intended to protect the slumberer from the December chill. The sun-streaked hair was disarranged as if from sleep, and the generous mouth was relaxed in what almost appeared to be a smile. Pickett was seized with the absurd notion that at any moment his father would sit bolt upright, throwing off the cloth and shouting "Surprise!"

He choked back a bark of slightly hysterical laughter at the thought. This was not the first time he had been called upon to examine a body, he reminded himself sternly, ignoring the little voice—a voice that sounded suspiciously like Mr. Colquhoun's—that pointed out he had been summoned for the purpose of identification, not investigation. He took a deep breath and forced himself to look again at the body lying on the table, trying to see it as if it were that of a complete stranger.

"It's him," he said tersely, then addressed himself to the coroner. "If you will turn him over, I should like to see the wound, please."

Mr. Colquhoun made a faint noise of protest, but Pickett's air of clinical detachment (which was in fact something akin to an emotional stupor, had the coroner but known it) was not without its effect. The coroner took the body by the shoulder and arm and turned it onto its side, revealing the back of a coat that bore a jagged cut some four inches long in its center, the slightly raveled edges of which were dark with blood. The ragged edge of the buff-colored waistcoat could just be seen, and, beneath that, the white shirt. These too were drenched in blood, especially the shirt, which, lying against the dead man's skin, had got the worst of it.

Pickett looked up at the coroner. "And the murder weapon?"

The answer to this inquiry was provided not by the coroner, but by one of the two youths. Upon receiving a nudge from his confederate, along with a whispered urge to "give it to him, Ned!," he withdrew the object from inside his coat and held it out for Pickett's inspection.

It was a knife; that much, at least, was certain. But it was a knife unlike any that Pickett—no stranger to the variety of implements with which one might do away with one's fellow man—had ever seen before. It was scarcely more than six inches long from the tip of the blade to the oddly misshapen haft, and the double-edged blade had been carved from stone rather than struck from steel. The haft was made of some material Pickett could not identify, and although it was hardly more than a lump encasing the last two inches of the blade, presumably to protect the hand of the user, its crude form was obviously intentional, and not the result of some error that had occurred during its manufacture, if the pattern of brownish-red stripes adorning it were anything to judge by—stripes, Pickett noted, very similar in color to the dried blood staining the business end of the blade

"I'm afraid this will have to be kept as evidence," Pickett told Ned, albeit not without sympathy. It was a curious weapon, and one which any lad still in his teens would be pleased to call his own. Removing the handkerchief from the breast pocket of his coat, Pickett shook it out and spread it out on the table, then placed the knife on it, folded the corners of the handkerchief around it, and rolled it up before turning his attention back to the boy.

"Are you the one who discovered him, Ned? Where was he—it—the body?"

"He were in Gin Alley," the youth answered promptly, apparently seeing nothing to wonder at in the fact that the victim's son had taken over the investigation right under the coroner's nose.

As Pickett's early days as a pickpocket had rarely taken him so far east as Limehouse, he was unsure whether Gin Alley was an actual street, or if the boy was speaking metaphorically and telling him that his father had been drunk at the time of his death. Pickett glanced somewhat uncertainly to the proprietor of the pub for confirmation.

"Just east of here. A dogleg passage connecting Narrow and Queen Streets," the publican explained. "It's dark and shadowy even during daylight hours. For myself, I wouldn't care to venture down it alone this time of night."

Alone, he'd said. But what if his father hadn't been alone? What if someone had arranged to meet him there as a means of luring him to his death? What if he'd gone to the rendezvous to meet one person, only to find someone else lying in wait for him?

"Aye, and such places tend to attract criminals of every sort," the coroner was saying. "Your father isn't the first to meet his end there, and probably won't be the last—although I realize this is but cold comfort," he added sympathetically.

Pickett, however, had already turned back to Ned and his companion. "And he was already dead when you found him? He spoke no last words that might give some idea as to who—"

Mr. Colquhoun, having obtained the information for which he had originally summoned his young protégé, interrupted this line of questioning. "The coroner can handle matters from here, John," the magistrate said in a voice that brooked no argument. "I'll take you home now."

Pickett might have protested this high-handed treatment, but as he had his own reasons for not wanting to linger, he raised his hand to his mouth as if to cover a yawn, offering no resistance when Mr. Colquhoun took him firmly by the arm and led him outside, where the hackney driver, having been ordered to wait, was walking his horses.

They climbed aboard, and had hardly completed the westward turn into Broad Street when Mr. Colquhoun said, with steel in his voice, "I'll expect that thing to be returned before the inquest."

Pickett had been slumped in his seat, leaning his head against the window and gazing out upon the slumbering city, but upon recognizing the veiled accusation behind the magistrate's words, sat upright and turned to regard his mentor with limpid brown eyes. "Sir?"

Mr. Colquhoun was not deceived. "Save that innocent act for someone who hasn't known you for the last ten years and more," he recommended. "I know full well you've got that knife secreted somewhere about your person—up your sleeve, unless I miss my guess."

Pickett opened his mouth to refute this charge, then, acknowledging the futility of such a gesture, reached inside the cuff of his shirtsleeve with a sigh of resignation, withdrew the curious weapon, and placed it in the magistrate's waiting hand.

Mr. Colquhoun unwrapped the knife and turned it over in his hands, inspecting it as best he could in the feeble light of the carriage lamps.

"How did you know, sir?" asked Pickett, much chastened.

"Aside from long experience with your particular skills, you mean? When you're interrogating witnesses one moment—something I strictly forbade you to do, if memory serves—and then in the next moment falling asleep on your feet, let's just say I had my suspicions. It seemed to me that you were hoping for me to intervene. I trust I did not disappoint?"

"No, sir," Pickett said sheepishly. "It's heavy for its small size—you can feel that for yourself—and I wasn't sure how long I could keep it from falling out. Raising my hand to cover a yawn pushed it back to my elbow, but only temporarily. As soon as I lowered my arm, it was going to fall right back down to my wrist, and I wasn't sure my cuff would hold it."

"Then, too, there was always the possibility that you might accidentally slit your wrist," observed the magistrate. "Awkward for you."

"I never intended to keep it," Pickett insisted. "It's just that—I have a feeling I may know who it belongs to."

Mr. Colquhoun's bushy white eyebrows lowered thoughtfully. "Oh?" He waited expectantly for Pickett to enlarge upon this theme, but when no further explanation was forthcoming, he gave the odd little knife one last look before returning it to his protégé, saying sternly, "I trust you know what you're doing. I still don't like it, mind you, and I meant what I said about returning it in time for the inquest. Perhaps you'd best give it to me right before the proceedings begin. I'll tell the coroner you'd suffered a nasty shock, and put it into your pocket without thinking. I daresay it won't be far from the truth," he added, regarding Pickett with an appraising look.

"Perhaps not." Pickett shook his head as if to clear it. "Truth to tell, I can't quite believe he's really gone. I don't know why not; it's a wonder someone didn't take him out years ago. If ever a man was 'born to be hanged,' as the saying goes, it was Da."

"I'm sorry, John," the magistrate said quietly.

"It's not your fault, sir. God knows he tempted fate often enough."

Mr. Colquhoun continued as if he hadn't spoken. "I deprived you of a father at an age when you badly needed one."

"I never blamed you for that," Pickett insisted, taken aback by this admission. "You might have sentenced him to the gallows."

"The end result was the same, so far as you were concerned. To a lad of fourteen, a father ten thousand miles away might as well be dead. I might have commuted his sentence at any time over the last ten years; I certainly should have done these last five." The magistrate sighed. "The truth, I suppose, is that I envied the man too much."

"You, envy Da? Why should you?"

"Because he possessed the one thing I never could, and held it so cheaply," was the cryptic reply.

"Oh?" Pickett asked, bewildered. "What was that?"

The Scotsman shook his head. "Never mind."

Pickett did not dwell for long on this conundrum, for his mind was filled with other things. Suddenly he burst out, "I've never had any illusions about who or what I was—the son of Gentleman Jack Pickett, by gad! A pickpocket, an occasional mudlark, and a thief—and a damned good one, thanks to my father. But all this time, I knew nothing! Nothing at all! I have a grandfather, did you know?" he asked, causing the magistrate to blink at this sudden *non sequitur*. "He's a marquess; Da was once his footman!"

Seeing that Mr. Colquhoun appeared to be as stunned by this revelation as he had been himself, Pickett launched into explanation, recounting the whole story of his parents' doomed romance and clandestine marriage, his own birth, and his mother's illness and death, and, finally, his abduction in Covent Garden and the revelation to which it had led.

"God bless my soul!" breathed the magistrate at the conclusion of this narrative. "And Lord Melrose? What has he to say to all this?"

Pickett gave a bitter laugh. "He ignored my existence completely until his only son died without issue. Then he needed an heir, and whatever my deficiencies, it seems I'm better than nothing. He's even petitioning the Crown to allow me to inherit the title through my mother!"

But that, if his suspicions were correct, was not the worst of it. According to Da, Lord Melrose had known of his grandson's existence since the day of Pickett's own birth, more or less, but had chosen not to acknowledge him. And then, after a silence of twenty-five years, he'd not only acknowledged him, but had even had him abducted off the street. And at almost the same moment, Gentleman Jack Pickett, newly returned from Botany Bay, was making his own presence known in Curzon Street. Two men, his only living ancestors, who despised each other and who had not been in communication with each other for a quarter of a century. And now, less than twenty-four hours later, one of them was dead. It couldn't be a coincidence…could it?

"Look here," he said abruptly, as the gaslit streets of Mayfair came into view, "will you object to setting me down now? It isn't far to Curzon Street, and I could use a brisk walk in the cold air. It's—it's been a lot to take in, all at once."

Mr. Colquhoun regarded his young protégé with a long, measuring look, then rapped on the roof and gave the order.

"Thank you, sir."

As the vehicle slowed, Pickett opened the door and leaped down without waiting for it to come to a complete stop, then raised his hand in farewell as the hackney bore the magistrate away.

7

In Which John Pickett Makes a Tactical Error

Although Pickett had been quick to absolve the magistrate of any responsibility, even indirectly, for his father's murder, there was another toward whom he was not prepared to offer the same forbearance. And so, once the magistrate and his hired conveyance were well out of sight, Pickett turned his steps in quite the wrong direction for anyone wishing to reach Curzon Street. By the time he reached the elegant Park Lane house that was his intended destination, the guilt of its primary occupant had taken such firm possession of his mind that he ignored the brass knocker and began to pound on the door with his fist.

"Open up!" he bellowed, heedless of the lateness of the hour and the slumbering residents of the adjacent dwellings. "I know you're in there! Open up, you bloody bastard!"

A moment later the door opened and a butler, somehow contriving to appear stately in spite of the nightcap askew over his disheveled gray hair, glared at him with acute dislike.

"I regret to inform you, sir," he began, although regret was clearly not the emotion uppermost in his mind, "that Lord Melrose is asleep in bed. Perhaps if you call tomorrow, at a more auspicious time—"

This eminently reasonable suggestion fell on empty air, for Pickett had brushed past him and was taking the stairs two at a time on his way to the upper floors where he knew the marquess's bedchamber would be located. "Where are you?" he demanded, shedding his hard-won vowels with every step he climbed. "Don't think you can 'ide from me, your bleedin' lordship! I know wot you did, and I'll demolish this 'ouse brick by brick, if that's wot it takes to flush out a rat that walks like a man! I'll—"

He had just reached the second-floor landing when a pair of gilt-paneled double doors at the end of the corridor were flung open to reveal the marquess, resplendent in a quilted dressing gown of emerald-green satin.

"What the devil—?" he demanded. Upon recognizing the invader, he said, "Oh, so it's you, is it? And cupshot into the bargain. Well, don't think I'll allow you to make a drunken fool of yourself, not while I'm calling the tune!"

Pickett, ignoring a claim that contained more than one entirely erroneous assumption, launched into a stream of invectives he hadn't even been aware that he knew, much less had ever before directed at a fellow human being, concluding with, "You murdered my father!"

"What the devil are you going on about?"

"As if you don't know! I've just been to identify Da's

body after he was murdered in the street—knifed in the back, no less, by a man too cowardly to confront him face to face!"

"And so naturally you think his killer must have been me," his lordship observed, his cold rationality a stark contrast to his grandson's emotional accusations. "Believe me, sirrah, if I'd had any such inclination, I would not have waited twenty-five years to accomplish my purpose."

"Better late than never, I daresay," retorted Pickett. "How did you know he'd returned to London? Did you think to manipulate me more easily if you eliminated him first?"

"I've never heard anything so preposterous in my life! The very idea that I would kill anyone, even such a one as—"

"Oh, of course not!" Pickett agreed bitterly. "You'd never sully your lily-white hands with anything so ugly as murder, would you? No, you hire others to do your dirty work for you—as I have cause to know! Tell me, was it the same precious pair who abducted me off the street this very afternoon? They have had a busy day, haven't they? I hope they were well paid for their trouble!"

"Oh, good God," grumbled the marquess, tightening the braided cord of his dressing gown about his waist in the manner of one girding himself for battle. "I can't have you standing there shrieking blue murder loud enough for all the world to hear! If you won't stubble it and go home, you might as well come in and have a drop of brandy. God knows you look like you could use it."

"I thank you for your gracious hospitality, your lordship," said Pickett, sounding anything but grateful, "but I'm afraid I must decline to partake of anything under your roof. I'm sure I would choke on it."

The effect of this speech was considerably diminished by the fact that even as he spoke, Lord Melrose seized his coat sleeve and pulled him through the door into a small sitting room connected to the bedchamber. Pickett was fully a head taller than his grandfather, but as the older man outweighed him by at least five stone, he was compelled perforce to follow.

"Now, sit down!" barked the marquess, indicating with a nod the two velvet-upholstered chairs positioned before the fire from which, though banked for the night, some warmth still emanated. Without waiting to see if Pickett obeyed this command, he crossed the room to a small table on which stood two pot-bellied glasses and a decanter of golden-brown liquid. He poured a generous dollop from the decanter into both glasses, and handed one to his grandson.

Pickett's fury had considerably abated by now, for his was not a temperament given to prolonged fits of rage, and he realized he could not resist his lordship's orders without causing a scene which would no doubt be as futile as it was undignified. Perhaps more to the point, he discovered that the prospect of brandy, even brandy provided by his grandfather and consumed beneath that gentleman's scowling gaze, held considerable appeal. He meekly accepted the glass proffered by his lordship and drank deeply from it.

"Better?" asked the marquess, and although it would be an exaggeration to say there was kindness in his voice, Pickett recognized a slight lessening of the brusqueness with which the man had addressed him thus far.

"Yes," Pickett said, belatedly adding, "Thank you."

"Now"—Lord Melrose sank into the chair adjacent to his—"what's all this about your father?"

"Mr. Colquhoun—Patrick Colquhoun, that is; he is—was—my magistrate at Bow Street. I was a principal officer there until quite recently—"

"Yes, I know. It's a comfort to know that you operate on the right side of the law, in any case—which is more than can be said for your father," he added darkly.

Pickett refrained from informing his grandfather that this had not always been the case, correctly supposing that the marquess would be considerably less enchanted with his raid on the Bank of England than his father had been.

"Anyway," he continued, "Mr. Colquhoun came to my house tonight and said he needed me to come and formally identify my father's body. He—my father, that is, not Mr. Colquhoun—he'd been discovered in Gin Alley in Limehouse. He'd taken a room in a boardinghouse there after arriving in London. He'd been stabbed in the back."

"And you leapt to the conclusion that I must be behind the murder, even if it hadn't been my hand holding the knife."

Pickett bristled at this charge, all the more so because he feared his lordship might have a valid point. "You must own that you have no shortage of weapons at your disposal for just such a purpose. Any one of that collection in your study would have been more than sufficient to the task."

"Dare I indulge the hope that you intend to favor me with a description of this knife so that I may weigh it against those in my own possession, or is it more in your style to fling unwarranted accusations without allowing the accused to offer exonerating evidence?"

The second half of this speech made Pickett's face burn with mortification, but he refused to be drawn. "I can do more than that." He withdrew the handkerchief-wrapped weapon from the inside pocket of his coat. "I have the knife in my possession. The blade is still stained with my father's blood."

He drew back the folds of linen to reveal the primitive knife, then surrendered it, handkerchief and all, for the marquess's inspection.

"Quite a collector's piece," Lord Melrose observed with interest, turning it over and back again so as to study it from all sides before handing it back to Pickett. "Not only do I *not* possess such a knife, I cannot recall ever having seen one like it. If I were inclined to stab anyone to death, you may be sure I would not choose to do so with a weapon better suited to the hallowed halls of the British Museum than the back alleys of Limehouse."

Feeling compelled to offer some defense of a course of action that had gone rather glaringly abroad, Pickett rushed into speech. "When I returned home after you—after our interview"—he could think of better words for it, but this hardly seemed the time to quibble over what seemed at the moment a minor point—"I found my father waiting for me. I hadn't seen him in more than ten years. He'd just returned to England after serving a sentence in Botany Bay. I'd just heard from your own lips how my mother had eloped from this house with your footman, and then, for the first time in my life, Da told me the truth about my mother. Save for the matter of perspective, it matched in every particular the account I'd just heard from you. I knew you and Da had no cause to love each other, so when he was murdered only a few hours later, well—"

"It might interest you to know," the marquess interrupted brusquely, "that I have been at home all night long. If you desire proof—"

He stretched out his hand for the bell pull and gave it a tug. A moment later, the butler entered the room, the same man who had tried without success to deny Pickett the house. He was looking rather less disheveled now, having abandoned his nightcap and changed his nightshirt and hastily donned breeches for the dark suit he'd been wearing when Pickett had first been brought to the house.

"You rang, your lordship?" he asked, quite as if his master entertaining raving lunatics in his private sitting room in the middle of the night were an ordinary occurrence.

"You will please describe for my grandson my movements this evening."

"Yes, sir." Without betraying by so much as a flicker of the eyelash that he recognized his lordship's grandson as the same person he had tried without success to evict from the premises, he turned to Pickett and intoned, "After spending the afternoon at his club, his lordship repaired to his study to write letters. He remained there until time to dress for dinner, at which time he retired to his bedchamber to change into his evening clothes. By the time he came downstairs again, the dinner gong sounded, whereupon he partook of the evening meal in the dining room. He lingered at the table over port, after which time he entertained Sir Matthew Whitby for an evening of cards. After Sir Matthew's departure, he withdrew to this very room in order to read for a time before seeking his bed."

"Thank you," the marquess said, then turned to Pickett. "Oh, but I was to have made use of henchmen who actually did the deed upon my orders, was I not? The 'precious pair,' I believe you called them. In fact, they are footmen, just as your father was."

"I—I—never—I didn't—" Picket stammered, but was ignored. Lord Melrose turned back to address the butler.

"Pray have James and Charles attend me here, Simmons."

Simmons was betrayed into protest. "They'll be in bed asleep, your lordship."

"Exactly the point," said the marquess, inclining his head.

"Yes, sir."

Simmons left the room, and Pickett turned to his grandfather, whose expression was inscrutable.

"You've made your point," he said. In fact, he was ashamed of his earlier outburst, and his humiliation was not lessened by his grandfather's determination to rub his nose in it. "You needn't drag those poor fellows from their beds."

The marquess made no reply, but watched the door expectantly. It opened a short time later to admit two tall young men wearing sleepy expressions and nightshirts whose tails had been hastily stuffed into their breeches.

"Yes, your lordship?" asked one, the same fellow who

had advised his colleague against silencing Pickett's protests with his fist.

"James, Charles, have either of you gone to Limehouse this evening?"

"Limehouse?" The more aggressive of the pair echoed incredulously. "What the dev—er, what would we be doing in Limehouse, your lordship?"

"Murdering my grandson's father," the marquess answered without so much as a blink.

"*Murdering*—? That's what he says, is it?" James regarded Pickett with an expression that suggested he now regretted his earlier restraint, be the fellow his nibs's grandson or no.

"No," Pickett put in hastily. "I only—I meant—"

"Very well," Lord Melrose continued, "just what were you doing, then?"

The question was put to the two footmen equally, but after the pair exchanged a quick glance, Charles spoke for both.

"After we fetched this fellow—your grandson, that is— we went back to our regular duties here. Your lordship will remember sending me with a message to Sir Matthew Whitby, inviting him for an evening of cards after dinner, and when I came back to Park Lane with his acceptance, you put the pair of us to work getting the study ready for Sir Matthew's arrival: setting up the card table and chairs, making sure glasses were at the ready, and so forth. Then after helping Mr. Simmons serve your lordship's dinner, we fetched the dirty dishes back down to the kitchen before eating our own meal and then helping clean up the lot. Mr. Simmons gave James a couple of bottles—one of brandy and another of port"—he glanced for confirmation at James, who nodded in agreement—"and had him set them out in readiness for your lordship's guest, while I lit the fire in the study. And then Mr. Simmons said as how we could go up to our bedchambers, so long as we held ourselves in readiness to clean up the study after Sir Matthew had gone. And after that, I guess we both went to bed. Of course, I read my Bible and said my prayers first," he added with a saintly air.

Alas, this display of piety was lost on his employer. "And what time would you say that was?" asked the marquess.

Another glance at one another for confirmation, and Charles said, "Midnight or thereabouts, your lordship."

Lord Melrose addressed himself to Pickett. "Which, I'm sure you will agree, would hardly allow them sufficient time to walk to Limehouse—for I would certainly not wish to be wish to be linked to the crime by the unhappy coincidence of someone recognizing my crest on the carriage door—locate your father from my description of a man I have not seen in more than a quarter of a century, lure that man into a back alley and stab him, then walk back to this house, dispose of any bloodstained garments, and climb into bed in time to be awakened by my butler and summoned to this room."

As Pickett could hardly dispute the matter, he was obliged to sit seething in silence while Lord Melrose thanked the two, begged their pardon for having unnecessarily roused them from their slumbers, and gave them permission to return to their beds.

"I said you'd made your point," Pickett reiterated once he and his grandfather were alone. "Did you really have to humiliate me in front of the household staff?"

"If you choose to barge into the house throwing about accusations of murder without first ascertaining the facts, I feel no obligation to shield you from the consequences of your own folly," replied the marquess, unrepentant.

Pickett had the lowering conviction that Mr. Colquhoun would be in complete agreement with his lordship on this point, and so made no attempt to defend actions he knew in retrospect to be indefensible.

"I—I beg your pardon," he said stiffly, trying not to choke on the words. "I can only say that I had just endured the crowning blow to a day of unwelcome surprises, although of course that is no excuse." He set aside his empty glass and rose to take his leave. "As you pointed out, it's very late. I'll trespass no longer on your—" *Your what?* "Hospitality" was hardly the word for it. "—your time," he concluded, then executed an excruciatingly correct bow and betook himself from the room.

"Not at all," his lordship said mockingly, accompanying him as far as the top of the stairs. "I daresay you acted with great courage. Who knows but what I might have decided to mete out to you the same fate that I dealt your father?"

Pickett paused on the stairs and turned back to address the marquess. "On the contrary, I knew myself to be quite safe with your lordship—unless and until some other claimant to the title turns up."

And on this Parthian shot, he descended the stairs with

his head held high, feeling the eyes of one marquess, one butler, and two footmen upon him as he retraced his steps to the front door and stepped out into the cold December night.

* * *

When he reached Curzon Street, he found that the house was dark, save for a single candle burning on a small table at the foot of the stairs; Rogers, it appeared, had not waited up for him. Pickett could not but be relieved. He didn't want to face anyone at the moment, not even his wife. If he was very quiet, he thought, taking the candle to light his way up the stairs, perhaps he could undress and slip into the camp bed without waking her.

In this, he was doomed to disappointment.

"John?" Julia asked sleepily, "did you go out, or was I dreaming?"

He was sorely tempted to deny it, to agree that she must have been dreaming and urge her to go back to sleep; after all, it could hardly be good for her to be burdened with images of violence and murder when she was so near to her confinement, but if he had learned anything in nine months of marriage, it was that his gently-born bride had no very high opinion of his withholding from her the more brutal aspects of his profession for her own good. No, he would be obliged to tell her the truth in the morning in any case, so sparing her now would only delay the inevitable.

On one aspect of his nocturnal activities, however, he was determined to remain silent. With any luck, she need never know of his invasion of his grandfather's Park Lane residence or his accusations of murder. He wasn't quite ready to absolve Lord Melrose entirely, but the combination of brandy and a brisk walk in the cold night air had brought home to him the realization that he had gone about it in the worst possible way. No, he would say nothing to Julia on that subject, but he would go about establishing the guilt or innocence of Lord Melrose just as he would that of any other suspect. After all, the man was nothing to him.

"Yes, I had to go out. Mr. Colquhoun came by; he needed me to come with him and—and identify a body. Sweetheart, my father was found dead. He's been murdered."

"Oh John, no!" She sat up in bed at once, and reached out to him. Hastily revising his plans, he slipped not into the despised camp bed, but into her arms. "And after you'd just got him back! How did it happen? Who could have done such a thing?"

"He was taken by surprise—stabbed in the back. As for who, well, I don't know. But"—his jaw tightened, and the determined set of his chin was one which his grandfather would have instantly recognized—"I intend to find out."

"Darling, are you sure that's wise, with you being so closely involved? After all, he *is* your father, and the investigation might turn up elements of his recent past that could only distress you."

"No one could tell me much about Da that I don't already know," he said, but even as he spoke the words, he knew they weren't true. Less than twelve hours earlier, he'd heard from his father's own lips things he'd never even imagined.

"Be that as it may," Julia persisted, "I'm a bit surprised that Mr. Colquhoun would countenance your involvement in the investigation, when you are so intimately connected to its subject."

Pickett readily conceded the point. "He didn't. But I'm not with Bow Street anymore and no longer accountable to Mr. Colquhoun. In other words," Pickett concluded with the faintest hint of a smile, "he can't stop me."

8

*In Which John Pickett Seeks Cultural Enlightenment
while Julia Receives a Caller*

Pickett awoke the next morning to a lingering sense of
nightmare that had nothing to do with the camp bed and
its hard, lumpy mattress. In fact, he realized as his sleep-
befogged brain swam into consciousness, he wasn't in the
camp bed at all. Suddenly all the upheavals of the last twenty-
four hours came rushing back: his abduction from Covent
Garden, followed by the discovery of the grandfather he'd not
known had existed; the unexpected reappearance of his father,
newly returned from Botany Bay; the crowded back room of
a Limehouse pub, and a white cloth drawn back to reveal the
still, lifeless form laid out on a table; and, finally, his own
half-crazed invasion of his grandfather's house and wild
accusations of murder, based on no more solid evidence than
a decades-old grudge and a collection of knives displayed in
a gentleman's study.

Squeezing his eyes shut, he rolled over with a groan, unwilling to face the memory of all he had said and done. What had he been thinking?

The answer was not far to seek. He *hadn't* been thinking, not to any noticeable degree. His had been a purely visceral reaction based on shock and, perhaps, exacerbated by his ambivalence toward the man who had sired him. Anger, even rage, was easier to summon than grief for the father who had been absent from his life for more than a decade, and easier still than to admit the guilt produced by the lack of any finer feelings.

But there was another whose grief would be unmixed with any more complicated emotion. Kit would have to be told, and the prospect of this conversation filled him with dread. He dashed a hand over his eyes and forced himself to open them.

"Awake so soon?" asked a solicitous feminine voice.

There were certainly worse sights to wake up to. Julia sat beside him looking fresh and lovely, with pillows at her back and a tray across her knees. She must have been awake for some time, while he'd slept through the usual morning sounds of servants rebuilding the fire in the grate and serving the mistress of the house her breakfast.

"I'd hoped you would be able to sleep later," she continued. "You must have been out most of the night."

Determined to make as little of the night's interruptions as possible, Pickett forced himself up to a sitting position and leaned over to kiss her good morning. As he bent over her, an untidy lock of brown hair fell over his forehead, and when

Julia reached up a hand to brush it back, he captured the hand and kissed it too.

"I'm sorry all my coming and going disturbed you," he said contritely. "I know you haven't been sleeping well lately."

"You did what you had to do," she said firmly, then on a lighter note added, "As for my sleeping difficulties, it shouldn't be much longer now. Every morning, I wake up thinking, 'This could be the day!' And every night I go to bed disappointed."

Pickett could sympathize; she wasn't the only one going to bed disappointed, albeit for a different (if not entirely unrelated) reason. He reminded himself that he'd had to be content with expressing his love for her in nonphysical ways long before he'd ever had cause to hope for more; he could do so again, for as long as it took. Even lying in bed with her in his arms, as he'd done the previous night—a short reprieve from the camp bed—was more than he'd ever dreamed possible only a year ago. He only hoped that, if she found childbirth too excruciating to risk a second pregnancy, she would at least allow him to sleep in the same bed, even if she didn't want him to touch her while they were there.

"Would you like your breakfast brought up?" she asked, reaching for the bell pull. "I can ring for a second tray, if you wish."

He shook his head, albeit with considerable regret. "Thank you, love, but I'd best not. I want to be downstairs before Kit comes down."

"John," she said, her tone suddenly grown serious, "if

you would prefer that I be the one to break the news to him, you have only to say the word. He and I became quite close, you know, while you were at the Larches."

He shook his head. "You're sweet to offer, but that's something I have to do myself." He sighed. "Why didn't I let him keep that blasted watch?"

"You can give it back to him after you've retrieved your father's belongings," she pointed out. "You can say with all honesty that your father wanted him to have it."

"I suppose I'll be responsible for disposing of all Da's things." He had not considered this prospect before, and now he could feel the weight of these new and unwanted responsibilities settling on his shoulders like the sacks of coal he'd hauled long ago in exchange for room and board. "Even if he made a will—which I doubt—Kit won't be mentioned in it. Da didn't even know he existed before yesterday, and illegitimate children have no rights under the law. Granted, Da wouldn't have left much, but it's the principle of the thing: I was born within the bonds of matrimony; he wasn't. It's a rotten deal for him, but there it is."

"What's a rotten deal?" asked Kit, bounding into the room at that moment, already fully dressed and breakfasted, if the smear of black currant jam on the corner of his mouth was anything to judge by. "John, d'you know where Da is? He's not downstairs, and his bed isn't even mussed! Has he gone out already, or did he stay out all night?"

Pickett heaved a sigh. The time, it seemed, was at hand. "Come here, Kit, and sit down." He patted a spot on the mattress beside him.

Kit, suddenly wary, looked at his brother and sister-in-law in turn, then crawled onto the bed and sat down where Pickett had indicated.

"Something's wrong. It's Da, isn't it." It was a statement, not a question.

"Well, yes," Pickett confessed. "Sometime after Da left yesterday, he suffered a—" *A what?* An accident? No one was "accidentally" stabbed in the back. The truth, he decided, would have to do. "He suffered an—an attack, of sorts, and was badly injured."

"Is he dead?" asked Kit, never one to mince words.

Pickett took a deep breath. "Yes, I'm afraid he is."

Kit stared into his brother's face for a long moment, then leapt down from the bed and darted from the room. In the next instant, Pickett heard the pounding of footsteps on the stairs.

He sighed. "That went well."

Julia put her hand over his and gave it a squeeze. "Give him time."

In fact, Kit required even less time than she had anticipated. Only a few minutes later, the sound of footsteps on the stairs heralded his return, this time accompanied by the *clink-clink* of metal on porcelain. Kit entered the bedchamber a moment later, holding in his hands a hollow porcelain pig with a cork plug in place of a tail. He squirmed back onto the bed, then pulled out the cork tail with a *pop!* and turned the ceramic swine upside-down. A stream of copper coins poured out—chunky "cartwheel" tuppences and shiny new pennies, along with a quantity of humbler ha'pennies and farthings—all the wealth of which a ten-year-old boy was possessed, piled together in a mound that gleamed dully against the pristine fabric of the counterpane.

"This is for you," Kit said in a rush. "I want to hire you to find out who killed Da."

"Kit, you don't have to—" Pickett began, then stopped. *You don't have to pay me for what I already intend to do*, he'd meant to say. But to deny his young half-brother the opportunity to participate in bringing their father's killer to justice would only serve to emphasize Kit's inferior standing as Gentleman Jack's "other," son: illegitimate, his very existence unknown to their father until just yesterday, forever "less than" his elder brother. He knew enough of the Pickett pride to recognize that Kit would someday have to wrestle his own demons, once he was old enough to realize that the dubious circumstances of his birth, which never raised an eyebrow in St. Giles and its environs, were regarded very differently in the eyes of society and the law. Anything he might do now to confirm his brother's place within the family could only ease the boy's way later on.

And so he spread the coins and studied them for a long moment—in fact, he was tallying them up in his head and calculating the smallest amount he might take without arousing his brother's suspicions, but Kit didn't have to know that—then counted out coins amounting to just over half the boy's total savings.

"I think this should be enough to go on with," he said at last.

Kit let out a long breath, and Pickett was rather touched to realize that his brother had feared he would not have the wherewithal to retain the services of so exalted an investigator as John Pickett of Bow Street.

"And you'll let me know how you're doing?" asked Kit, attempting with mixed success to pour his remaining coins back into his pig's rump.

"I'll give you weekly progress reports," Pickett said, briskly businesslike. "Although if at any time you have questions, you may require me to render a full accounting. Is that agreeable?"

Kit was understood to say that it was.

"Well, then," Pickett said, scooping up his fee, "take the rest of your money back upstairs before it falls off the mattress and rolls under the bed."

As Kit hurried off to obey this command, Pickett turned and found Julia regarding him quizzically.

"What?" he asked, all at sea.

She leaned over to kiss him. "I love you, John Pickett. You know that, don't you?"

"I do," he said. "But someday, after this baby is born, I shall require you to render a full accounting."

* * *

Given that his father's murder had taken place late at night, and the coroner summoned later still, Pickett thought it unlikely that the inquest would take place before midafternoon. Granted, Mr. Colquhoun had borne him away before this topic had been raised—not that he'd complained at the time—but Pickett thought it unlikely that the coroner had gone door to door rousing the neighborhood until he'd enlisted the requisite seven to twelve men to serve as jurors.

Then, too, while the Grapes had been a convenient place for the body to be brought until other arrangements could be made, the pub's narrow frontage precluded its having a room large enough for holding the inquest, meaning the coroner would be obliged to locate a larger public house whose proprietor would be willing to host the proceedings.

All of which meant he had a few hours' grace in which to learn what he could about the murder weapon before surrendering it to the magistrate. And so, after he'd breakfasted downstairs with Kit, he returned to his bedchamber to brush his teeth and shave.

"Sweetheart"—his eyes met Julia's in the mirror over the washstand—"what do you know about the British Museum?"

She had known that he meant to go out immediately after breakfast, but she had assumed he had in mind some errand connected to his father's death, either as the son of the deceased or as an independent agent making inquiries into the murder. That he should choose this of all possible times to go on a pleasure outing left her nonplussed.

"I've never given it much thought," she said, trying not to sound as bewildered as she felt. "Why do you ask?"

"I'm wondering if someone there might be able to tell me something about that knife."

He had shown it to her as soon as they could be certain that Kit would not interrupt, and now she wrinkled her nose at the thought of the curious knife with its bloodstained blade of sharpened stone.

"I daresay they will know as much about it as anyone else."

"There's one problem solved, then."

Having finished his ablutions, he wiped his face with a towel and crossed the room to the clothes-press, where he stood regarding its contents for a long moment.

"Now, what's the most suitable thing to wear to a museum?" he asked.

"Surely you don't intend to go today!"

He turned away from his contemplation of the clothes-press and its contents. "Sweetheart, I can't keep a valuable piece of evidence indefinitely. I'll have to return it before the inquest."

"Yes, but have you considered that perhaps Kit needs you?" she suggested gently.

"It's for Kit's sake that I have to go. Remember," he added with a hint of a smile, "he's paying me nine pence."

"Very well, then," Julia said, changing tactics, have you thought that perhaps *I* need you?"

This suggestion had the effect of wiping the smile from his face as his gaze fell to the bulge of her abdomen. "Are you—? Is it—?"

"Not the baby, no," she assured him hastily. "Perhaps it would be more accurate to say that I thought *you* might need *me*."

"Always." Abandoning, at least for the nonce, the question of dress, he strode across the room to the bed and took her in his arms, drawing her as close as their child would permit.

She leaned her head against his chest with a sigh of contentment. "I know you want to find your father's killer, but there's nothing wrong with taking a little time to mourn your loss first. The British Museum will still be there."

"Very likely," he agreed without hesitation. "But the knife won't. I have to give it back to Mr. Colquhoun, remember?"

"I could make you a sketch of it," she suggested. "You could take that to the museum instead."

His arms tightened around her. He dropped a kiss onto the top of her head, but said, "It's kind of you to offer, sweetheart. But my father went to his death believing I'd betrayed him by working for Mr. Colquhoun. If I don't at least use the things I learned at Bow Street to bring Da's killer to justice, then—well, I'd say he was right."

From this stance he would not be moved. Conceding defeat, Julia made suitable suggestions as to what he might wear, then watched with an appreciative eye as he stripped off his dressing gown and nightshirt and arrayed himself in these garments. She lifted her face for his goodbye kiss, then listened for his footsteps descending the stairs and the sound of the front door opening and closing behind him.

She hoped the museum would yield the information he sought, but she suspected it was not love so much as guilt that drove him.

Obeying a sudden impulse, she threw back the counterpane and eased herself carefully out of bed, then padded in her bare feet to the elegant rosewood writing desk beneath the window. She dipped a quill in the inkwell and scrawled a few words, then folded the note, returned with it to the bed, and gave a tug to the bellpull.

* * *

"Oh, Emily, thank heaven!" Reasoning that she had defied doctor's orders enough during the last twenty-four hours, Julia did not rise to greet her visitor, but held out her hand as if reaching for a lifeline. "I was so afraid you might have gone out!"

"Surely I wasn't so tardy as all that!" Breezing past the butler who had just announced her, Lady Dunnington took Julia's hand and gave it a reassuring squeeze. "I came as soon as I received your note."

"I knew you would, if only you were at home," Julia said warmly. "I daresay it only seems like a long time because of everything that has happened since yesterday—but never mind that! Rogers, if you will be so good as to set a chair for Lady Dunnington, I shan't keep you any longer."

"Very good, madam." He picked up the nearest of the two wing chairs facing the fire and moved it to his mistress's bedside, positioning it at an angle that would allow Julia to converse easily with anyone seated in it. "Do you wish for some refreshment? I believe there are freshly-baked fairy cakes to be had, in addition to tea or perhaps sherry."

"Then do let's have them, for I'm famished!" put in Emily, addressing the butler over her shoulder as she settled herself in the chair he had placed for her.

"Yes, please, Rogers," Julia concurred, smiling at him. "We would not want poor Lady Dunnington to starve. Oh, and pray make sure some are taken upstairs to Kit, as well."

"Begging your pardon, madam, but I believe Master Kit is in the kitchen assisting Cook with their preparation."

"Oh, is he? In that case, let us have them at once, while there are still some to be had! The last twenty-four hours have been trying for all of us," she said to Lady Dunnington after Rogers had gone, "and Kit has been particularly affected—"

She broke off abruptly, for Lady Dunnington was no longer listening. Instead, Emily stared off to the left in wide-eyed astonishment. Following the line of her gaze, Julia realized the object of her amazement was the camp bed that took up a great deal too much of the dressing room.

"No, no, it isn't that," she said, laughing. "I haven't banished John from my bed. Did you think I had summoned you to commiserate with me after a quarrel? Nothing of the sort, I assure you. In fact, the current sleeping arrangements were not my idea, but the midwife's. And then, only a few days later, Dr. Gilroy put me on bed rest until my confinement. I—I was bleeding a little," she confessed in a much more serious vein.

Lady Dunnington's astonishment turned to dismay. "Julia!"

"Not much, you understand, and only for a day or two," she put in hastily. "But Dr. Gilroy thought it best not to take unnecessary chances. As for the camp bed, it is certainly not ideal, but better by far than requiring poor John to remove to the best guest chamber."

"It would be useless, I suppose," mused Lady Dunnington, "to point out that separate bedchambers are the norm rather than the exception in most noble households."

"Indeed it would, for that was precisely the arrangement that Frederick and I had for years," Julia agreed. "And yet, there is—at least, there *was*—something so very pleasant in knowing one has only to reach out one's hand to—that is, even if it doesn't lead to—rather, if nothing of an—an amorous nature is likely to—to—"

"Pray, say no more," interrupted Lady Dunnington, seeing her friend foundering in a sea of connubial recollections. "We shall take it as read, then, that it was not for any reason pertaining to marital strife that you wished to see me. What was it, then? Sheer boredom, or something else entirely?"

"Something else." Julia put a hand to her forehead in the manner of one quite overwhelmed. "Oh Emily, I scarcely know where to start! First of all, do you remember telling me a few weeks ago about Lord Melrose's grandson?"

"Of course I do! Granted, I have no great liking for Lord Melrose, but one can't help but pity him. It must go very hard with so proud a man, being obliged to beg the king for the privilege of seeing his titles and estates devolve upon a fellow who very likely eats with his knife. Can you imagine?"

In fact, Julia could imagine entirely too well, but she said only, "I can assure you that Lord Melrose's grandson does *not* eat with his knife."

"Oh?" Lady Dunnington's eyebrows rose in the manner of one who scents a particularly juicy *on dit*. "How do you know?"

"Because he's John."

"I beg your pardon?" asked Lady Dunnington, all at sea.

"He's John," Julia repeated. "*My* John. He's Lord Melrose's grandson."

At this revelation, Lady Dunnington's eyebrows all but disappeared into her hairline. Her jaw dropped, giving Julia a brief glimpse of her parted lips before she pressed both hands to her mouth. A moment later her shoulders began to shake, and Julia realized with some indignation that she was laughing.

"I should like to know what you find so funny about it," she said testily.

"I'm—sorry," Lady Dunnington said in between gales of laughter. "It's just that—I'm sure I wish King George many years of good health, but I can't help thinking of someday when he is gone, and Prinny becomes king, and—and—"

She went off into another paroxysm, and Julia was obliged to wait until she regained control of her mirth before she could discover just what it was that her friend found so amusing.

"—And at the coronation, your Mr. Pickett will take precedence over Lord Fieldhurst!"

"Oh, heavens!" Far from taking offense, Julia found herself smiling at the picture conjured by Lady Dunnington's words. "In crimson velvet and ermine, with a coronet of gold strawberry leaves. The poor darling!"

Lady Dunnington shook her head. "In general, I believe it is wise to humor a lady in the final stages of childbearing, but honesty compels me to point out that 'poor' is the very *last* word most people would choose to describe such a change in status."

"Very likely," Julia agreed. "But then, John is not 'most people.' He doesn't want it, you see."

"If we were speaking of anyone else, I would say he was putting on airs to be interesting, but in the case of your husband, I can readily believe it. What, pray, are his objections?"

Julia considered this question for a long moment before answering. "Quite aside from the fact that he would be completely out of his depth, he doesn't want to be beholden to Lord Melrose in any way, for anything. Which brings me to the second upheaval of the past twenty-four hours."

It was at that moment that Rogers returned with the tea tray, so Julia was obliged to hold her tongue while tea was poured and fairy cakes were served. Once the butler had left the two ladies alone, however, she described for Lady Dunnington the unexpected return of Gentleman Jack Pickett from Botany Bay and his disclosures regarding her husband's parentage, followed by his violent death that very night. Lady Dunnington listened in silence, the creases in her usually smooth brow deepening with each new revelation.

"And you say all of this was the very same day that Lord Melrose made himself known to your Mr. Pickett?" she asked at the end of this recital. "Did he know about Mr. Pickett Senior—I say, may I call him Gentleman Jack? All these 'Mr. Picketts' are confusing." Receiving an answer in the affirmative, she rephrased the question. "Did Lord Melrose know Gentleman Jack had returned to England, do you suppose?"

"I think he must have done." There was no one else near enough to overhear their conversation, Julia lowered her voice nonetheless. She had not known until Lady Dunnington had swept into the room just how badly she had needed to confide in someone—someone who, unlike her husband, was not personally connected to any of the players, and therefore could not be distressed by any speculations regarding them. "John's father and grandfather—two men who haven't been in contact with one another for twenty-five years—turning up not only on the same day, but within a few hours of each other? It seems a very unlikely coincidence."

"Perhaps not so much as it appears at first glance," countered Lady Dunnington. "If Lord Melrose knew that Gentleman Jack had been given a ten-year sentence, he must have known that those ten years are now up, and that Gentleman Jack might well be returning to England."

"Yes, but on the very same day that he had John snatched off the street and brought to him in Park Lane?"

The countess shrugged. "Why not? If Lord Melrose has kept up with his grandson's whereabouts all these years, would it be so unusual for him to have arranged for some obliging stevedore to notify him of any ships arriving from New South Wales?" Her eyes narrowed in sudden suspicion. "But that's not what's really troubling you, is it? What you're really wondering is whether Lord Melrose, having learned of Gentleman Jack's return, arranged for him to be killed."

Julia took a deep breath. "Yes, that's it. John hasn't mentioned such a possibility, and I'll admit it sounds absurd when one says it out loud, but—well, *someone* killed him, and barring the possibility of his merely having the misfortune to have been in the wrong place at the wrong time, that someone must have had a reason."

"And that reason is?" prompted Lady Dunnington.

"Having made up his mind to lick John into shape to succeed him, Lord Melrose might have thought he could be more easily manipulated without his father near at hand to exert an opposing influence—not that it would work, of course, for John is not so easily led." She shook her head as if to clear it. "But this is mere conjecture on my part. Truth to tell, Emily, I'm not sufficiently well acquainted with Lord Melrose to form any opinion as to what he might or might not do."

She could not have guessed just how soon this state of affairs was about to be remedied.

* * *

Whatever his motivation for making inquiries at the British Museum—whether love, or guilt, or some uneasy mix of the two—Pickett was fortunate in that recent changes to the policies of that establishment made it no longer necessary to apply to the porter for a ticket allowing one to return to the museum at a designated time. Instead, he was able to enter the building without any hindrance beyond the baleful looks cast down upon him by the stuffed giraffes on display at the top of the stairs. Undaunted by these silent witnesses, he mounted the stairs, but upon reaching the upper floor, he realized he had no idea of what, or whom, he was looking for. Fortunately, it was not long before a middle-aged man of scholarly mien took pity upon him.

"Pardon me, sir," he said, approaching Pickett just as that young man had paused to stare in morbid fascination at an Egyptian mummy, resolving to introduce Kit to these exotic wonders at no very distant date. "May I be of some assistance? My name is Oliphant; I have the honor of being one of the caretakers of these wonderful objects."

"Yes, please, Mr. Oliphant." Pickett said, withdrawing the bulky handkerchief once more from the inside pocket of his coat. "John Pickett, of—of Curzon Street." How long would it be, he wondered, before the impulse to say "of Bow Street" was finally banished?

But he had no time to ponder the question now. Under the curator's interested gaze, he unfolded the handkerchief to expose the curious weapon within. "I was wondering if someone here could tell me about—this."

"Dear me." Mr. Oliphant leaned forward, adjusting his spectacles for a better look. "Dear me."

"Do you know what it is?" Recognizing the idiocy of this question, Pickett hastily corrected himself. "That is, I know it's a knife, but it's unlike any knife I've ever seen before. Can you tell me anything about it? Where it may have come from, who might possess such a weapon—anything, really."

Mr. Oliphant took the knife from Pickett, being careful to handle it only by the handkerchief enfolding it.

"As a matter of fact," Mr. Oliphant said, straightening himself to regard Pickett with a hint of a smile, "I can. Not because of anything in the museum's collection, you understand, but because I have a cousin who for several years held an administrative position in our colony in Port Jackson."

Pickett's expressive brown eyes lit with recognition. "Oh?"

The curator nodded. "That is the collective name for the

penal colony of Botany Bay and its environs." He gestured toward the knife in its cradle of white linen. "The proper name for this particular weapon is a leilira knife. The double-edged blade is struck from stone, and the handle, if one can call it that, is made of resin and painted with red ochre. It is but one example of many such knives made and used by the aboriginal tribes of that region."

"You're sure of this?" Pickett asked, but even as he asked the question, he knew no doubt.

"Oh, quite sure. My cousin brought back many similar curiosities when he returned to England upon his retirement." His brow wrinkled as he studied the dried brown flakes clinging to the sharp edges of the blade. "Although since it appears that this one has been used recently, I sincerely hope it is not one of his."

Pickett shook his head. "It was found in an alley in Limehouse."

Of course, it had been lodged in his father's back at the time, but he saw no reason to divulge this rather gruesome detail. Instead, he thanked Mr. Oliphant for his assistance, and returned to Curzon Street, where a note from the coroner had been delivered only half an hour earlier, informing him that the inquest had been scheduled for that afternoon at three o'clock at the Chalk and Cheese in Limehouse.

9

In Which Is Held an Inquest
into the Death of Gentleman Jack Pickett

It seemed strange, Pickett thought, to think that he would be attending an inquest not as an investigating officer, but as the subject's next of kin. Stripping off the fashionable coat he had worn for his interview at the British Museum, he dug into the recesses of the clothes-press and pulled out the sober black coat (a relic of the days before his marriage) that he'd worn during his three miserable weeks as a clerk in the City.

"I suppose," Julia said thoughtfully, affixing a black armband to his left sleeve just above the elbow, "that I had best select a couple of gowns for Betsy to dye. I should think one for now and one for later, after the baby is born, would be sufficient."

"Sufficient for what?" asked Pickett, studying the effects of her labor in the mirror over her dressing table.

"For mourning," she pointed out, as if this should have

been obvious—as indeed it would have been, had he been less distracted by his own thoughts. "He *was* your father, after all, and I would not wish to appear disrespectful—"

"Do you mean," demanded Pickett, his wife having got his full attention at last, "that you intend to go into *mourning?*"

"Why, yes, of course," Julia said, puzzled by his vehemence. "It is customary, you know—"

"I don't care a button for 'customary'! Sweetheart, the day after we met, you went into mourning for Lord Fieldhurst. From that day until the night of the Drury Lane Theatre fire— almost a year, all told—I saw you in nothing but black. I hope never to see you wear black again."

"But John, pray consider how very odd it would look," protested Julia, albeit halfheartedly. In truth, she had spent much of the first year of their acquaintance chafing under the knowledge that her newly widowed state prevented her from looking her best before the young Bow Street Runner whose good opinion she coveted for reasons she'd not dared examine too closely. "People would say—"

"People have been saying one thing or another about us for the last nine months, most of it unflattering," he pointed out with unassailable logic. "Besides, since you're bedridden, at least for the nonce, no one sees you anyway. Who's to know?"

"*I'll* know," she said, although the element of doubt that had crept into her voice suggested she was wavering.

She completed her operation on his sleeve, and as she released it, he put his now-unencumbered arm around her waist and drew her close. "If there is one thing that can be said of my father, it is that he knew how to appreciate a beautiful woman. Trust me, love. He would agree with me on this."

* * *

As Limehouse was some distance east of the City, and still further east of Mayfair, Pickett hired a hackney to convey him to the Chalk and Cheese, the public house where the inquest was to be held. He was set down before this establishment some ten minutes before the proceedings were set to begin, and when he entered the room that had been pressed into service in the cause of justice, he was not surprised to see Mr. Colquhoun was already there. If anything was needed to convince him he had done the right thing in taking the murder weapon to the British Museum that morning, it came in the haste with which the magistrate approached him. Clearly, he was not going to be allowed to retain possession of the murder weapon any longer than absolutely necessary.

"I'll take that knife from you now," Mr. Colquhoun said by way of greeting, holding out his hand in expectation. "Did you learn anything from it?"

"My original theory was, um, disproven," Pickett confessed, inwardly cringing at the memory of his invasion of Lord Melrose's house in Park Lane. "But I did learn something about its provenance. It's a leilira knife, made by the aboriginal people of the Antipodes. So it appears my father was murdered by someone he knew there, or someone he met on the ship during the voyage home."

"Not necessarily," the magistrate cautioned. "Bear in

mind that almost everyone who lives and works in Limehouse is connected with the sea trade in some capacity. There might be any number of people who have come into possession of such curiosities through buying or bartering for them, or even having been given one as a gift, without ever setting foot on colonial soil. The possibility of your father's having had the misfortune to be in the wrong place at the wrong time can't be dismissed."

"Yes, sir," Pickett agreed, although privately he doubted it. It had always seemed to him that his father had the devil's own luck. Before he could point out this contradiction, however, the proceedings were called to order, and he was obliged to take his seat.

In fact, he was fortunate to find a seat at all, for the room was so crammed with people that several of those present were obliged to stand. Looking about, Pickett recognized several of the men he had seen the previous evening: the coroner, the physician, and the magistrate within whose jurisdiction the body had been found, along with the two youths who had found it—Ned and his compatriot, whose name, if Pickett had heard it at all, he could not remember.

The seven members of the jury were unknown to him, but this was hardly surprising: he'd rarely had cause to venture this far east of the City, even in his Bow Street days.

As for the remainder of those present, many—perhaps most—were probably mere curiosity-seekers. After a five-year career with Bow Street, Pickett no longer wondered how word of the inquest had spread so quickly; Londoners appeared to have some sixth sense where spectacular crimes were concerned. Still, he wasn't quite certain how many of the people had flocked to the Chalk and Cheese in order to satisfy a morbid fascination for violent death, and how many had come specifically because it was Gentleman Jack Pickett who had in this instance been the victim; his father's checkered career had rarely (if ever) taken him so far east as Limehouse, but Gentleman Jack's reputation was widely known amongst a certain set—descendants, no doubt, of the same persons who had so eagerly followed Jack Sheppard's misadventures a century earlier.

And yet, a few of those present didn't seem to fit into either of these categories. Their countenances wore expressions too sober to suggest a taste for lurid entertainment, their overall appearances too respectable to be old acquaintances of his father come to pay their last respects.

In the third row sat a tall, thin man of about forty whose rusty black tailcoat, stooped shoulders, and wire-rimmed spectacles forcibly recalled to Pickett's mind some of the more senior clerks in the counting-house of Ludlow & Ludlow. The one rather glaring difference was the fact that this man's spectacles perched on a nose that was pink and peeling, as if, after a lifetime spent largely indoors, he had at some time in the not-to-distant past been subjected to prolonged exposure to the sun.

Seated in the center of the next row was a man who gave Pickett the impression of a sea-farer, although he could not say on what, exactly, this impression was based, save for the weathered brown face that also made the man's age impossible to estimate with any expectation of accuracy.

Directly behind him sat a lady wearing a bonnet heavily trimmed with black lace, including a veil that covered most of her face. Pickett wondered what made him so certain that she was a lady, instead of some lesser-born female, and decided it was her posture: Her spine never touched the back of her chair, as if she feared contamination from so low an establishment—which raised the question of why, then, she had chosen to attend at all. Pickett put her age at somewhere in her thirties, and the evidence supporting this estimation was not far to seek: The fact that she seemed to be unaccompanied by either a servant or a spouse suggested a certain age, and yet the chin under which the ribbons of her bonnet were tied still appeared smooth and firm.

He recalled his father having mentioned a lady—he had called her a lady, hadn't he?—with whom he had become acquainted on the ship and in whom he had expressed an amorous interest, and wondered if this woman might be she. In any case, Pickett supposed he shouldn't wonder at there being a woman present at his father's inquest; the only real surprise was that there weren't more.

This thought led, not unnaturally, to Moll, of whom there was no sign. In truth, Pickett was not quite certain whether to be sorry or glad of her absence. Granted, he could very happily live the rest of his life without ever again seeing the woman who, according to his father, had been set in his mother's place out of necessity, and who had failed in that rôle so abysmally. Moll's absence suggested that she was as yet unaware of her former cully's death, quite possibly unaware that he had returned to England at all. If that was the case, did he have a moral obligation to call on her to inform her of the fact? He hoped not; the last time he had seen Moll, she had proposed that he, now that he was grown to manhood, should take his father's place in that capacity. Pickett shuddered at the memory. There wasn't enough Blue Ruin in all of St. Giles to make him consider the prospect with anything but revulsion. Still, Moll had loved his father, in her way. More to the point, she had borne him a second son: his own half-brother, Kit, of whose existence his father had been wholly ignorant scarcely more than twenty-four hours earlier. Surely that fact alone was obligation enough—or wasn't it?

This moral dilemma was interrupted as the coroner addressed his opening remarks to the jury, and it was with some relief that Pickett turned his thoughts to the matter at hand.

"Let me remind you," the coroner instructed the seven men who comprised the jury, "that this is an inquest, not a trial. It is not your responsibility to determine whose hand held the knife, nor should you indulge in any speculation as to that point. Your duty is merely to determine the cause of death, whether by accident or misadventure, suicide, or intentional murder by person or persons unknown. This, and *only* this, is the question you must consider as you hear the facts of the case."

The facts, such as they were, offered little enough to go on. Pickett himself was the first person called upon to testify, primarily for the purpose of identifying the deceased and giving a brief account of his father's last day of life: his return to London from the penal colony of Botany Bay, his setting out that evening for Limehouse with the expressed intention of returning to his son's house in Curzon Street, albeit at an unspecified time, and, finally, his own visit from the Bow Street magistrate with news of his father's death. Pickett couldn't help noticing that, although he played a much more passive rôle in this inquest than in any of the dozens of such proceedings he had attended over his five-year career with Bow Street, he was treated with far more respect than in any of those other inquests at which his testimony had been of much more significance so far as the law was concerned. He reflected rather cynically that he might have had "Bereaved Son" tattooed on his forehead.

After he was invited to return to his seat, however, the first of the two boys who had discovered the body was summoned, and the mood in the crowded pub changed from solemn condolence to something akin to eager anticipation.

When questioned, Ned Mullins, stiff and uncomfortable in his Sunday-best clothes, recounted having left the Grapes in Narrow Street some few minutes before midnight with his boon companion, Bob Pendleton, and had cut through Gin Alley to Queen Street.

"It bein' the quickest way to get to the Rope Walk, where I lives with my aunt and uncle," Ned explained.

They'd made as if to pass a man lying in street, assuming he was the worse for drink, until Bob had noticed a trickle of blood coming from the corner of his mouth. Even then, it hadn't occurred to them that the man was dead, only that he'd been beaten up and perhaps robbed by someone belonging to the rougher element usually to be found loitering about the waterfront late at night.

"So we went to see if we could be of any help to the fellow," Ned recalled, "only when Bob shook him by the shoulder—him not meaning any disrespect, mind, but not getting any response any other way, y'see—his head sort of flopped back, limp as a rag doll. And then I caught a glimpse of something dark on the back of the fellow's coat, only it wasn't a shadow, for Bob had a lantern with him, what with his mum bein' a widow who don't like him to be out so late at night. So I told Bob to roll him over, which he did, and we seen the back of his coat cut open and all drenched in blood, and there underneath him a knife like none I've ever seen in all my born days! We reckoned somebody must'a stuck it in his back, right between his shoulder blades."

"Yes, Mr. Mullins, that will do," said the coroner, cutting off this bit of deduction lest the jury be influenced by it. "You are to tell only what you saw or heard, not what you thought."

"Yessir." Ned, much chastened, dipped his head in acknowledgement. "Only there weren't much to hear, since the fellow was as near to bein' dead as made no odds. He only spoke the one word."

"Oh?" the coroner's voice sharpened. "You said nothing of this last night. What one word did he say?"

"It didn't seem to mean nothin'," Ned insisted. "It was so soft I wasn't sure at first that I really heard it at all, not 'til Bob said he heard it, too."

"And what was it that you and Bob both heard?"

"It was a woman's name," recalled Ned. "It weren't nothing but a whisper, really."

Pickett glanced toward the veiled lady in the fifth row. If her posture had been erect before, she was stiff as a ramrod now. He could practically feel the tension emanating from her halfway across the room.

"And just what, precisely, was this woman's name?" the coroner asked, his patience obviously wearing thin.

" 'Lydia,' " the boy said at last. "Just that...Lydia. And then he was gone."

The veiled lady suddenly slumped in evident relief, and Pickett realized she had feared it might be her own name that had been spoken by the dying man. His father's shipboard inamorata, perhaps? It would certainly go a long way toward explaining her presence at the inquest, but who was she? Clearly, it behooved him to obtain a look at the ship's manifest; this document, as he had learned during his brief career as a counting-house clerk, would list the names of the ship's passengers as well as itemizing its cargo.

Upon being called to give his evidence, Bob Pendleton corroborated Ned's testimony, although he was less forthcoming than Ned had been, and so the coroner did not detain him for long. He sent the boy back to his seat and summoned the doctor, the same man Pickett had seen in the back room of the Grapes the previous night.

"Will you please state your name and profession for the jury?" prompted the coroner.

"Jonathan Carstairs, physician and surgeon," came the reply.

"You examined the body of the deceased last night?"

The doctor inclined his head. "I did."

"And what did you deduce from your examination?"

The doctor launched into a description so larded with technical jargon as to be virtually incomprehensible to the layman. The coroner allowed him to continue until at last he ran down, then said, "Once again, if you please, in plain English this time."

"In short, the deceased suffered a stab wound to the back. Although one cannot be certain without an autopsy, it appears that the blade punctured the right lung. He would have died within a very short time, and as the lungs filled with blood, he would have been unable to draw sufficient breath to shout for help."

"In your opinion, could such a wound have been the result of an accident?"

The doctor's eyebrows rose, and he blinked in surprise. "If it was, then I can only say that the victim must have been prodigiously unlucky. In order to puncture the lung, the flat of the blade"—he demonstrated with his hand held palm down— "must have passed between the ribs. To intentionally strike with such accuracy would be difficult enough; to do so as a result of random chance—well, it staggers the imagination," the doctor concluded, shaking his head in disbelief.

"Very well, then, do you suppose such a wound could have been self-inflicted?"

"In other words, could the deceased have committed suicide? The obvious answer, of course, is no; that is, it would have been impossible for him to reach behind his back"— once again he demonstrated, closing his fist about the hilt of an imaginary knife and stretching his arm behind his own back—"and stab himself with sufficient force to penetrate three layers of clothing, a dense layer of skin and muscle, and finally a lung—aside from the fact that it would be a damned silly way to go about the thing, even if he were so inclined. Although…" The doctor's voice trailed off, and he frowned thoughtfully.

"Go on," urged the coroner.

"It seems to me that if a man is tired of living and yet can't quite bring himself to do the deed, he might deliberately put himself in harm's way, and trust to some obliging member of the criminal classes to do the rest. One can't help but wonder why he was alone in such an insalubrious spot at so late an hour."

"Have you any reason to suspect he might have done such a thing?" asked the coroner, clearly taken aback.

"None at all," the doctor hastily demurred. "I had never laid eyes on the man until last night, after he was already dead. I would not presume to make any such judgment on his state of mind."

"Nor are you"—the coroner turned to issue a caveat to the jury—"to engage in any such speculations. If you believe the hand that held the knife to have been anyone's but the deceased's own, then suicide is not a legitimate verdict, no matter what the deceased may have thought or hoped."

And with this stern warning ringing in their ears, the jury withdrew to begin their deliberations.

* * *

Having tried and failed to persuade Kit that he would have been bored to tears had he prevailed upon his brother to take him to the inquest—an argument which she then inadvertently destroyed by assuring him that John would certainly tell him anything interesting that had been revealed during this procedure—Julia had seized upon the happy notion of inviting him to sit cross-legged on the foot of her bed and read aloud to her from Malory's tales of King Arthur. In a little more than a month, Kit would be going off to school, and while she could do nothing about his complete lack of Latin, she could at least see to it that he was as literate as possible in his native language. She was well aware of the attraction the stories of Camelot and its knights held for boys, for she remembered her brother-in-law, Jamie Pennington, at the age of twelve, and how any stick discovered lying on the ground was instantly transformed into the sword Excalibur in his hand. Kit, only a little younger than Jamie had been, would very likely prove to be equally susceptible.

The young Arthur had scarcely pulled the sword from the stone, however, when they were interrupted by a light scratching at the door, and a moment later Rogers peered into the room.

"Begging your pardon, madam, but Lord Melrose is below, and is quite insistent upon seeing you."

"Me?" asked Julia in some surprise. "You are quite certain it was not Mr. Pickett he wished to see?"

Rogers inclined his head. "Quite certain, ma'am. I told him the young master was not at home, and he said he had not come to call on that—well, never mind his exact words. Suffice it to say that he described the young master in the most unflattering terms, and said he wished to see the lady of the house."

"Oh, dear," she said with a sigh. It was hardly surprising that, having made himself known to his grandson, Lord Melrose should wish to make the acquaintance of that grandson's wife—his "St. Giles wench," as she recalled—but she had neither expected nor desired that meeting to take place so soon. "I shall have to see him, Rogers, but I will *not* do it here! Show him into the drawing room and offer him something to drink—preferably something that will put him in a mellow mood—and tell him I shall be down in ten minutes. No, best make it fifteen."

She punctuated this last by giving a sharp tug to the bell pull which would summon her lady's maid, Betsy, who would be charged with the task of making her presentable to receive her husband's exalted relation. After sending Kit upstairs to his room, she once again addressed the butler, this time in hushed accents in spite of the fact that they were alone in the room.

"I daresay you will hear it soon enough, Rogers, so I might as well tell you that Lord Melrose is Mr. Pickett's maternal grandfather. I have no intention of toad-eating him, but nor do I wish to put Mr. Pickett to the blush."

If Rogers was surprised at all by this revelation, he hid it admirably. "Very good, madam, I believe I know just the thing to do the young master proud and make Lord Melrose, er, mellow."

She gave him a conspiratorial smile. "Somehow I thought you would." In a more serious tone, she added, "I have never thanked you properly for the way you have accepted Mr. Pickett as master. Please know that you have my eternal gratitude."

"I assure you, ma'am, young Mr. Pickett has always been a pleasure to serve."

"That I can readily believe, for I have never known a man with a sweeter disposition! Still, I suspect you may have much to bear amongst your fellows at the Silver Tray, particularly those who know you were previously in service to a viscount." She frowned uncertainly. "It is the Silver Tray, is it not? The pub where butlers tend to congregate on their half-days?"

"It is, ma'am. But I pay no heed to the idle talk of vulgar persons, well aware that there are those in service to demanding aristocrats who secretly envy me. And while I would never stoop to gossip, I can think of more than one underbutler who will be obliged to eat his words once the young master's true parentage becomes known. I am sure Mr. Pickett deserves every bit of his good fortune."

Julia made a wry face. "Yes, but at the moment, it remains to be seen whether Lord Melrose will prove to be good fortune or no."

Their hushed conversation was interrupted at this point by the entrance of Betsy through the jib door. "You rang, ma'am?"

Rogers bowed and then took himself off in search of the spirits that would have so beneficial an effect upon his lordship's temperament. Scarcely twelve minutes later, Julia entered the drawing room, her golden hair simply coiffed and her figure clad in an elegantly simple morning gown of soft blue wool with a high waist and skirts cut full enough to accommodate her swollen midriff.

"Lord Melrose," she said, making a very credible curtsy. "An unexpected pleasure."

The marquess put down his glass and rose, returning the briefest of bows and saying without preamble, "I daresay your husband must have told you that he's my heir."

"Those are not quite the words he used, but yes, I'm aware that you are his maternal grandfather. Have you come to buy me off, then?" she asked, a hint of mischief in her eyes. "He tells me you have your own plans for his marriage, and I confess, I'm curious to know how much you intend to offer me."

"You are impertinent, miss!"

"Am I? But then, *I'm* not the one arranging other people's marriages. Nor am I a 'miss,' for that matter. But how rude of me!" she exclaimed in quite a different voice as she sank gracefully onto the sofa. "We must not quarrel, since it appears we are to be family! Do sit down, and let us get to know one another. I'm sorry John is not here to receive you."

"Well, I'm not," Lord Melrose said bluntly, returning to his seat. "It was to see you that I came."

"Oh?" The slight lift of her eyebrows invited him to explain.

"I suppose he's told you that I'm petitioning the crown to allow my title to pass through the female line if there is no male heir. If my petition is granted, your husband will become the Marquess of Melrose upon my death, with all the properties and privileges that entails."

She nodded. "Yes, I'm aware of how the laws of

succession work. My first husband was the Viscount Fieldhurst."

"Exactly!" The marquess slapped his knee for emphasis. "Although I should like to know what it is about these Pickett fellows that make otherwise sensible women of good breeding —but that's neither here nor there. Having come from an aristocratic background yourself, you are well aware of the advantages that come with such a position. Can't you do something to make him see reason?"

"I am certainly aware of the advantages that come with a lofty title," she agreed in measured tones, "and I'm not unsympathetic to your desire to prevent its falling into abeyance. But I must caution you to go gently. John has the sweetest temperament of any man I've ever known, but don't mistake it for weakness. He won't be driven. Any attempt on your part to do so will only set up his back."

"Hmph! I daresay it was sweetness of temperament that led him to barge into my house in the middle of the night accusing me of murder!"

"Did he do so?" she asked, taken aback by this revelation. But then, she supposed she shouldn't be; if she and Emily Dunnington had wondered if perhaps Lord Melrose had taken a belated revenge against his despised son-in-law, then surely John, with five years' experience with Bow Street under his belt, must have considered the same possibility. The only real surprise was that he had not mentioned his confrontation with his grandfather to her himself. "I confess, that doesn't sound at all like something he would do. But then, only consider what a day he'd had: he'd only just learned of your existence—and what possessed you to have him abducted from Covent Garden, I can't imagine—and then he came home and what should he find but his father, for whom his feelings are ambiguous at best, returned from Botany Bay, only to be awakened a few hours later in the middle of the night and obliged to identify his father's body, stabbed to death in a back alley in Limehouse."

Lord Melrose made an impatient motion with his hand. "You need not tell me that. I know all about it."

"Then, too," she continued as if he had not spoken, "he has little enough cause to love you, and every reason to resent you."

The marquess took instant umbrage at this suggestion. "What the devil—I'd never even laid eyes on the fellow!"

She nodded sagely. "Exactly. He has no memory of his mother, you see, and his father had only just told him about the circumstances of their marriage and her death."

Lord Melrose gave a derisive snort. "How old is he now, twenty-four? Twenty-five? And he was about four years old at the time, so she's been gone twenty years at the least reckoning. It's all water under the bridge now—ancient history!"

"To you, perhaps, but not to him. You see, he has lived with the consequences of Lady Lydia's death every day of his life."

"Nonsense!"

"Not at all. It was to buy medicine for her that Jack stole from his employer, and after that, when the theft made it impossible for him to find honest work, he—and, later,

John—was obliged to steal for a living."

"But—well, but damn it all, what does he expect me to do about it now?" he demanded, and beneath the combative tone, Julia caught a glimpse of a very lonely man who had lived with deeply buried regrets for more than twenty years.

"May I make a suggestion?" she asked gently.

"I wish you would," he grumbled in a tone that suggested quite the opposite.

"Abandon any talk of titles and estates for the nonce, and just get to know him—not as the baseborn heir you'd thought to mold to your satisfaction as if he were a lump of clay, but as the rather remarkable man he is." She smiled. "You may find you like him a good deal more than the paragon of your imagination."

10

Which Concerns the Contents of the Dead Man's Pockets

The jury was not long in reaching a verdict, for if ever there was a clear case of intentional murder by person or persons unknown, this was it. Pickett squeezed his way through the motley crowd, eager to catch up with any one of the three persons whom he had judged the most likely to have made the voyage back to England with his father.

If he were to offer to buy the woman a glass of sherry, he wondered, would she think him some sort of pervert? *Very likely*, he thought, abandoning this promising lead with some reluctance. *What's more, Julia wouldn't be enthusiastic about the idea, either.*

No, the pink-nosed clerk was probably his best source of information regarding his father's time on board ship. In any case, any questions he were to ask would be less open to misinterpretation.

Even the seaman (if seaman he was) might be a useful

source of information. After all, Gentleman Jack was not the sort of man who went unnoticed, by persons of either sex—although men's impressions of him were generally less favorable than were their female counterparts'.

Alas, he was thwarted in his objective. Having worked closely with Mr. Colquhoun for six years, he was resigned yet unsurprised to hear himself hailed in a familiar Scots brogue.

"Ach, here he is! Mr. Pickett, come and let me introduce you to my colleague. Mr. Tomlinson, this is Mr. Pickett, a principal officer at Bow Street until quite recently, when he left us to become an independent agent. Mr. Pickett, Mr. Isaiah Tomlinson, the magistrate for the district of Limehouse, who will oversee the investigation."

"How do you do, Mr. Tomlinson?" Pickett took the proffered hand of a short, stout man with kind blue eyes behind wire-rimmed spectacles.

"Mr. Pickett." Mr. Colquhoun's fellow magistrate shook him warmly by the hand. "I can assure you that no effort will be spared in bringing your father's killer to justice. Can't have my department looking no-account to a Bow Street man, you know," he added with as jovial a tone as was permissible at so solemn an occasion.

"That's very good of you, sir," Pickett said. "I'm sure—"

At that moment the coroner approached, carrying a small bundle wrapped in brown paper and tied with string. "Your father's effects," he explained, placing the bundle in Pickett's arms. "Everything he had on him at the time of his death, excepting, of course, the clothes he was wearing, which may be needed as evidence should the case come to trial. Now that the inquest is concluded, I'm releasing the body for burial, so you may go ahead and notify the woman who is to lay him out."

Burial? Laying out? It occurred to Pickett that, although he had seen dozens of recently-deceased bodies over the course of a six-year career at Bow Street, he hadn't the slightest notion of how to arrange for his father's interment. He supposed Julia must have some idea, having gone through a similar procedure after the murder of her first husband less than two years earlier, but he suspected the obsequies due a viscount were quite different to those appropriate for a convicted felon newly returned to the land of his birth after a decade in a penal colony.

"Yes—er—thank you—I—um—"

"I'll see to it," Mr. Colquhoun put in, earning a grateful look from his former principal officer.

By the time Pickett said all that was proper to the magistrate, the coroner, the physician, and the three members of the jury he discovered in the tap room rewarding themselves with foaming pints for having performed their civic duty, he was not surprised to find that most of the crowd had dispersed, and the three people he had hoped to interview were nowhere in sight. Great, therefore, was his surprise when he stepped out of the Chalk and Cheese and into the street only to find the pink-nosed clerk (Pickett's brain refused to think of him in any other way) clearly lying in wait for him.

"I—I s-say," the man stammered, plucking at Pickett's sleeve. "You're J-Jack's son, aren't you? Of c-course you are;

they said so at the trial, didn't they?" he added, answering his own question with a nervous giggle.

It had been an inquest, not a trial, but this seemed a minor point at the moment. "Yes, I'm Jack's son," Pickett said. "What can I do for you?"

"Oh, n-nothing, nothing! It's just that—I've got your father's things, y'see." His gaze fell on the paper-wrapped bundle in Pickett's hands, and he made a hasty correction. "His valise, I mean. The one he brought with him on the ship."

Enlightenment dawned. "You're Sully."

"That's it." He grinned broadly, exposed a mouth full of teeth. One top tooth was markedly crooked, but this imperfection had the curious effect of making his smile all the more engaging. "Sullivan Bradley's the name, but most p-people call me Sully. I would've b-brought the bag to the inquest today, excepting that I didn't know you'd b-be there, or if I'd recognize you even if you were."

"Look here," Pickett said impulsively, "can I buy you a drink? I should like to hear more about my father's time abroad, if you please."

"Buy me a drink?" Sully's face turned even pinker. "But you d-don't even know me!"

"No, but my father considered you a friend," Pickett said. "That's good enough for me."

Sully yielded with a good grace, but observed, quite accurately, that his friend's son had probably had enough of the Chalk and Cheese to last him for some time to come. Pickett might have told him that the Grapes held even less appeal. But as he had no desire to conjure horrors, he said nothing beyond agreeing to the other man's suggestion that they look in at a pub called the Bell and Anchor.

As its name implied, this establishment catered to the men who made their living on the river. It was an ancient building whose plastered ceiling was so low that both Pickett and his companion were obliged to duck their heads every time they passed beneath one of the thick black beams that supported it. Still, the fire in its inglenook was warm and welcoming, and the pub had the further advantage of being completely unconnected, so far as he knew, with anything having to do with his father's death.

Once they were settled inside, however, it became clear that there was one point on which his companion was determined to have his way. Not only did Sully flatly refuse to allow Pickett to pay for the two pints of ale, he even insisted upon paying for them himself, claiming it as his privilege to perform what he called a last act of kindness for his old friend. Pickett, knowing quite well that he himself could have stood drinks for everyone in the house without making so much as a dent in his own household's income, was forced, albeit reluctantly, to let the man have his way, but he was more than a little embarrassed, and not for the first time, by the prosperity that had come to him upon his marriage.

"So, how did you know my father?" he asked, accepting one of the two foaming tankards. "Did you meet on board ship, or had you known him before?"

"I'd known him for s-seven years by the time we b-boarded the ship back to England." Answering the question Pickett had not quite known how to ask, he added, "I'd b-been a b-bank clerk. Ac-c-cused of having my hand in the t-till."

Accused of, Pickett thought, noting that Sully had neither admitted his guilt or protested his innocence. Which one was it? Of course, to hear the convicts themselves tell it, Botany Bay was awash with innocent men. His best bet, he decided, was to be sympathetic without expressing either skepticism nor belief.

"I was employed for a time as a counting-house clerk," he said, his voice carefully neutral. "It can be tedious work— easy enough to make a mistake now and again."

"Aye, that it is. *They* don't s-see it that way, though."

Pickett wondered fleetingly if "they" referred to the bank's governing board, or the judge and jury who had convicted and sentenced him, and decided that, for his purposes, at least, it didn't really matter. "So you would have been transported in '02."

"That's it." Sully paused and took a long pull from his tankard. "When I arrived at B-Botany Bay, your d-da had already been there for three years. He helped me settle in— showed me the r-ropes, you m-might say."

"He spoke well of you, too." Even as he spoke the words, Pickett realized they weren't entirely true. His father had said that he and Sully had taken a room together at a boardinghouse, but he'd said nothing about the man's character at all. Still, it was unlikely that he would have been willing to live even temporarily with a man he distrusted, so this was a safe enough assumption that Pickett felt no qualms in making the claim.

Sully, at least, saw nothing in it to cavil at. "And d-don't you worry about anything that d-doctor might say! I never knew a fellow less likely to wish himself d-dead than Gentleman Jack Pickett!"

"He seemed to be in prime twig when I saw him," Pickett observed.

Sully chuckled. "He was, at that. Always had s-some new scheme afoot, most of 'em 'guaranteed' to m-make us b-both rich." His smile faded, and he gazed unseeing at the tankard in his hands. "When he set out yesterday morning to look you up, I never d-dreamed that I'd never see him alive again."

"Then he never made it back to the boardinghouse at all." And yet his father had still been alive when Bob and Ned had come across him hours later. What had he been doing in the interim?

Sully shook his head. "I'm afraid not. When he hadn't come b-back by midnight, I reckoned he was spending the night at your place, so I went to b-bed. And all the time, only a few yards away, he was—he was—" Overcome with emotion, Sully sought recourse to his tankard.

"He told me he was going to the boardinghouse to get his things and then come back," Pickett said haltingly. "I'd—I'd told him he could stay at my place for a few days, until he could make more permanent arrangements."

Saying it out loud brought home to him just how ungracious he must have sounded. And if it hadn't been for Julia's insistence, he wouldn't have been willing to offer even this grudging hospitality.

"Look here," he burst out impatiently, "what was he doing in Gin Alley in the first place? He made a joking reference to an assignation with a lady, but even if he'd meant it, he wouldn't have had any reason to go down that passage, certainly not alone and in the middle of the night!"

Sully's narrow shoulders rose and fell in a shrug that communicated his complete ignorance. "I wish I could t-tell you." He sighed. "Truth to tell, I d-don't like to think of Jack that way. I'd rather remember him as I knew him b-back in B-Botany Bay."

Pickett could not argue with this sentiment, but knew he hadn't the luxury of being similarly selective. Still, Kit might like to know something of his father's life, assuming Sully's anecdotes were suitable for a child's ears, and so he encouraged the clerk to share his recollections.

Sully didn't have to be asked twice. He launched into a long and amusing account of Gentleman Jack's time in Botany Bay, and Pickett noted that as he became caught up in his tale, his stammer grew much less pronounced. According to Sully, felons in the penal colony were given a good deal more freedom than their counterparts in Newgate (after all, even if they escaped, where could they go?), and it appeared his father had taken full advantage of his opportunities. To hear Sully tell it, Jack's life there had been a series of adventures—some financial, some romantic, and some a combination of the two.

And I'd imagined him poverty-stricken and starving, Pickett thought, hardly sure whether to be amused or indignant at the thought of all the money he'd sent his father over the last five years. They must have made an odd pair, his smooth-talking father and this bashful and stammering clerk with the oddly engaging smile.

"I know you've a lot to d-do in the coming d-days, what with b-burying your father," Sully said in a more serious vein, having exhausted his supply of stories, "but whenever you want to stop and fetch your d-da's valise, it'll be there waiting for you. Did J-Jack give you the d-direction of the b-boardinghouse? No? It's in Narrow Street, just a few d-doors down from the Grapes. Just ask for M-Mrs. Huggins."

Pickett promised to do so, relieved that the man hadn't suggested he return to the boardinghouse and fetch the valise then and there. Of course, it would mean another trip to a part of London that was quite out of his way, but no matter; it had been a full and, in many ways, a difficult day, and at the moment he wanted nothing more but to go back home to his wife.

* * *

Nor did she disappoint. As soon as he opened his own front door, Julia emerged from the drawing room to meet him.

"I'm glad you're home," she said, putting her arms around him and drawing him close. "Was it too dreadful, darling?"

"Murder by person or persons unknown, which was no surprise." He returned her embrace, but asked with mock severity, "Are you out of bed *again*?"

"I'm afraid so," she confessed. "I had a caller who couldn't be put off."

His gaze shifted over her head to what could be seen of the drawing room from his vantage point in the foyer. Everything looked in order there, with the exception of a crystal decanter of amber-colored liquid and an almost-empty tumbler, both positioned on a small table within easy reach of anyone seated on the sofa. Clearly, the caller, whoever it was, had been male.

"Not my father again, obviously," Pickett said.

"No, not your father." Seeing him at a loss, she said, "Your grandfather."

If she had hoped to surprise him, she succeeded. "*Lord Melrose?*"

"If you have another grandfather, I'm not aware of him."

"As far as I know, I've only the one—and in my opinion, he's one too many. What the devil did he want?"

"I think he wants me to try and talk sense into you," she said, determined to make light of the subject for his sake. "I'm sorry to say, he never did tell me how much he'd intended to pay to buy me off. But never mind him! What do you have there?"

He glanced down at the package, which he'd tucked under his arm in order to embrace her and all but forgotten. "My father's personal effects. The coroner said this is everything Da had on him when he died. I've no idea what's in it."

"Perhaps you'd best examine the contents in privacy," she suggested. "If your father's life was even half so colorful as you say, there may be things Kit ought not to see."

Pickett saw nothing to dispute in this proposal, adding only the proviso that she should join him in this grim task—a condition to which she readily agreed.

"And speaking of Kit," he said as they slowly climbed

the stairs, his arm steadying her, "Do you think I should allow him to follow the coffin along with me?"

"It can surely be no worse than allowing him to attend a public hanging, and you had no qualms about letting him do that," she said, grimacing at the memory. "You said at the time that children of the rookery haven't the luxury of being spared the realities of death. Besides, it might please him to be treated like his father's son, just as you are."

Pickett nodded. There it was again, the one big difference between the two brothers, of far more significance than the fifteen years that separated them, and of which Kit would certainly become aware as he grew older. It was perhaps fortunate that their father had never had two pennies to rub together, for it rendered the question of inheritance a moot point: Half of nothing was, after all, still nothing. There was no point in creating unnecessary distinctions between the two Pickett sons.

As far as any physical distress the boy might suffer from attending the funeral, Pickett thought it unlikely. The lid of the coffin would be nailed down long before the cortège set out for the burial ground, and even if it wasn't, the mortal blow had been struck in his father's back. Either way, Kit shouldn't see anything to upset him.

Pickett nodded. "All right, then, I'll talk to him in a little while. Let's take a look at this first, shall we? With any luck, there'll be something in here"—he indicated the parcel in his hand—"to shed some light on the last few hours of his life."

"John, if you would prefer to do this in privacy—"

"I'd rather have you with me," he insisted. "You might

catch something I miss."

Which was true, of course, so far as it went. But there was more to it than that. He had not seen his father in more than a decade, during which he had gained a wise and compassionate mentor, a wife he loved deeply and who loved him in return, an engaging half-brother, and, soon, a son or daughter of his own. And yet, seeing his father's lifeless body stretched out on a table in the back room of the Grapes, and then hearing his death discussed so dispassionately at the inquest, had left him feeling as utterly abandoned as he had at fourteen, watching his father led off to the convict ship bound for Plymouth and thence halfway 'round the world to Botany Bay. Even Da's last, dying thoughts had not been for the son with whom he had just been reunited after a ten-year separation, or even for the second, unexpected child he had only just met. No, his last words had been for the young wife he had lost twenty years earlier.

It was absurd to be jealous of his own mother, but there it was. Perhaps Kit was not the only one to cherish long-buried dreams. Whatever the reason, he found he could not face the prospect of sorting through his father's belongings alone. And Julia must have understood his dilemma, for she did not press the issue.

Having reached the bedchamber and closed the door against the bright eyes of a curious ten-year-old, Pickett placed the package on the bed, then untied the string and spread open the paper wrappings. Within the creased folds lay a coin purse, a small brass key, a handkerchief, a penknife in need of trimming, a small scrap of paper and a somewhat larger one folded in half, and the watch with its engraved initials, the same watch he had taken away from Kit. The glass that covered its face was now cracked, and no ticking sound emanated from it. Pickett, noting its hands stood at some seven or eight minutes until twelve, wondered if it simply needed winding, or if it was a silent testimony to the exact time at which his father had died. Either way, his father's body could not have been lying there for long, else the watch, the coin purse, and anything else of value would have been stripped—which, now that he thought of it, would appear to eliminate robbery as a motive for the murder.

He tried winding the watch, but the shaft spun loosely beneath his fingers; the thing was well and truly broken. He resolved to have it repaired for Kit as soon as possible. Had it really been only twenty-four hours earlier that he had snatched it out of the boy's hand? It seemed a lifetime ago. *It was*, a voice in his head chided him. *Your father's life, to be exact.*

Pushing aside the thought, he tugged open the purse's drawstring, then dumped out and counted the contents. They amounted to one half-crown piece, two shillings, and four pence—just under five shillings, all told.

" A 'man of property,' " Pickett echoed bitterly, surveying the meager collection. "Four and ten. It's not much, is it, to show for more than forty years of life?"

"He left a valise, too, back in his room at the boardinghouse," Julia reminded him, unaware that he had recently spent half an hour in a tête-à-tête with the bag's temporary custodian. Before he could inform her of this new development, however, she added firmly, "Although I must dispute the idea that he left little to show for his life. No one who produced you—yes, and Kit, too—can be said to have lived in vain."

He acknowledged this with a little smile, but his mind was on the piece of paper, on which were scrawled the words *91 Chancery Lane* in a firm hand. Wordlessly, he held the paper out to her.

" '91 Chancery Lane,' " she read aloud. "Who, or what, lives there?"

"I don't know, but it shouldn't be difficult to—"

As Julia examined the small scrap of paper, Pickett had picked up the larger one and unfolded it, and now stared down at it in dismay.

"What have you found?" Julia asked, leaning toward him to see for herself.

"It's confirmation of Da's passage. He sailed on the *Queen of the Seas*."

Julia regarded him in bewilderment. "But that's good, isn't it? You'll know exactly where to go to look for a list of passengers."

He gave a humorless laugh. "Oh, I know exactly where to go, all right."

"Well, then—"

"The *Queen of the Seas*," he explained bleakly, "belongs to the firm of Ludlow & Ludlow, Importers."

* * *

A return to the poorly-lit and insufficiently-heated office where he had endured almost a month of misery as a counting-house clerk was not a prospect Pickett could regard with anything other than dread. As he recalled, Mr. Ludlow's last words to him had been something along the lines of "—and don't come back." He had been more than willing to obey this stricture at the time, since it had been prompted by Julia's coming to fetch him home to meet with his first real client as an independent investigator.

In any case, he did not expect a warm welcome from his former employer, which was no doubt a good thing, since it meant he was not disappointed when Mr. Ludlow greeted him with, "So it's you again, is it? I believe I told you that if you walked out the door, you need not bother walking back in. You had your chance and you threw it away, so you're wasting your time, coming here pleading for your old position back—"

Why is it, Pickett wondered, *that suddenly every man I meet expects me to come back to him begging for a favor?*

Aloud, he merely said, "I haven't come seeking a position." He darted a quick, sympathetic glance at the nervous-looking young man seated at the desk that had once been his, then began to explain the reason for his return to a place in which he'd never wanted to set foot again. "A murder took place in Limehouse recently—"

"Only one?" retorted Mr. Ludlow in mock surprise. "Must've been a slow night in the East End."

"—concerning a man who had only just arrived in England," Pickett continued, as if he had not spoken. "I have been engaged to discover who killed him, and to bring the killer to justice." He saw no reason to divulge the fact that his client was only ten years old, nor that the victim was his own as well as his "client"'s father.

"What this can possibly have to do with me, I cannot imagine," his former employer said in a voice that dared Pickett to contradict him.

"The victim of the crime," explained Pickett, unfazed, "had disembarked from your own ship *Queen of the Seas* less than twenty-four hours earlier. I should like to see the ship's manifest, if you will be so kind."

"Why the devil should I?" demanded Mr. Ludlow. "You are well aware, or should be, that the *Queen of the Seas* is a merchant ship. She takes only a handful of passengers as space permits, and once those passengers disembark, this firm assumes no further responsibility for them. However tragic the fate of this unfortunate man, it can have nothing to do with me."

Having anticipated this response, Pickett heaved a sigh of regret. "I understand, sir."

"Good," said Mr. Ludlow, although his expression grew wary, as if he mistrusted Pickett's ready capitulation.

"I had hoped," confessed Pickett, his downcast eyes communicating the depth of his disappointment, "that you might be amenable to cooperating with an independent agent who promises his clients discretion, but I'm sure you know your own business best. You need not trouble yourself, sir. I'll wait until Bow Street serves you with a search warrant, and then get the information I need directly from them."

He bade Mr. Ludlow a meek "good day," then turned and retraced his steps to the door, counting under his breath. *One...two...three...*

"Wait!"

Ten minutes later, he quitted the premises with a neatly transcribed passenger list in his coat pocket and a rather smug smile on his face.

11

In Which Gentleman Jack Pickett Is Laid to Rest

Before he could begin his investigation in earnest, however, there was his father's funeral to be got through. A note send round from Mr. Colquhoun had informed him that all was arranged, and he had only to present himself at St. Paul's Church in Covent Garden the following morning at eleven o'clock. His invitation to Kit to join him in their father's funeral cortège had been accepted with an enthusiasm not entirely appropriate to the solemnity of the occasion, and so after partaking of a rather sober breakfast, the two brothers had set out for the church, both clad in black coats with armbands on the right sleeves and sprigs of rosemary tied with black ribbons pinned to their left lapels.

While Pickett's feelings toward his father were ambivalent at best, Kit knew no such indecision. "And I'd only just got him!" he complained bitterly. "He was going to tell me all about the Antipodes. Da says—said—the seasons are all mixed up there, that it's winter in July and you can go sea-bathing on Boxing Day!"

"Did he?" Pickett asked, feigning an interest he did not feel.

"And," Kit continued, "he said they have all kinds of funny animals that we don't have here."

"Do they?"

At least Kit's constant chatter spared him the necessity of speech, for the boy required no response beyond a vague acknowledgement, just enough to convince him that his elder brother was still listening.

"I showed Da the horse I drew," Kit continued, when the topic of the Antipodes and its peculiarities had been exhausted, "and he said I might get to where I can draw even better than your mum could. D'you s'pose my mum could draw?" After a contemplative pause, he indirectly conceded the superiority of his brother's claim in this regard, offering as an alternative, "But Mum can down a whole bottle of Blue Ruin without belching even once, so I guess that's something, isn't it?"

Pickett had no opinion to put forth on this subject, so Kit continued his monologue uninterrupted until they reached the church.

Mr. Colquhoun had assumed, quite correctly, that Pickett would not want his father's body laid out in the drawing room of the house in Curzon Street. Pickett was almost certain the old superstition about pregnant women not viewing dead bodies was exactly that—a superstition—but there was no need in tempting fate, especially now that Julia's confinement was so near at hand. Instead, the magistrate had arranged for the coffin to be conveyed to St. Paul's Church in Covent Garden, adjacent to the market where the deceased had once plied his dubious trade.

Pickett opened the door of the church, and the scent of lilies filled his nostrils. The coffin lid had not yet been put in place, but a large bouquet of the trumpet-shaped white flowers lay at the base of its bier, ready to adorn the top of the coffin once it was closed. Kit's voice trailed into silence, and a small hand slipped into Pickett's.

"Do I have to look at him?" Kit asked, his voice a near-whisper.

"No, of course not," Pickett assured him. "Not unless you want to."

"It'll be my last chance to see him," the boy said doubtfully.

"I'll go first, shall I?" Pickett suggested. "Then I can tell you what he looks like, and you can decide for yourself if you want to see."

Kit nodded in agreement, and Pickett approached the coffin alone. Since the knife wound had been in the back, and the crust of dried blood at the corner of his mouth had been washed away by the woman who had laid out the body for burial, there were no visible signs of trauma, let alone violence. In fact, Pickett was struck by how very young his father looked. The lines on his face that had testified to a hard life were now smoothed out in death, and he appeared fully ten years younger than the forty-five years he'd had in his dish. *He said 'Lydia,'* the boy who'd found the body had testified. Pickett found himself thinking not of the transported felon, but of the gallant young footman who had eloped with his master's daughter in order to save her from an unwanted marriage. To his surprise, he found himself wishing he'd had the chance to know that Jack Pickett better; the Pickett men, it seemed, had a knack for marrying above themselves.

He caught a movement out of the corner of his eye, and in the next instant, Kit stood beside him.

"He just looks like he's asleep," the boy said with patent relief.

"He does," Pickett agreed, adding, perhaps unwisely, "Not scary at all."

Kit bristled with indignation. "Who said I was scared? I'm not afraid of my own da!"

"No, of course not," Pickett said hastily, scrambling to retrieve his position. "What was I thinking?"

Having corrected this patently false implication of cowardice on his part, Kit readily forgave Pickett for his lapse. "You were probably thinking there would be blood and all," he allowed generously. "But there isn't, is there?"

"None at all," Pickett concurred, keeping to himself the observation that there had been a great deal of blood at first, until the body had been laid out for burial.

"In fact—" Kit looked from his father's earthly remains to the elder brother who was very much alive, and back again. "In fact," he said, much struck, "he looks a lot like you." Realizing this assessment was hardly flattering, he hastily amended it. "I mean, he looks like you would look, if you were dead."

A smile tugged at Pickett's lips. "Well, that's a relief," he told his young half-brother. "You had me worried for a minute."

"I trust everything has been done to your satisfaction?"

Pickett turned at the sound of the familiar Scots burr, and saw Mr. Colquhoun walking up the aisle.

"Mr. Colquhoun!" Kit, sensing a gift of coinage in the offing, cried with an eagerness quite unsuited to the occasion, the gleeful exclamation echoing off the walls of the nave.

He was not disappointed. "Well met, young Kit," said the magistrate, offering the boy a handshake as a guise for slipping something into the palm of his hand. "Well, John?"

"Yes, sir, very—very satisfactory," Pickett said gratefully, thinking how inadequate the word seemed. "If you will give me an accounting of the extent of my obligation, I will repay—" He broke off, reading in his former magistrate's face the unlikelihood of his being allowed to reimburse the expenses, which surely must have been considerable, incurred on his behalf. "But, sir, why should you be obliged to pay for my father's funeral? You may be sure he would not have done the same for you, although—forgive me—he would have been pleased enough by the occasion that warranted it."

Mr. Colquhoun chuckled. "No doubt, and can you wonder at it? You might say I owe it to the man," he added in a more serious vein.

"Nonsense! He willingly broke the law, not only once, but repeatedly. No one would have thought it unduly harsh if you had sent him to the gallows. By sentencing him to be transported instead, you granted him a mercy many would say was undeserved."

"Aye, and in the process, I denied him the chance to see his son grow to manhood."

A quick glance at Kit, who had polished the large copper coin on the sleeve of his coat and was now holding it up to the figure in the coffin as if presenting it for his inspection, served to remind Pickett that his father's sentence had also denied him the knowledge of his second son at all.

Having made his point, the magistrate continued. "Perhaps worse, I claimed that privilege for myself."

"And if you hadn't, there is every chance I would not have lived to manhood in any case. If you'll recall, Da was not the only one breaking the law."

Mr. Colquhoun needed no reminder. Even after eleven years, he still retained a vivid recollection of the night John Pickett had first made his acquaintance, having been hauled into the Bow Street Public Office for stealing an apple from the fruit and vegetable market at Covent Garden. He had been a gangly and undernourished fourteen-year-old at the time, and yet the officer who made the arrest had apparently felt it necessary to black the lad's eye and break his nose in order to subdue him. Blood had still been oozing from the boy's nostrils, but more compelling than his injuries had been the fear in his eyes (or, rather, his eye, as one of the two was swollen almost completely shut), contrasted with defiant tilt of his chin as he regarded the magistrate who possessed the power to sentence him to hang. Mr. Colquhoun had not done so. In fact, he had not charged the lad with any crime at all. Instead, he had taken young John to a pub and bought him something to eat—a ham sandwich, as he recalled, which had disappeared with all the speed of which an adolescent male is capable—after which he had called in a favor and persuaded an old acquaintance, a coal merchant, to take the boy on as an apprentice. Five years later, he had bought the remaining two years of nineteen-year-old John's contract of apprenticeship out of his own pocket, and had brought him to Bow Street.

And still, at twenty-five, his young protégé felt himself indebted to his mentor for this checkered career, when Mr. Colquhoun regularly cursed himself for his lack of foresight in failing to send him to school, where his natural intelligence, combined with whatever influence the magistrate could wield, might well have earned him a scholarship to university.

The magistrate harrumphed to clear a throat that suddenly felt tight. "Be that as it may," he said impatiently, "there's a crowd waiting outside, so if you're ready, I'll be on my way. I hope you'll forgive me for not forming part of the cortège; I suspect my presence would be an unwelcome distraction amongst your father's former set."

Pickett had been aware of a muted roar from outside, but he had assumed it to be an especially lively market day in the piazza. To his surprise, the doors flew open and a crowd descended upon the nave, all clad in what he recognized to be their best clothes. Since these garments had been augmented with whatever black adornments they could contrive, from black bands affixed to sleeves to black ribbons fluttering from bonnets, the purpose of their presence was clear. He wasn't quite sure how word of Gentleman Jack Pickett's murder in Limehouse had made its way to Covent Garden, but that it had done so could not be denied. Pickett, who had assumed that his father would be mostly forgotten after an absence of more than a decade, was touched. He took a deep breath and stepped into the crowd, prepared to receive the condolences of his father's friends and acquaintances.

And then the rector took his place at the altar, and the funeral began. Since the service as outlined in the Book of Common Prayer followed a set form, the rector was spared the challenge of representing a notorious felon as a pattern-card of virtue. Even so, it was not long before the service was over and the crowd departed the church and spilled out onto the piazza, separating themselves into those who intended to form part of the cortège and those who did not.

"And after I'd raised him as if he were my own son—"

A querulous voice cut through the babel, a voice Pickett recognized at once. He scanned the crowd and soon located Moll, clearly in her element. Somehow she'd contrived to procure a slightly faded gown of black satin cut in what must have been the latest fashion twenty years earlier. It appeared she had cast herself in the rôle of grieving widow, never mind the fact that her union with his father—whom she had not seen in ten years, and whose place had been filled with a succession of men in the interim—had never been blessed by a parson.

"And then what must he do but take my boy away from me—*me*, that cared for him like a mother—"

Pickett felt a tug at his sleeve. "John," Kit said timidly, "will I have to go back and live with Mum, now that she's seen me?"

Pickett might have assured him that Moll had no real

desire to have her son returned to her, as no mere human child could take the place that Blue Ruin held in her affection. But surely no child would want to hear such a thing, even if the child knew it to be true.

"No," he said firmly. "You can go and say good morning to her, if you feel you ought to, but if she wants you to stay with her, just tell her that I won't let you go." Moll would like that, as it would appear to confirm the tales she was pouring into the ears of her cronies. In the meantime, it would serve to distract Kit from any sounds he might hear from within the church as the coffin lid was put in place and nailed down. Now that he thought of it, he wouldn't mind having something to distract him from those sounds, as well.

At last it was time to depart for the burial ground where Mr. Colquhoun had arranged for his father to be interred. The coffin had been loaded onto a hearse and draped with a black pall, while the horses hitched to the vehicle were similarly garbed in black, their elegant headdresses of black ostrich plumes fluttering with their every movement. As the hearse turned into Bedford Street, the church bell began its mournful toll—another funeral custom for which Mr. Colquhoun would have borne the expense—and it occurred to Pickett that his father had achieved in death a dignity that he had never possessed in life.

As the chief mourners, Pickett and Kit followed behind the hearse. Rather to Pickett's surprise, Moll did not accompany them, and he breathed a silent thanks to whoever had dissuaded her. He wondered if someone had pointed out that Gentleman Jack's lawfully wedded wife—a lady born and bred, albeit one who had been in her grave these twenty years and more—would never have done anything so vulgar as attend a funeral; he couldn't imagine any other argument that might have had the power to move her.

They had not gone far when it began to rain, a cold, steady stream that trickled down the back of Pickett's neck and caused the horses' handsome feathers to droop. And yet none of the mourners abandoned the procession; on the contrary, several bystanders, upon being told who it was whose body was being laid to rest, had joined the cortège, giving the proceedings an almost festive air.

Gradually, however, Pickett became aware of a disturbance somewhere behind him. He turned to identify the source of the confusion, and saw a carriage being forced past the procession, a sleek black carriage with—yes, Pickett was almost certain there was a crest on the door. The mourners were compelled to make way, lest they fall afoul of the coachman's whip, and so it did not take long for the vehicle to draw abreast. The coachman slowed his team to a walk in order to keep pace with the cortège, and it struck Pickett that the matched black horses might be mistaken for part of the funeral procession themselves.

And so, in a way, they were. For the carriage door was flung open, and a curt voice from inside commanded, "Get in."

The interior of the vehicle was lost in shadow, but Pickett recognized the voice at once, and did not hesitate to reply, "No, thank you."

"Don't be a fool, boy!" Lord Melrose snapped. "D'you

think your freezing to death will punish me? Well, it won't."

Pickett might have asked why, if that were the case, his lordship had bothered to seek out his father's funeral cortège at all. Instead, he glanced hesitantly at Kit. The boy was following the exchange with interest, but his cheeks were red, his nose was dripping, and he was shivering so violently that his teeth chattered with cold.

"All right, then. Come on, Kit," he called to his young brother, prepared to hoist him bodily into a carriage whose step was not lowered. "Up you go."

"Not him. You."

"I beg your pardon?" Pickett asked, certain he could not have heard aright.

"The boy is nothing to me. Just because I choose not to have my grandson making a spectacle of himself don't mean I intend to do the same by every tag, rag, and bobtail who has a fancy to stay warm and dry."

"In that case, I thank you, but I would prefer to walk." Turning to his young brother, he said bracingly, "Chin up, Kit. Not much farther now."

In fact, he had no idea how much farther they had to walk. Still, he had no intention of riding comfortably in his grandfather's carriage and allowing a ten-year-old boy to follow his father's coffin alone, no matter how inclement the weather.

"Oh, have it your way," Lord Melrose grumbled. "Let the brat ride; it's nothing to me."

Had it been merely his own comfort at issue, Pickett would have taken great pleasure in flinging his grandfather's unwilling generosity back in his teeth. One look at Kit's misery, however, was enough to put paid to this tempting prospect.

"I'm obliged to you," Pickett said in accents every bit as grudging as his grandfather's had been, then boosted Kit up into the carriage and climbed in after him, closing the door behind him.

"Who are you?" Kit inquired artlessly of his reluctant rescuer, bouncing experimentally on the elegantly upholstered and well-sprung squabs.

"Lord Melrose, this is my half-brother, Christopher, familiarly known as Kit," Pickett put in quickly, before his lordship could annihilate the boy with a brutal snub. "Kit, Lord Melrose. He's—well, it looks like he's my grandfather."

"Oh." Far from being awed by his brother's exalted connection, Kit took this revelation in his stride. "Are you my grandfather, too?"

"I thank God, no," said his lordship in crushing accents.

"Is this your carriage?" continued Kit, undaunted. "Julia—John's wife, you know—she has a carriage, too, but hers doesn't have that—that *thing* on the door." Kit's hands described the shield shape of the Melrose coat of arms emblazoned on the panel of his lordship's carriage.

"She used to," Pickett told him, unwilling for Julia to appear in any way inferior to his lordship. "When her first husband was still alive."

"Do you have to be very rich to have one of those things?" Kit's inquisition of Lord Melrose continued. "Is that why you have one and Julia doesn't anymore?"

Lord Melrose did not answer either of these questions directly, only observed that if his petition should prove successful, Kit's sister-in-law might someday have a crest on her own carriage doors.

"Will she?" Kit turned to his brother for confirmation. "Why?"

"Let's—we'll talk about it later, shall we?" Pickett suggested, avoiding his grandfather's eye.

Some time later, standing with his arm about Kit's shoulders beside the hole dug to receive their father's coffin, Pickett was hard-pressed to pay attention to the rector reading the burial service, so conscious was he of his grandfather's carriage waiting some distance away. Lord Melrose did not join the mourners at the graveside, but Pickett had been so certain that the marquess would quit the premises as soon as he had delivered his passengers to the burial ground that he could hardly have been more surprised if his grandfather had personally delivered the eulogy.

At last the coffin was lowered into the ground, and the brothers Pickett removed the black-ribboned sprigs of rosemary from their lapels and tossed them onto the lid of the coffin. Pickett promptly led Kit away from the grave, wishing to spare the boy the grim sight of the sexton and his assistant shoveling dirt onto the casket containing their father's body.

If he had any doubts that he—and, by default, Kit—were to ride back to Curzon Street in the marquess's carriage, these were settled by the sight of his lordship's coachman climbing down from the box, opening the carriage door, and lowering the step. Boarding the vehicle was considerably easier when it was standing still, and so it was not long before they were threading their way through the dispersing mourners. If any of these resented the fact that Pickett and Kit were being conveyed to and from their father's funeral while they were obliged to trudge back to Covent Garden or its environs in the rain, this was not apparent in the friendly waves or respectful tugging of forelocks directed toward them. Pickett acknowledged these with a sober yet grateful nod, but when he imagined what the situation might have been had Moll decided to accompany her former cully's coffin, he could not quite suppress a smile at the thought of Lord Melrose's discomfiture had he insisted that she, too, be offered a seat in the carriage.

The conversation on the return to Mayfair was strained, even Kit having been cowed into uncharacteristic silence, until at last the vehicle came to a stop before the tall, narrow house of which he had become master upon his marriage. Pickett gripped Kit's sleeve to prevent the boy from opening the door and jumping down to the pavement as was his usual habit, while the coachman climbed down from the box to open the door and lower the step—tasks that Andrew, Pickett's own footman, might have performed, had he any reason to expect Mr. Pickett and young Master Kit would be not be returning on foot, just as they had set out.

Once his sleeve was released, Kit lost no time in bounding down from the carriage and bolting into the house, eager to tell Rogers that he had been given a ride in a carriage, one with a "thing" on the door, by his half-grandfather—a relationship that Lord Melrose must surely have found appalling, had he been privy to it.

Pickett's own disembarkation was rather more sedate. He said nothing as he exited the vehicle, but upon reaching the pavement, he turned back to address the one remaining passenger.

"I—I'm obliged to you, sir," he said stiffly.

Lord Melrose harrumphed in a manner that might have signified anything, or nothing at all, and then the driver raised the step, closed the door, and climbed onto the box. A moment later, the carriage was bowling smartly down the street and around the curve that hid it from view.

Suddenly feeling very tired, Pickett heaved a sigh, then climbed the two shallow steps onto the portico and entered the house, closing the door behind him.

12

In Which John Pickett's Investigation Begins

A nd the worst part," Pickett complained to Julia upon his return to Curzon Street, "is that except for Sully—Mr. Sullivan Bradley, that is—I have no idea where to find any of these people!"

Having buried his father, Pickett had plunged headlong into the work of investigation, starting with the list of the *Queen of the Seas*'s passengers and crew he had wrung from the unwilling Mr. Ludlow. At least, that had been his intention, until he had encountered this rather daunting obstacle.

"Were they not obliged to state their place of residence when they booked passage?" Julia, sitting up in bed, leaned in for a better look at the neat column of names, written in a curiously slanting hand with which she had become very familiar over the last nine months.

"No, for none of them appears to have a permanent

residence in London—or anywhere else, for that matter. They would have given up their colonial residences before sailing, and no doubt had intended to find housing after they arrived."

"What about this one?" Julia pointed to a name listed near the top. " 'Sir Horace Stapleton, Undersecretary to the Governor of His Majesty's Colony of New South Wales.' He should be easy enough to run to ground."

Pickett looked doubtful. "Should he?"

"Of course! You have only to go to the War and Colonial Office in Whitehall and start asking for him. Government circles are surprisingly small. Sooner or later, you're going to run into someone who can tell you where to find him."

Pickett jotted down the name of this entity in the margin next to Sir Horace's name. He hated being beholden to Julia's first husband for anything, but there was no denying the fact that the late Lord Fieldhurst's government connections, and the knowledge Julia had gleaned from them over her six-year marriage to the viscount, had their uses.

"I'm assuming Lady Stapleton is his wife," he said, moving down to the next name on the list. "I wonder if she's also the veiled lady at the inquest." He closed the notebook and returned it to the inside pocket of his coat. "I think that will do to be going on with. I'm going to the docks first, to talk to the captain of the ship. While I'm about it, I'll look up Sully's boardinghouse and collect Da's valise. With any luck, I'll find something in it that will give me a lead."

The weather had not noticeably warmed since the funeral on the previous day, and in concession to the cold—to say nothing of the fact that he would be obliged to make the return journey carrying a valise of unknown weight and size—Pickett hired a hackney instead of making the seven-mile trek to the Isle of Dogs on foot.

No island in the literal sense, the Isle of Dogs was a marshy peninsula enclosed on three sides by a deep meander in the River Thames. No one could say how or when the peninsula had got its name, but over the past ten years, the area had become an island indeed with the construction of the City Canal, the West India Docks, and, most recently, the East India Docks intersecting it roughly east to west. Along its western boundary, the opposite shore of the river was punctuated at intervals with a series of smaller, more established but less ambitious docks.

Pickett, stepping down from the hackney, tugged the brim of his hat down over his ears and turned up the collar of his coat against the cold wind coming off the water, then took a moment to survey his surroundings. He was no sailor—he had discovered this fact a year earlier, when a short pleasure cruise on a Scottish fishing boat had left him hanging his head over the gunwale—but he had to admit there was something impressive about the sight. Here were watercraft of all kinds, from enormous East Indiamen with their exotic cargoes of tea and spices to small wherries that conveyed passengers across the river. If the framed aquatints adorning the walls of their offices were to be believed, the half-dozen merchant ships belonging to Ludlow & Ludlow, Importers, fell somewhere between these two extremes.

Unfortunately, trying to locate one specific ship amongst the dozens of vessels tied up along the wharves or riding at anchor on the river was very likely to prove a fool's errand. He needed to narrow the field by seeking information from someone more familiar with the maritime aspects of international commerce than he'd become as a mere knight of the quill.

It soon became apparent, however, that finding this individual was likely to prove more challenging than he'd anticipated. The dock swarmed with males ranging in age from beardless youths to old "tars" with grizzled hair and lined, weathered faces, but he could form no impression of which men were in charge, and therefore more able to answer his queries. Unlike their counterparts in the Royal Navy, the officers of merchant ships did not wear uniforms or indeed any form of insignia that might allow the casual observer to distinguish them from the men under their command. All of them seemed to be dressed more or less the same, in loose trousers and shirts of blue or white cotton worn open at the neck, many with red or blue kerchiefs knotted loosely about their necks. Some wore knitted wool caps pulled down over their ears. A few were coatless even in the December chill, but most wore short, double-breasted coats of dark blue wool.

In the end, Pickett was obliged to make his selection based on the dubious measure of age—older men, he reasoned, would be more likely to have achieved the higher ranks—as well as their general bearing toward their fellow men. The bow-legged man terrorizing two younger men as they labored over a canvas sail, for instance, appeared a likely candidate for an officer, but Pickett, noting the cowering sailors under his supervision, wasn't at all sure he wanted to approach a man who looked like he would have little enough patience with questions from able seamen, much less ignorant landlubbers.

At last he settled on a man of perhaps forty-five—presumably old enough to have climbed the chain of command, but seemingly of a considerably mellower temperament than his fellow, although this was quite possibly due to the beneficent effect of the long-stemmed clay pipe clenched between his teeth.

"Excuse me," he said, approaching this promising source of information, "I'm looking for a merchant ship called the *Queen of the Seas*. She belongs to the Ludlow fleet. Do you have any idea where she might be berthed?" *Berthed?* he thought. *Is that the right word?* In any case, it was out now, and couldn't be called back.

The sailor cupped his hand around the bowl of his pipe and removed it from his mouth, then blew out a long plume of smoke while he regarded Pickett appraisingly.

"Thinking of going to sea, are you?"

"Um, no," Pickett said, adding apologetically, "I'm afraid I would make a very poor job of it if I did. But my father just returned to London as a passenger on the *Queen*, only to die less than twenty-four hours after disembarking—"

"Illness?" the sailor asked sharply.

"No," Pickett said hastily, realizing he feared the *Queen of the Seas* had brought with her some contagious disease that would now run rampant through the ranks of these men who lived for months at a time in very close quarters. "Not illness; murder. He was stabbed in the back with a leilira knife."

"God bless my soul!" The man's fingers instinctively closed around the edge of his collar, the sailors' ancient gesture of protection against evil.

"So you can see why I would like to discover what I can about my father's time on a ship sailing from the very place these weapons are made," Pickett concluded.

"Surely you don't think one of the ship's crew stalked him onto land and killed him! Why, it's preposterous!"

"How so?"

"Because, frankly, no sailor making port after so long a voyage would have the time! There are only a few days in which to repair any damage the ship might have suffered rounding the cape, and to revictual her before setting sail again. Then, too, the men want a little time for counterpane-hurdling while they're in port. While they're at sea, they often go months at a time without seeing a woman."

The *Queen of the Seas*, Pickett knew, had numbered two women among its passengers, for all the good it did the ship's crew; both of these ladies had been accompanied by their husbands.

"I see your point," he conceded. "Still, I should like to speak with the captain of the *Queen of the Seas*, if you will tell me where I can find him."

"First of all, this ain't the Royal Navy. The man in charge of a merchant ship is rated 'master,' not 'captain,' and you'll get a lot forrarder with Josiah Tubbs if you address him as such. As for where the *Queen* is berthed, you'll most likely find her over there—Commercial Dock number four." He stretched out his arm and pointed a calloused finger toward the warehouses clinging to the opposite shore.

"On the other side of the river," Pickett said in a flat voice.

The sailor took a long drag from his pipe. "Aye, that's it. There's any number of watermen who'll row you across for a shilling. Only look out for a fellow in a red knitted cap with a blue cockade. Folks on the river call him Barnacle Ben, on account of how once he latches onto you, you're stuck with him. He'll take you halfway across, then when you're in the middle of the river he'll pull a muscle in his arm or some such thing, and won't row another stroke until you cross his palm with silver, same as with any gypsy crone. What's more, he can spot a greenhorn at twenty paces."

Pickett didn't ask why he should be taken for a greenhorn; he had no doubt it stuck out all over him. Sure enough, as he descended the Mill Wall Stairs to the water's edge, no fewer than three watermen began loudly extolling the virtues of his own wherry, as well as the skill and speed with which he could convey his passenger across the water. A fourth man was bent over his boat, a man wearing a striped jumper and a greasy red knitted cap from beneath which a long, thin braid of graying hair hung, unflatteringly reminiscent of a rat's tail. As his fellows raised the hawkers' cry for custom, he straightened and turned toward Pickett, revealing a blue cockade affixed to the ribbed band of his cap as he added his own voice to the cacophony.

"Barnacle Ben, is it?" Pickett asked as he neared the boats tied up on the foreshore.

"Aye, that's m'name." Ben's smile revealed a set of

yellowed teeth from which a few were missing. Pickett noticed that the other men had fallen silent, expectantly watching the negotiations with broad if somewhat envious grins. "Take you across, guv?" He jerked his thumb toward the water and, presumably, the opposite shore.

Pickett shook his head. "I'm afraid your reputation has preceded you, Ben. *You, there!*"

He called to one of the other watermen, who looked surprised and gratified to have stolen a march on one whose exploits on the river were in a fair way to becoming legendary. In a very short time, Pickett was settled in the wherry, and the waterman untied his craft, pushed it off the strip of exposed foreshore and into the water, and climbed aboard.

Pickett's few excursions on the water had not been all bliss, and the river crossing ran true to form, with the added discomforts of the December chill in the air and the cold wind off the water. At last, however, they reached the other side. The waterman stepped over the gunwale into the shallow water, then dragged the wherry onto the foreshore, allowing Pickett to step out of the boat onto dry land. He thanked the man (he might, after all, have fallen victim to Barnacle Ben, had he not been warned in advance), then asked the way to Commercial Dock number four.

Armed with this information, and after walking some considerable distance, he eventually came upon that part of the dock where several of the Ludlow ships lay at port, looking oddly naked with their sails furled and tied fast to the spars, whereas the framed aquatints adorning the walls of the counting-house depicted the ships with sails billowing so convincingly that one could (if one's work that day were particularly tedious) almost feel the wind in one's hair.

Here, too, the dock swarmed with activity: the *Mary Katherine* was being loaded for her outbound journey, the tall crane lowering a stack of crates into the cargo hold while a few members of her crew stood next to the open hatch, ready to guide the load down the hatch to the hold below. Other sailors swabbed the decks, while still others packed the seams of her hull with fresh oakum, thoughtfully provided by the residents of London's workhouses and prisons, who were required to pick the fibers of rope apart as a condition of their residence in the former case, or of their punishment in the latter.

He passed the *Mary Katherine* and soon came to the much larger *Queen of the Seas*. He recognized its master at once as the same man he'd noticed at the inquest. Seen here in his proper context, it was easy to identify the markers of the sailor: the wide stance and rolling gait that allowed him to keep his balance on a pitching and tossing deck and yet looked so odd on land, as he was now; the tanned and weathered face of a man exposed to the elements for long periods of time; even the dark blue, double-breasted coat that so many sailors favored—all identified Josiah Tubbs as a man whose life had been spent on the water.

As he drew nearer, Pickett realized that he was the object of a similar appraisal by his quarry.

"Thought it wouldn't be long before you showed up," the ship's master said as soon as Pickett was within earshot.

"Oh?" responded Pickett, determined not to be put off by

this unpromising welcome. "Why is that?"

"Saw you at the inquest. Realized at once that it was your father I had the dubious honor of hosting on the *Queen*." Receiving no immediate answer, he challenged, "Well? Am I right?"

"Quite right, cap—er, sir. I was wondering if—"

"Well, I won't say he deserved what happened to him— no one does, for that matter—but I won't deny I was glad to see the back of him."

"Troublemaker, was he?" Pickett asked, trying to sound sympathetic.

Mr. Tubbs gave a short bark of humorless laughter. "That's putting it mildly!"

"I understand he and one of the ladies on board had a bit of a flirtation going on."

"If Sir Horace Stapleton can't keep his household in order, that's his own lookout. My responsibility is to the ship and her crew."

"Surely Da didn't try to interfere with your running of the ship!" exclaimed Pickett, startled into thoughtless speech.

"O-ho, didn't he just?" retorted Mr. Tubbs. "Tell me, Mr. Pickett, what d'you think this ship runs on?"

"Er, um, the wind, I suppose," stammered Pickett, caught off guard by this frontal attack.

"Discipline!" Mr. Tubbs answered as if he had not spoken, driving one fist into the palm of his other hand for emphasis. "Discipline, Mr. Pickett! The passage from New South Wales is a long one, and crew as well as passengers can become bored. Where there is boredom, discipline breaks down, and where discipline breaks down—well, only look at the H. M. S. *Bounty* for an example. One night my first mate discovered several of the *Queen*'s ordinary seamen down in the cargo hold playing 'penny up the wall'—and your father leading the pack."

"And you don't allow gambling on board," Pickett deduced, nodding in understanding.

"Not at all!" protested Mr. Tubbs, bristling at this implied criticism. "I enjoy a civilized game of whist as much as the next man. In fact, on nights with a clear sky and a fair sea, I often invite a few of the more genteel passengers to join me and some of my senior officers for a night of cards."

"So gambling is permitted for the officers, but not for the men beneath them," Pickett said, without a trace of irony.

"Just so," pronounced the ship's master, rocking back on his heels. "It's a moral failing, you know, amongst the lower classes."

That's rich, Pickett thought, *especially coming from a man who's hardly Almack's material himself.* He could show Mr. Tubbs places in London where the flower of English aristocracy could lose more money in a single night than an ordinary seaman on a merchant ship would earn in his entire life.

At the moment, however, he had more immediate concerns.

"Were there any of the men who might have borne him a grudge?" he asked. "Someone who lost money to him, perhaps?"

Mr. Tubbs scratched his bristly chin. "From what I

understand, he had quite a run of luck. But most of the men were using farthings, so the amount of money changing hands was actually quite small." In a more severe tone, he added, "Excepting, of course, for Bowen, but as I told him at the time, if he wasn't prepared to lose his father's watch, he never should've staked it. They knew they weren't supposed to be gambling, so if any man arrived in port with pockets to let, he has no one to blame but himself."

Pickett's ears pricked up. "One of your men lost a watch? What was his name?"

"Aye. Ordinary Seaman Bowen. That fellow there." His stubby finger pointed toward one of the mop-wielding sailors on the *Queen of the Seas*'s main deck.

"Forgive me, but what is his given name?" Pickett asked, seeing in his mind's eye a watch with a cracked face and the letters *H. B.* engraved on its case.

"Henry," Mr. Tubbs said, regarding him curiously. "Henry Bowen. Mean anything to you?"

"I found a watch amongst my father's effects," Pickett said. "The initials *H. B.* are engraved on the front of its case. Would you object to my having a word with Ordinary Seaman Bowen?"

"As long as you don't prevent him from doing his work," said the ship's master, "you can talk to any man you like." Mr. Tubbs waved a hand toward his ship in a gesture usually associated with the words *Be my guest*.

Pickett didn't wait for a second invitation. He thanked the ship's master and strode up the gangplank. As he approached the sailor, Bowen's mop grew still. He assumed a stiff, almost hostile stance curiously at odds with the wariness in his face. Pickett wondered how much he had heard about Gentleman Jack's murder.

"I don't know nothing," he said as soon as Pickett was in earshot. "I paid him his winnings, and if I grumbled a bit afterwards, well, what does that prove?"

"I believe you accused him of cheating," said Pickett, drawing a bow at a venture. "That's a bit more than mere grumbling, don't you think?"

"And nobody ever said anything in his cups that he wouldn't say when he was sober as a judge, did he?" retorted Bowen, stepping neatly into the trap laid for him. "Anyways, I never saw Jack again once he left the ship, and nobody can say otherwise."

"Can anyone say where you were on the night after he left the ship? Oh, and keep mopping, will you? I don't think Mr. Tubbs will be happy with either one of us if he sees you shirking on the job."

Bowen began to ply his mop once more, but gave Pickett a look that said he would have much preferred to beat him about the head with it. "If you must know," he said mulishly, I was with a girl named Cat. She lives in a house across from the ropewalk."

Pickett didn't have to ask about Cat's profession, or the nature of the house in which she resided. He filed the information away for future reference in case it should be needed, and came to the point for which he had sought Ordinary Seaman Bowen out.

"I understand my father won a watch from you, a watch

with a certain sentimental value." He didn't intend to tell Bowen that it held a certain sentimental value to Kit, too, as it represented the only gift he was ever given—the only gift he would ever be given—by his father; Bowen would only assert, quite accurately, his own prior claim. Still, he thought—hoped—there was a way to resolve the quandary in a way that would make them both happy. "I would be happy to return it to you—Da should never have accepted such a stake in the first place—but I'm afraid it's broken. I daresay he must have landed on it when he fell. In any case, since I can't give you the watch"—he withdrew a large silver coin from the inside pocket of his coat—"I wonder if you would be willing to accept half a crown for it."

Pickett had fully expected him to try to negotiate a higher price, so he was taken completely by surprise when Bowen took a step backwards, raising his hand as if to ward off a blow. "That's not—you don't need to—Jack won it fair and square, God's truth!"

Scared, thought Pickett, regarding him in some amazement. The belligerence Bowen had shown when Pickett had first approached him had been nothing but a big show, when all the time he was so terrified of being connected to the death of Gentleman Jack that he wouldn't even accept reimbursement for the watch he had lost at honest, if unauthorized, play. It might be interesting to see what Cat of the Ropewalk would have to say about her clientele on the night in question.

Unfortunately, he hadn't the time to pursue this potential lead today. He still had to fetch his father's valise from Sully's boardinghouse, and the return trip from the docks was going to be rather more circuitous, since he was going to have to make his way westward along the river until he came to the nearest bridge, he having no intention of being rowed back across the water in an open boat.

The boardinghouse was not hard to find. A building of considerable antiquity, it had once been the home of a prosperous merchant who had made his fortune on the river some two centuries previously. Its best days were clearly behind it, but the well-scrubbed front stoop and front window hung with cheap lace curtains testified to the current owner's efforts to convey a homelike appearance even in the coarse environs of the waterfront.

He lifted the brass door knocker, wincing at the screech of neglected hinges. Moments later, the door was opened by a stout middle-aged woman in a starched apron and mobcap who gave him to understand that, yes, she'd had a lodger by the name of Jack Pickett, but if the visitor had hoped to see him, then he was out of luck.

"For he's dead now," she concluded. "Dead only two days hence, and he as pleasant-spoken a man as I've met in many a long day. What the world's a-comin' to these days, I'm sure I don't know! Why, just yesterday old Tom Mason, him that lives just two doors down—"

"Yes, I know Jack Pickett is dead," said that man's son, cutting off what threatened to be a lengthy account of not only the unknown Tom Mason, but the state of the world in general. "He is—he was—my father. I've come to collect his things."

"O-ho!" she said, peering at him with the squinted eyes of the short-sighted. "Well, you've got the look of him about you, and no mistake! Mind you, I wouldn't let just anyone come in and make off with one of my lodgers' bits and bobs without him having got permission first, for there's no denying there's folks in this world that don't think twice about taking what they've no right to, such is the way of the world these days, what with—but that's neither here nor there." To Pickett's relief, she interrupted herself in the middle of what was apparently a favorite topic of conversation. "As I say, I wouldn't in the ordinary way be lettin' you make off with one of my boarders' things without him having first given permission, but besides the fact that you can't get permission from one what's already dead, it's plain as a pikestaff that he was your da, for the pair of you's as like as two peas in a pod."

Pickett nodded. "So I've often been told," he said, adding with a glance at the narrow staircase that gave access to the upper floors, "if you'll tell me which room was his, I'll remove his things so you won't be obliged to store them any longer."

It was a tactical error. Her eyes suddenly gleamed with avarice. "I won't deny it's a burden, having space taken up by someone's things what won't never pay the rent he owes, he bein' cold in his grave," she said with the air of one shouldering a load too heavy to be borne. "Still, it's not like he was askin' to get hisself done in, only that's the world we live in these days..."

Pickett, recognizing his cue, reached into his coat pocket for his coin purse. He might have pointed out that since his father had shared the room with one of his fellow passengers from the ship, the room would not have been vacant in any case. Still, he'd walked into that one when he should have known what would be the inevitable result, so he supposed having his pocket picked (figuratively speaking) was no more than he deserved. Resolving to be more careful in the future, he gave the woman a shilling for her supposed inconvenience. After biting the coin to make sure the silver was real, she started for the stairs, giving him to understand that he was to follow her.

She climbed two flights, and was puffing slightly by the time she stopped before a closed door at the back of the house, presumably overlooking the river. The door was warped with age, and rattled against the jamb as she rapped her knuckles against a panel that would have been the better for a coat of fresh paint.

"Mr. Bradley, are you in there? Here's Mr. Pickett's boy, come to fetch his da's things."

The faint vibration of footsteps within found their echo in the tremor of the door against its frame, and a moment later it was opened by the same man who'd bought him a pint after the coroner's inquest.

"Won't you c-come in?" Sully stepped aside, allowing Pickett to enter. "I t-trust you had no t-trouble finding the house?"

"None at all," Pickett assured him, accepting Sully's proffered hand.

"I'm sure I c-can find enough t-tea to offer you a cup or two, and I'll be glad to answer any q-questions you may have thought of since the inquest." As if suddenly aware of a very interested audience, he shifted his gaze from Pickett to the woman standing just outside the door, her ears all but quivering as she strained to take in every word. "But I mustn't k-keep Mrs. Huggins from her d-duties, knowing how hard she works to k-keep a respectable house."

Mrs. Huggins opened her mouth as if to protest this cavalier dismissal, but was forestalled from making any objection when Mr. Bradley gently but firmly closed the door in her face. Pickett hadn't anticipated staying for tea—he'd been gone from Curzon Street too long already—but realized he could hardly grab his father's valise and go without so much as a by-your-leave.

While his host busied himself with putting water on to heat, Pickett seated himself on a nearby straight chair and said haltingly, "I'm afraid I never thanked you properly the other day—after the inquest, I mean—"

"No need for that," Sully assured him. "Glad to d-do a good t-turn for Jack's boy. Besides, it was j-just a p-pint of ale. Anyone would d-do the same."

"I think we both know it was a good deal more than that," Pickett said. "I'm glad to know he had such a good friend, anyway."

"There was a p-peculiar charm about Jack," Sully observed with a faraway look in his eye. "Not with j-just the ladies, n-neither. Men liked him, t-too. He had a gift for making friends."

"And enemies," Pickett added darkly.

"Then you d-don't hold with the theory that it might have

b-been a random attack—a matter of b-being in the wrong place at the wrong t-time?"

Pickett shrugged, lifting his hands in a gesture of helpless frustration. "I don't see how it could be! The time and the place, perhaps, but what of the weapon? That knife doesn't lend itself to explanations of mere happenstance. Even if it belonged to Da, it would be a very odd sort of murderer who would attack a man while unarmed, trusting to find a deadly weapon conveniently placed on his victim's person—to say nothing of being able to wrest it away from him in the struggle. Still, I suppose the possibility must be considered. Did my father own such a knife?"

Sully pondered the question for a moment before answering. "I d-don't know," he said at last. "You must understand, that k-kind of knife is used mostly for ceremonial purposes—ritual scarring, that sort of thing—in other words, t-too important to the t-tribe's c-culture to sell to Europeans as mere curiosities. Still, as I said, your father c-could exercise a certain charm; it's quite p-possible that he persuaded some t-tribesman to part with one in exchange for coin, or else by t-trading it for some object of his own. Still, if he owned a knife like that, I n-never saw it."

"I keep coming back to that woman," Pickett said, hoping a different approach might jog some memory in Sully's brain. "Da hinted at a shipboard flirtation, and I had no reason to doubt him; it fits so well with what I remember of him before he was transported. Is it possible that the lady wanted more than a shipboard dalliance, and was displeased when he broke it off once they made port? 'Hell hath no fury,' you know."

His face fell as he recognized the flaw in this promising theory. "No, for no woman would venture out alone at such an hour, even to avenge herself on a faithless lover. A trusted servant, perhaps? Or what about her husband? Was Sir Horace aware of his wife's intrigues?"

"Sir Horace?" Sully echoed in surprise.

Pickett was momentarily taken aback. "We are talking about Sir Horace and Lady Stapleton, aren't we?"

"What m-makes you think so?"

"Only two women are listed on the ship's manifest: Lady Stapleton and Mrs. Harriet Marsh, wife of the Reverend Edwin Marsh. If my father was engaged in a flirtation with a woman on the ship, it isn't difficult to guess which one was his inamorata through a simple process of elimination. She was at the inquest, too, wasn't she?"

"Aye, with her face covered," Sully said, nodding. "Seems to me that she'd have d-done better to t-try and b-blend in, rather than swathe herself in veils."

Pickett nodded distractedly. The picture he was forming of Lady Stapleton—a woman carrying on an intrigue right under husband's nose, then appearing at her murdered lover's inquest in a garb guaranteed to draw all eyes—was that of a woman who enjoyed creating little dramas in which she, naturally, was the leading actress. Such a woman would relish being at the center of a love triangle, and the possibility of her husband's discovering her *in flagrante delicto* would very likely add spice to the amorous encounters.

It appeared Sully's thoughts were running along similar lines. "As for whether S-Sir Horace knew about his wife's indiscretions—to be honest, I d-don't see how he could've *not* known. A merchant ship doesn't offer much in the way of privacy, you know."

"And he didn't seem to object? You never heard any quarrel, or any threats of violence?"

"No, but I said there wasn't m-much privacy; I never said there was n-no privacy at all. They might have f-fought like f-fishwives, as long as they k-kept their voices down while below deck, or stood d-downwind on the d-deck, where their voices wouldn't c-carry. In any case, I reckoned your father knew his own business best. I had no d-dog in the f-fight, so to speak."

"All right, let's set aside the Stapletons for now. Was there anyone else on the ship who might have been nursing a grudge against Da? You need not hesitate to tell me anything to his discredit," Pickett added hastily. "Remember, I lived with him for fourteen years; I know exactly what kind of man he was."

But even as he said the words, he had a nagging feeling that they weren't entirely true.

13

In Which John Pickett Claims a Valise

Behind the wire-rimmed spectacles perched on his pink and peeling nose, Sully's light blue eyes wore an expression of almost comic dismay. "Nursing a g-grudge is one thing; committing m-murder is quite another!"

"But someone felt he—or she—had cause," Pickett said.

"Not n-necessarily," protested Sully. "Life is cheap along the w-waterfront; a man who's looking for t-trouble can usually f-find it, w-with or without a reason."

"Still, it's curious that Da's pockets weren't rifled. His coin purse didn't contain a fortune, but it surely must have been worth someone's while to nab. Then, too, his watch would have been good for something, even with its face cracked. If you're going to go to the trouble of killing a man, you might as well make it worth your while."

"By God, you're a cold-blooded f-fellow!" exclaimed Sully, regarding Pickett with something like revulsion.

"I'm only trying to see Da's murder from his killer's perspective," Pickett insisted. "And I can't imagine any situation in which a random attack makes sense. Which brings us back to the *Queen of the Seas*."

Sully conceded the point with a sigh of resignation, and Pickett withdrew the small notebook from his coat pocket, flipping its pages until he came to the list of names.

"I've just come from the docks at Rotherhithe, where I talked to the ship's master and a member of her crew." Pickett gave his host a mischievous smile. "Tell me, did you get in on any of the penny-pitching?"

Sully's answering grin was somewhat sheepish. "Oh, I p-pocketed my f-fair share, but I never had anything to equal J-Jack's skill."

"So," Pickett began, once again consulting his notebook, "we've got illicit gambling in the cargo hold, and a clandestine love affair in the—wherever they could find a quiet, dark corner, I suppose. What about the Reverend Mr. Edwin Marsh and his wife? What did they think of all these immoral goings-on? Might one of them—or both—have thought to play the part of divine retribution?"

"In f-fairness to the reverend, one c-couldn't expect him to approve of Jack's c-conduct on board ship, never m-mind the actions that had g-got him t-transported in the first place," Sully allowed generously. "Still, he d-did his b-best to t-take people as he f-found them. Pity the same c-can't be said for his wife, Harriet. Harriet? Harridan, more like, who d-disapproves of everybody and everything. Mind you, I think it was mostly j-jealousy. It was Lady Stapleton who had all the men j-jumping to set a chair for her, or c-catching her shawl when the wind t-tried to take it, or lending her a spyglass so she c-could see the whales—"

Pickett looked up in sudden interest from the notes he was jotting in the margins. "Whales? Were there whales? No, don't answer that," he said, wrenching his mind back to the business at hand. "It'll have to be the valise, then, since the passenger list doesn't appear to be much help."

"Oh, right," Sully said hastily, setting aside his cup and rising to his feet. "We shoved our b-bags under the b-bed, so as not to c-clutter up the room."

In proof of this statement, he knelt on the rag rug beside the bed, then reached underneath and dragged out a somewhat worn leather valise with brass fittings, including, Pickett noticed with interest, a lock. Sully set the valise on the bed— an act which would no doubt bring Mrs. Huggins's wrath down upon his head when she saw the counterpane white with dust from beneath the bed—and turned to address Pickett over his shoulder.

"I'm afraid it's locked," he said apologetically, "and I d- don't know what your father d-did with the key."

Pickett recalled the small brass key that had been amongst the detritus of his father's life, all wrapped in brown paper and given to him by the coroner, and wondered if this lock was its match. Had his father carried it on his person simply as a matter of principle, or had he wanted to be sure his crony could not rifle through his belongings in his absence? And, if it had been the latter, exactly what was it that his father had not wanted Sullivan Bradley to see or, perhaps, to confiscate?

He looked up from his examination to query Sully. "Have you something long and narrow that I can borrow?"

"Do you mean to say you can d-do that, t-too?"

Sully's voice was filled with admiration. *Too much admiration?* Pickett wondered.

"I d-don't think the lock exists that Jack c-couldn't get into," he continued. "He showed me the t-trick of it more than once, b-but I was never able to m-master it."

Though not for lack of trying, Pickett thought, noting the faint scratches around the keyhole. He chided himself for the thought. If his father had bought the valise at second hand, the scratches might have been there all along. Or his father might have accidentally locked the key inside, and been obliged to pick his own lock in order to retrieve it. He was forced to abandon this theory, however; if Gentleman Jack had picked the lock, there would be no scratches, nor any other indications of clandestine entry.

Of course, these scratches might be the result of those lessons which Sully readily owned had been unsuccessful.

Or Sully might have had a go at it in the hope of discovering something that might prove important the inquest.

Or he might have thought to discover the whereabouts of Jack Pickett's son, in order to inform him of his father's death.

Or he might have tried to force the lock out of lurid curiosity.

In any case, no real harm had been done, and lurid curiosity, after all, was no crime.

While Pickett considered these possibilities, Sully pulled

open the top drawer of a rickety chest which rocked on its slightly uneven legs, and returned with a somewhat showy cravat pin comprising a large ruby in an ornate setting of gold.

He accepted this offering with assurances to Sully that it would not be damaged, and inserted it into the lock. A moment later, he heard the satisfying *click* of the lock as it yielded.

What followed was, he was forced to concede, a disappointment. He wasn't quite sure what he'd expected to find in his father's valise, but whatever it was, he'd not found it there. In fact, there was nothing in the valise that could not have belonged to a hundred other men: a straight razor and a shaving brush, a cravat, two pairs of stockings, two shirts of dingy white linen, a waistcoat with one of its mother-of-pearl buttons missing, a dark brown double-breasted tailcoat with sleeves rather worn at the elbows, a small glass vial filled with what appeared to be dirt, and a small stack of letters tied with a narrow blue ribbon. Looking over his father's meager wardrobe, Pickett realized he'd donned his best clothes before seeking out the now-grown son he hadn't seen in more than a decade, and was oddly touched.

He let the coat fall back into the valise, picked up the letters, and pulled the end of the ribbon until the knot gave. There were three of them, all with wax seals broken, and it was clear that they had not been delivered by the post; they bore no direction at all, only the single word *Jack* written in a flowing script. Frowning, Pickett raised one of the letters to his nose. The heady scent of jasmine filled his nostrils. He was not quite certain whether he ought to read them or not; he was not at all sure he wanted to know about his father's shipboard escapades, and yet, if he himself had any obligation to the lady...

One thing, at least, was certain: he had no intention of reading them here, under the curious gaze of a third party. He put the letters and their accompanying ribbon back into the valise and turned his attention to the glass vial. He turned it over in his hand, studying its contents for a long moment, then withdrew the cork plug and shook some of the substance into his hand and touched it to his tongue. *Yes*, he thought, grimacing. *Definitely dirt.*

"Is that what it looks like?" asked Sully, peering at it.

"If you think it looks like dirt, then yes, it is," Pickett said, then added, "although why Da decided to bottle it and bring it halfway 'round the world escapes me. I wouldn't have thought his memories of Botany Bay were so pleasant as to make him want a permanent reminder."

I've become a man of property... Surely even one of so optimistic a temperament as his father would find it difficult to believe that a small glass bottle filled with dirt could be considered "property," by any definition of the word. Unless...

"Tell me," he said aloud, "did you ever hear my father say anything about acquiring property—real estate, I mean?"

Sully's expression grew guarded. "So he told you about that, did he?"

"He made a few cryptic boasts about becoming a man of property, which I took to mean land, but he never said how he acquired it." *Because I never asked*, Pickett silently chided himself. *Because I was so certain it was an idle boast that I changed the subject every time he brought it up.* And now, for his sins, he was left with the responsibility of discovering exactly what mischief his father had been up to, and making it right. "If he swindled it off some poor sap—"

"No, not a b-bit of it," Sully assured him hastily. "I should say it was more likely that he was the victim of such a scheme, rather than the perpetrator. I don't know how familiar you are with that part of the world—"

"Hardly at all," put in Pickett.

"Nor was J-Jack, else he would have known the land in the interior is p-practically worthless, f-full of wild men and w-weird animals."

"In fact, the biter bit," Pickett observed dryly. "What a pity he didn't live long enough to realize he'd been had! It might have done him a world of good."

"Now, now, m-mustn't speak ill of the d-dead, you know," Sully chided him gently.

"What I don't understand," Pickett said, ignoring this caveat, "is how he had the money to buy it in the first place. He never had two farthings to rub together!"

"I b-believe there was s-someone in England who sent him m-money from time to time."

"It was me!" Pickett said, indignation causing him to lose his grasp of grammar. For almost six years, he'd sent half of his earnings to his father, partly out of some sense of filial duty, and half to assuage a guilty conscience, knowing that they were the fruits of an occupation his father would have deplored, and paid out by the same man who had sentenced him to be transported. And all the while, his father had been throwing it away on land speculation.

"Ah, well," Sully was saying, shaking his head sadly, "maybe it's b-best that he never knew he'd been p-played for a f-fool."

Pickett could not agree, but made no response beyond a skeptical look before saying, "Look here, you and Da are much of a size. Would you like to have any of his things?"

"That's very generous of you, J-John—may I c-call you John? I realize I'm a c-complete stranger to you, but I f-feel as if I've known you for m-many years." Upon being granted this liberty, Sully continued. "As I said, it's very generous of you, b-but are you sure you w-won't wish to k-keep them?"

Pickett nodded. "Yes, quite sure."

As he recalled from his youth, Jack Pickett had prided himself on being quite nattily dressed, as much as was possible for a man of his uncertain means. Still, no man who had been fitted out by Julia, courtesy of Mr. Meyer of Conduit Street, would find anything in Gentleman Jack's wardrobe to tempt him.

"Very well, then, if you're sure you don't mind," Sully conceded, then selected one of the two shirts, the cravat, and, after a severe struggle with his conscience, the tailcoat. "Thank you, J-John. And if I can d-do anything to help you sort your f-father's affairs, please d-don't hesitate to ask."

"I might just take you up on that," Pickett warned him, then snapped the valise shut, hefted it off the bed, and took his leave.

14

Which Concerns the Contents of a Valise

Pickett entered the tall, narrow house in Curzon Street with valise in hand, and headed straight for the stairs, only to be halted halfway to the landing by Rogers, speaking in a low voice.

"Begging your pardon, sir—"

"Yes? What is it?" The significance of the butler's hushed tones dawned, bringing to mind all manner of hideous possibilities. "Julia—Mrs. Pickett? Is she—?"

Rogers hastened to reassure him. "There is no cause for concern. The doctor left not fifteen minutes ago, so Mrs. Pickett may well be sleeping. The midwife," he added, with a slight emphasis on this last word, "has not been sent for."

Pickett let out a long breath. If the doctor had not stayed and the midwife had not been summoned, Julia's confinement must not be imminent. He glanced at the staircase in the foyer and back again. "Can I go up to her?"

If Rogers saw anything unusual in the master of the house asking the butler's permission to visit his own wife in their shared bedchamber, he gave no sign. "There is certainly no reason why you should not, although I would suggest that if you should find Mrs. Pickett asleep, you might not wish to wake her."

"No, of course not," Pickett agreed, then continued up the stairs to the floor above.

Once outside the bedroom door, however, he hesitated. No sounds issued from within, but then, they wouldn't if she were alone in the room, sleeping or not. He turned the knob carefully and noiselessly, and pushed the door open just far enough to peer inside.

The fire had been burning long enough that the room was quite warm. None of the candles were lit, however, and the curtains were closed, casting the room into shadow. The bed curtains had not been closed, however, and the fire offered just enough illumination for him to make out Julia's recumbent figure beneath the counterpane. Her back was turned to him and her hair was unbound. The light from the fire glinted off the steel hairpins on the bedside table, and limned her hair in gold.

Something twisted deep inside him at the sight of her. What had he ever done to deserve such a woman? Backing out of the room, he pulled the door closed.

Just before the latch caught, however, she stirred and said sleepily, "John?"

"I'm sorry; I didn't mean to waken you."

"No, don't go," she protested, struggling to sit up. "I

wasn't asleep."

He rather doubted the truth of this statement, but entered the room nevertheless. He crossed the floor to the bed and gave her his arm for support until she had settled herself comfortably with the pillows at her back.

"Thank you." Making a moue of distaste, she added, "Sometimes I feel like a turtle stuck on its back."

"You make the prettiest turtle I've ever seen," he said, then kissed her warmly. Upon the completion of this mutually satisfactory exercise, her gaze fell to the bag he'd set down beside the bed in order to attend to more pressing matters.

"Is that your father's valise?"

"Yes. I think it may be the match for that key we found among his things. But Rogers says the doctor has been here," he said, dismissing the valise out of hand.

"Yes, but you need not look like that," she assured him, tracing one finger along the furrow in his brow. "It's only that my back has ached ever since I woke up this morning, and since both Emily and Claudia have mentioned backaches as a sign that the end is in sight, I thought perhaps I should at least notify Dr. Gilroy. You'll be pleased to know that he says everything is exactly as it should be at this point."

Pickett hardly heard the latter half of this speech, so concerned was he with the former. "You said nothing about it this morning."

She regarded him in some bewilderment. "No, for the doctor hadn't yet been here. Oh, I see. You mean about my back aching. No, I didn't mention it. In fact, there are many aches and pains I never mention, for if I did, I should be the most tiresome creature imaginable!"

"I'm glad to know there's no reason to be concerned, although I'm sorry it's been so uncomfortable for you." He frowned thoughtfully. *There are many aches and pains I never mention*... And this was in addition to the worst bit, which was yet to come. Did he have the right—did any man have the right—to ask such a thing of the woman he loved?

The silence stretched between them until at last Julia took his arm and drew him down to sit on the edge of the bed. "Such a fierce expression! Darling, what can you be thinking?"

"Julia," Pickett said slowly, struggling for words, "if you should find all this too much—too painful, I mean, or too distasteful—I wouldn't want—you have only to—"

This speech was perhaps mercifully cut short when Kit, finding the door open, came bounding in. "Why didn't you tell me you were back?" He broke off, eyes widening at the sight of the valise on the floor at his brother's feet. "What's that?"

"It's Da's valise," Pickett said, bending over to grasp its handle. "Would you like to see what's inside? Let's take it downstairs, so we won't bother Julia."

"Oh no, you don't!" As he stood up, Julia grabbed his coattails to detain him. "If you think to leave me lying here in bed while you two have all the fun, you will very soon learn your mistake! Only give me a moment to move over and make room, and you can put the valise here on the bed."

In fact, it took more than a moment, but eventually Julia succeeded in settling herself far enough from the edge of the bed that the valise could be placed beside her.

In the meantime, Pickett fetched the small paper parcel containing everything his father had carried on his person at the time of his death, including the small brass key which Pickett strongly suspected would open the lock on the valise. As he unfolded the thick brown paper, he remembered another item amongst his father's effects, and a task left undone. He withdrew his father's watch from its wrappings, and turned to address his young half-brother with a constraint in his manner that had not marked their interactions since very early in their acquaintance.

"Kit, Da wanted you to have this." He offered the timepiece to the boy, who snatched it up eagerly. "I'm sorry— I shouldn't have taken it from you. I'm afraid it's been broken since he first gave it to you, probably during the attack that killed him. I'll take it to a watchmaker and have it repaired, if you like."

Kit looked down at the watch, its hands still reading seven or eight minutes to twelve beneath the cracked glass covering its face. "D'you mean"—his gaze shifted from the face of the watch to that of his brother—"that it's showing the very same time that Da was killed?"

"We can't know for certain, but I think it's very possible."

Kit set his jaw in the manner of one who, having reached a difficult decision, is determined to see it through. "In that case, I think we should leave it as it is, at least until after the trial is over. It might be important."

"You seem very certain that someone will eventually be

brought to trial," Pickett said, regarding him with a quizzical little smile.

"I *am* certain," the boy insisted, then spoiled this vote of confidence by adding, "but if they're not, then I'll expect you to give me my money back."

"That'll show me," said Pickett, chastened. "Mind you, these things take time."

"I know *that*," Kit said scornfully, then rooted through the items in the parcel until he found the key. "Is this the key to Da's valise?" he asked, holding it up for his brother's inspection.

"I think it might be. Would you like to try it?"

Kit's face lit up. "Y'mean you'll let *me* open it?"

Pickett shrugged. "He was your father, too."

Kit, nothing loth, tried the key, and gave a shout of triumph when it turned easily in the lock. A moment later he had flung the valise open, only to be crestfallen upon discovering its scanty contents.

"There's hardly anything in it!"

"No, for I let Da's friend Sully—Sullivan Bradley, that is—have most of Da's clothes."

"Y'mean you've already opened it?" Kit demanded indignantly.

"Well, yes," Pickett confessed, taken aback by his apparent breach of the brotherly code of honor. "I thought he might recognize anything of significance that I might miss." He gave a bitter little laugh. "And did he ever."

"And who, pray, was the accommodating female who provided the hairpin for this little exercise in lock-picking?"

Julia asked in dulcet tones that warned him to supply the lady's name at his peril.

He grinned appreciatively at her. "No hairpin this time, just a cravat pin. Pinchbeck, with a red stone of colored glass, unless I miss my guess," he added. "Who'd have guessed Da would take up with the dandy set?"

"Then why'd you give Da's clothes to that Sully fellow?" Kit demanded, understanding just enough of this speech to fuel his indignation. "You could've given them to me!"

"Don't you think they would be a bit large for you?"

The answer to this question was self-evident, for even as he spoke, Kit removed the remaining shirt from the valise and tugged it over his head. The waistcoat followed, and soon the boy was peacocking before the mirror of Julia's dressing-table. Kit was tall for his age, much as his half-brother had been, but the sleeves of his father's shirt completely swallowed his hands, and its hem swept the floor.

"By the time you're tall enough for them, they would be quite out of fashion," Julia put in, attempting to pour oil over troubled waters.

They were hardly the height of fashion now, but Pickett knew better than to point out this home truth.

"Then John could wear them himself." Kit turned to his brother. "You don't care about stuff like that."

"Maybe not, but your sister-in-law does. Although"— over Kit's head, Pickett's eyes met Julia's with a hint of mischief in their brown depths—"I do miss my old brown coat."

Since the coat he was wearing at that moment was a

duplicate of its predecessor (albeit one of better cut and made from a superior grade of cloth, as well as being specifically tailored to his person), which he'd purchased at a secondhand clothing shop a year before he and Julia had first met, this stated preference was unexpected enough to make her eyebrows rise in dismayed inquiry. "Is this one not inconspicuous enough to serve the purpose? I know you didn't want to dress as if you were setting yourself above your colleagues at Bow Street, but surely they would not expect you to wear a coat with a bullet hole in one shoulder and bloodstains all down the lining of one sleeve!"

"No," Pickett said in mock sorrow. "But I could have worn it next time I call on my grandfather."

Julia smiled at this sally, but after nine months of marriage, she had become sufficiently acquainted with his rather sly wit to have no doubt he would have done just such a thing, had the garment in question still been in his possession. She did not, therefore, challenge him on this point, but instead asked with all seriousness, "Does that mean you intend to pursue the acquaintance? I thought you wanted nothing to do with him."

"I don't," Pickett said with feeling. "But he clearly intends to pursue an acquaintance with me, so I'd rather visit him occasionally on his turf than have him trying to invade mine."

By this time, Kit had lost interest in the conversation and turned his attention back to the valise. Upon discovering the vial of dirt, he snatched it up and examined its contents, then shook it thoroughly and examined it again.

"Will you teach me how to open locks with a pin?"

"Stop shaking that thing before the stopper comes out and you spray dirt all over the bed," Pickett said firmly, taking it from him.

"But John, is it really dirt?" Julia asked, bewildered. "Can I see?"

"Be careful with it," he cautioned, putting it into her outstretched hand. "That's my inheritance you're holding— the 'property' Da boasted of."

"It is rather pretty, isn't it?" she remarked, turning the vial over in her hand.

"Is it?"

"Oh, yes! Just look at the way the tiny flecks gleam in the light. What is the land like, do you suppose?"

"I have no idea, but knowing Da, I'm not optimistic. Sully—Mr. Bradley, I should say—tells me it comes from the interior, and the land there is more or less worthless. I wonder if he knows anyone who might be interested in buying it. Under the circumstances, it seems unlikely."

"*Will* you?" Kit asked again.

"Will I what?"

"Teach me how to open locks with a pin," Kit reminded him impatiently.

"I'll teach you when you're older."

This promise found no favor with his young half-brother. "I'll bet *you* knew how by the time *you* were ten!"

"You'd lose that bet," Pickett said. "I was twelve when Da taught me. And it wasn't some parlor trick I performed for fun; it was something I had to do if I wanted to eat." Seeing

Kit was unmoved by this argument, he added, "Besides, I can't answer for the consequences. Once a lady saw me open a locked door with her hairpin, and she was so impressed she grabbed me and kissed me, right then and there."

"It wasn't like that at all!" protested Julia, choking back her laughter. "We had to have some reason for poking about a locked room in the middle of the night! Besides, I don't remember hearing any complaints at the time!"

"And if that wasn't enough," Pickett continued, unfazed, "only a few months later, she followed me to Scotland and made me marry her."

"Yes, and look what it's got me," she retorted playfully. "Swollen ankles and an aching back."

"Along with the chance to be a marchioness and mistress of a vast estate in New South Wales," he reminded her. "You never dreamed you were making so lofty a match, did you?"

"On the contrary." She stretched out a hand to brush a brown curl back from his forehead, and he, anticipating her next move, very obligingly brought his lips within range. "I knew I'd got a prize from the very beginning."

"Oh, stuff!" Kit, holding no truck with displays of marital affection, returned to his exploration of the valise, and soon his attention as well as his hand alighted on the little stack of letters. "What's this?"

Pickett was dismayed to realize that the haste in which he had repacked them in the valise, while protecting them from Sullivan Bradley's potentially prying eyes, had left them vulnerable to Kit's instead.

"That," he said firmly, removing them from the boy's

grasp, "is none of your business."

"What lovely penmanship," Julia said, having seen her father-in-law's sobriquet written on the outside. "Have you read them? Are they love letters?"

"I haven't read them, and I'm not sure I want to," Pickett told her. "Do you think I should? If Da was under any sort of, let us say, obligation to the lady, moral or financial, it might be my duty to settle matters."

He glanced at Kit to gauge how much of the conversation the boy was taking in, and saw to his relief that his intrepid young brother had finished with the valise and returned to the brown paper parcel. Having examined the pen knife, unfolded the handkerchief, and counted the money in his father's coin purse, he discovered a small scrap of paper. " '91 Chancery Lane,' " he read aloud, although he pronounced the second "c" as a "k." "That's where all the lawyers are. Leastways, that's what Roger said once."

"Not all the lawyers, but a lot of them," Pickett agreed, then added tactfully, "But I think it's supposed to be 'Chancery,' not 'Chankery.' "

But Kit, it seemed, had little time to waste on phonics. "You'd better go to Chankery—I mean, *Chancery*—Lane and see what's at number 91."

Pickett nodded. "I agree." To Julia, he added, "I thought I would go first thing tomorrow morning."

"Only if it turns out to be nothing but a bunch of fusty old lawyers, it'll be the shabbiest trick ever!" put in Kit.

Pickett was inclined to agree. In fact, he had been more than a little afraid that Kit would beg to accompany him on a call that, however valuable the information it might yield, any ten-year-old boy would find dull. He could only be thankful that the prospect of spending the morning in an office full of fusty old lawyers was sufficient to squelch any such inclination on his brother's part.

But as it happened, his visit to Chancery Lane proved to be anything but dull.

15

In Which John Pickett Consults a Lawyer
...and Gets a Surprise

Chancery Lane, as its name implied, had been the legal center of London since the Middle Ages, home to venerated bastions of English law ranging from the Six Clerks' Office at 113 to the rarified environs of Lincoln's Inn, which occupied much of the western side of the street. Several solicitors' offices were also located here, along with a few commercial enterprises catering to those in the legal profession. Most prominent among these latter was one which had occupied the site of number 93 since 1689. This was the establishment of tailors Ede & Ravenscroft, makers of the judicial robes and white wigs that characterized British court proceedings as well as the scarlet, ermine-trimmed ceremonial robes of peers.

Pickett, slowing as he passed in order to survey the sampling of judicial accoutrements displayed in the storefront windows, had a sudden vision of himself clad in the robe and coronet of a marquess, and hurried past, shuddering.

As he approached his destination, however, it became clear that something was amiss at number 91. The pavement outside the building seemed to sparkle in the light, and the reason for this curious phenomenon soon became apparent. The front window had been shattered so thoroughly that not a single glass pane remained intact. The frame was smashed as well, creating a hole large enough that an adult could crawl through with relative ease. The door stood wide open, but this, Pickett recognized as he drew abreast of the establishment, was due to the young man—a clerk, if his sober clothing and harried expression were anything to judge by—sweeping the broken glass from inside with the aid of a broom. Looking beyond him into the shadowy interior, Pickett could see that every drawer and cabinet door was open wide, and the floor was littered with papers.

The Bow Street Runner who still lurked just beneath Pickett's consciousness instantly asserted himself. "What happened here?" he asked sharply.

Pausing in his task, the young man leaned on his broom. "Someone broke into the office during the night." He gestured toward the broken glass. "Came in through the window, as you can see."

"Was anything taken?"

"Let him in, Hawkins," a second man called from deeper within the office.

The clerk stepped aside and waved Pickett inside with a flourish, and the second man, clearly the superior of the two in both years and position, picked his way through the debris to greet him with hand outstretched.

"Good of you to come so promptly," he said, pumping Pickett's hand firmly.

"Oh?" asked Pickett, taken aback by the realization that he was expected.

"My clerk, Mr. Hawkins, came in at seven o'clock this morning to light the fires, and this"—his hand swept in a wide arc—"is what he found."

"You saw no one?" Pickett addressed himself to the clerk, who had abandoned his broom and didn't even pretend not to eavesdrop on his employer's conversation.

Hawkins shook his head. "No one at all."

Pickett turned back to the senior of the two. "Was anything taken?"

"It's hard to say. The petty cash is undisturbed, so the fellow obviously wasn't after money, but as for just what he *was* after—well, look at the mess he left behind." He sighed and shook his head. "It'll take days, perhaps weeks, to put everything back in order."

Pickett stooped, picked up a paper at random, and glanced at it. *...granted to the party of the first part...to be paid quarterly by the party of the second part...* He looked back up at the two men as recognition dawned. "It's a contract."

"One of many: contracts, deeds, wills—" The elder man shrugged. "The same sort of thing you would find in any solicitor's office."

"So this is a solicitor's office," Pickett said, glad to have one puzzle solved.

"Why, yes." The elder man, presumably the solicitor himself, frowned. "Why, yes, of course it is. Were you not informed?"

"I had only the street name and number," Pickett said with perfect truth, neatly sidestepping the question.

"Well, then," said the solicitor, clearly flustered, "let me rectify the omission at once. "Henry Watson, solicitor, your very obedient servant." Mr. Watson offered his hand, remembered the had already shaken hands, and contented himself with a nod.

"John Pickett." He returned the other man's nod. "I believe you had some dealings with my father—also named John Pickett, but usually called Jack."

"Ah, yes. I had the pleasure of assisting Mr.—let us say, Mr. John Pickett the Elder—only a few days ago. What a small world it is, to be sure!"

Pickett was still puzzling over this *non sequitur* when the clerk interrupted.

"They're here, Mr. Watson, sir!"

Messrs. Pickett and Watson turned as one, and saw a slender youth clad in the blue coat and red waistcoat of the Bow Street Foot Patrol enter the office, followed by a taller man in street clothes, an incredibly handsome man with windswept blond hair and blue eyes which were at that moment wide with amazement.

"Good God!" Pickett exclaimed. "*Harry?*"

"Why, it's Mr. Pickett!" cried the youth, flushing with pleasure. "Fancy our meeting you here!"

"Yates, isn't it?" asked Pickett smiling down at Harry Carson's young partner. "An unexpected pleasure."

Mr. Watson glanced in confusion from Pickett to the newcomers, and back again. "Good heavens! Are you *not*, then, the Bow Street Runner I sent for?"

"He is most certainly not!" put in Harry Carson, with feeling. "*I* am! That is, *we* are!" His gesture belatedly took in the youth beside him.

"I beg your pardon, Mr. Watson," Pickett said hastily, seeing the solicitor's brow lowering in growing indignation. "It was not my intention to deceive. In fact, I was with Bow Street for several years, until quite recently, so I suppose I— but that's neither here nor there. It's just that my father— died—a few days ago, and—"

"Oh, Mr. Pickett!" exclaimed Yates in ready sympathy. "I'm so sorry!"

Pickett acknowledged this expression of condolence with a little smile and a quick nod, but continued to placate the solicitor. "—And among the things found on his body when he died was a scrap of paper with your direction written on it. I'm trying to—to put his affairs in order, and thought perhaps you might have some idea of what he'd intended to call on you for."

"Oh, very well," Mr. Watson said, obviously torn. "I'll let Mr. Hawkins talk to these fellows—it was he, after all, who discovered the damage—and I'll tell you what I can about your father's situation. In fact, he consulted with me only a few days ago. If you'll just step into my office—you'll see that it has not escaped the destruction…"

Still decrying the condition of his place of business, he gestured for Pickett to precede him through a door at the back of the room. If it were possible, the havoc wreaked upon this inner office was even worse than the damage to the outer room. Here, too, the floor was littered with papers, but the drawers of the broad mahogany desk, instead of merely hanging open, had been pulled out and dumped onto the floor, and one of the doors of the tall cabinet against the far wall had been completely ripped from its hinges. Even the painting hanging on the wall behind the desk—a portrait depicting a man, most likely the ancestor of the office's current occupant, wearing a solicitor's black gown and holding a rolled-up paper tied with a black ribbon—hung at a drunken angle, suggesting a search for a safe or some other compartment hidden behind it. Pickett was struck by the thought that this was no wanton act of destruction for its own sake, but a frantic search for some specific object, even to the point of sounding the desk drawers for a false bottom.

He made this observation aloud to the solicitor, adding, "I suppose it's too soon to tell if anything is missing."

"Lord, yes!" said Mr. Watson, heaving a sigh. He picked his way through the litter to seat himself behind his desk, then motioned Pickett toward the room's only other chair. "All these documents will have to be sorted and filed, but even after everything has been put back in order, it may be months, even years, before I realize that something that should be here is gone."

"Are any of these documents"—he made a gesture that encompassed all the papers littering the floor—"valuable enough for someone to steal?"

Mr. Watson leaned over to pick up a collection of papers still stacked more or less neatly, and flipped idly through the pages. "Yes and no," he said. "The paper itself is of no particular value, although I won't deny that the vellum required for legal documents is quite costly. But many—I would not scruple to say most—legal documents represent considerable wealth, or its loss, for someone: a will, for instance, showing that a large fortune is not to be left as one or more of the potential legatees had hoped; the deed to a valuable tract of land, perhaps acquired through dubious means; a contract that requires one to pay a sum of money one can ill afford—need I go on, Mr. Pickett?"

"I see your point," Pickett said. "But you say my father came to see you only a few days ago. Can you tell me why?"

"Normally, of course, I would not discuss one of my clients or his affairs with a third party, but if he has died, as you say…"

His voice trailed off uncertainly, and Pickett nodded. "Stabbed in a back alley in Limehouse."

"Good God!" exclaimed Mr. Watson, pausing in the act of gathering up still more of the papers at his feet. "Is it possible that he knew—that he had cause to believe—"

"That he knew what?"

The words came out more sharply than Pickett had intended, but if the solicitor noticed, he took no offense.

"Forgive me. I only wondered if your father had any reason to suspect that his life was in danger."

"Not that I know of." But even as he refuted this

suggestion, Pickett's ears pricked up at the possibility. Nothing in his father's manner had suggested that he harbored any fears for his life, but then, he was beginning to question how much he knew, how much he had *ever* known, about the man who had sired him. "What makes you say so?"

Mr. Watson leaned forward, propping his elbows on his desk and steepling his fingers beneath his chin. "Because," the solicitor said, "he came to see me about his will."

16

Which Takes John Pickett
from Legal London to the Corridors of Power

A t the thought of his father consulting with a solicitor, Pickett's brain had instantly conjured images of a law-suit over a dubious land transaction, or, worse, co-respondent in a divorce—most probably that of his fellow passengers, Sir Horace and Lady Stapleton. The truth, though less morally reprehensible, was even more baffling.

"His *will?*" he echoed incredulously. "Why did he need to make out a will?"

Because he'd become a "man of property." Even as his brain supplied the answer, Pickett heard Sully's words: *Land in the interior, full of wild men and weird animals...*

Mr. Watson, being a lawyer, felt compelled to add a modifier. "I should say, rather, that he desired to ensure that the will he made while on the ship would be considered valid, should it be challenged. Given that he must have died only hours after his visit to my office, one can only wonder if he had some reason to expect to meet with violence."

Pickett shook his head. "If he had any fears for his life, he kept them well-hidden. But tell me about this will." He glanced about the debris littering the floor. "I'm guessing it's here somewhere?"

"No, for he charged me with procuring a safe deposit box at Coutts in his name. If you haven't discovered the will amongst his effects, I daresay you will find it there. Only let me know if you have any trouble persuading them to give you the key, and I—on second thought—*Mr. Hawkins!*"

This last, bellowed at full volume, was directed to the hapless clerk in the outer room. A moment later, the door opened, and Mr. Hawkins asked somewhat breathlessly, "You wanted me, sir?"

"Fetch me a sheet of paper and a quill. As you see, all of my desk drawers have been turned out."

"Yes, sir."

After a few minutes which were no doubt spent searching amongst the debris for the desired items, the clerk returned.

"Here you are, sir," the young man said, giving a blank sheet of paper, a quill pen, and an ink pot to his superior.

"Thank you." Silence fell, unbroken by anything but the scratching of the quill across the paper. Then Mr. Watson laid aside his pen, folded the paper in half, and handed it to Pickett. "That should get you in."

Pickett took the paper and folded it, then tucked it into the inside pocket of his coat. "Thank you, Mr. Watson. I'm obliged to you."

"I daresay there's no harm in my telling you that you are the sole beneficiary. I take it you are your father's only surviving offspring?"

"As a matter of fact, no. I'm not." Pickett fortified himself with a deep breath. "I might as well tell you that my father is—was—a convicted felon, only just returned to England after serving a ten-year sentence in Botany Bay. His mistress was pregnant at the time of his transportation, although I don't think either of them were aware of it. In any case, my father didn't know he had another son until he met Kit—my half-brother—shortly after leaving your office." He knew the answer already, but for Kit's sake, he had to ask. "I don't suppose—that is, I was wondering if—is there any way that he—"

"And you are sure this half-brother is illegitimate? You are quite certain your father didn't marry the woman? Dockside marriages are not unheard of, you know. The prospect of a long separation—" He broke off, seeing Pickett emphatically shaking his head in the negative.

"If Da had married her, she would have told me of it years ago."

"I see," said the solicitor, nonplussed by this unexpected development. "Well, it's a pity the boy must be cut out, but had he been born within the bonds of matrimony, he and his mother, assuming she is still living, could challenge the will—and would very likely win, leaving you with no more than one-third of your father's monetary assets, and very likely only one-fourth, with your step-mother receiving half and the other half divided equally between you and your half-brother.

In strictly legal terms, your half-brother's illegitimacy makes everything easier."

"Easier for you, maybe," Pickett retorted without malice. "My father left very little of value, so it's not like we're going to fall out over who inherits a fortune. But I don't want Kit— that's his name, short for Christopher—I don't want him to think I've served him a backhanded turn. I don't suppose you can do anything at this late date to…?" He trailed off, not quite sure how to word his query.

Mr. Watson, however, needed no words, and very quickly put a stop to this no doubt well-intentioned but, for him, professionally disastrous line of thinking. "For me to make any alterations to your father's will after his death would be highly unethical. Still, since you appear to be the boy's guardian, I daresay your father would have depended on you to do right by him. On the day that I saw him, he had nothing but praise for you."

"He hadn't even seen me since I was fourteen years old," Pickett objected. "How would *he* know?"

The solicitor gave him an avuncular smile. "Suffice it to say that fathers have an instinct for these things. Now, if you will excuse me," he said briskly, "I think I had best relieve Mr. Hawkins and have a word with these Bow Street men myself. Good luck to you, Mr. Pickett. Let me express my warmest condolences for your loss, and assure you that should anything pertaining to your father be discovered amongst the wreckage"—his gaze raked the documents littering the floor—"you will be notified at once."

Pickett expressed his thanks and took his leave. *If that*

isn't just like Da, he thought, picking his way back through the outer office, *choosing the one solicitor in all of London whose office would be ransacked only three days later.*

Once on the pavement outside, however, he paused, frowning. The vandalism of the solicitor's office was merely an unlucky coincidence; the two events could not possibly be related. Still, as he left legal London behind and headed for the government offices of Whitehall, he wasn't quite so sure.

* * *

Under different circumstances, Pickett might have found the stately corridors of the War and Colonial Office intimidating. After the chaos of the solicitor's office, however, they, came as a welcome change. Locating Sir Horace Stapleton was easy enough; Pickett merely buttonholed the first person he saw and inquired as to that gentleman's whereabouts, and received in return not only concise directions to Sir Horace's office, but also the information that, yes, he would find his quarry there, Sir Horace only just having returned to his office following a meeting with the Secretary regarding his next assignment, a change necessitated by the recent designation of the Scotsman Lachlan Macquarie as the new governor of the colony of New South Wales.

That Sir Horace was not yet fully settled into his new office was evident by the boxes stacked against the walls of the sparsely furnished room. As for the man himself, he was engaged in emptying the uppermost box and arranging its contents in the desk drawers to his satisfaction. The door to the office was open, giving Pickett a brief moment in which to assess the gentleman before making his presence known.

Sir Horace Stapleton was a stout man of about fifty, with unruly gray hair rather badly in need of a trim; Pickett could only assume that Sir Horace had not trusted whatever services the ship might have offered in the way of personal grooming. Like Sullivan Bradley's, his face was ruddy, but Pickett suspected that, unlike the clerk's sunburned countenance— the result, no doubt, of several months at sea—the robust color staining the public servant's somewhat jowly face was its normal condition. Pickett rapped on the doorframe, and when Sir Horace looked up from his task, his naturally ruddy complexion darkened to something akin to purple.

"Thought I'd seen the back of you when we disembarked," he growled, and rather pointedly turned back to his work. "Wasn't much I could do on board ship, short of throwing you overboard, but if you think I'll tolerate you sniffing about my wife now that—"

"Sir Horace," Pickett interrupted, "I think you have mistaken me for someone else."

The bureaucrat peered more closely at his visitor. "Eh? What's that?"

Pickett took a few steps into the room, and the light from the window behind the desk fell more directly on him. "I think you want my father."

"Hmmph. I won't deny I 'mistook' you for your father," Sir Horace conceded, albeit grudgingly. "It's an honest mistake, for you're as like to him as bedamned, and with you standing in the shadows—but that's neither here nor there. As for my sentiments toward that blackguard, I'll beg leave to tell you that 'wanting' him isn't anywhere close."

"What about stabbing him to death with a leilira knife?" Pickett suggested blandly. "Will that play?"

Sir Horace set the book in his hand down on the desk with more force than was strictly necessary. "Look here, just what are you accusing me of?"

Pickett answered the question with one of his own. "Do you mean to tell me you didn't know my father had been murdered within twenty-four hours of setting foot on his native soil?"

"The devil you say!" breathed the bureaucrat, his rude color fading to a sickly pallor even as his belligerence gave way to something resembling fear. "Is this true? How did it happen?"

"He was stabbed in the back. His body was discovered in a back alley in Limehouse."

"The man who attacks without facing his adversary is no better than a coward," Sir Horace pronounced loftily, "whether his weapon is a blade, a bullet, or a good hard shove over the taffrail."

"Not necessarily," objected Pickett. "A man who is old, or sick, or simply lacking in physical strength might attack from the rear if he knows his opponent could overpower him. Or a woman might do so, if she's desperate enough."

Sir Horace turned away from the open box whose contents he had been unpacking, having by this time abandoned all pretense of work. "Just what do you know about your father's pursuit of my wife? It's obvious you must have been told something, else why would you go to the trouble of seeking me out? What did he have the effrontery to say about her?"

"Nothing inappropriate, and he might not have been speaking of Lady Stapleton at all," Pickett assured him with perhaps less than perfect truth. "He only said he would like to become better acquainted with a lady he'd met during the voyage. Your wife was not the only lady on board, was she?"

"No, but if you think your father would prefer Mrs. Marsh to Lady Stapleton, you're a bigger fool than I took your for!"

Pickett swallowed the insult for the sake of expedience. "Mrs. Marsh?"

"Vicar's wife. More than forty years in her dish, and an expression on her face suggesting she'd just eaten a lemon. Not that she deserved what happened to her, poor woman."

"What *did* happen to her?" Pickett asked. Sully's description of the woman had been equally unflattering, but he couldn't recall his father's friend mentioning that anything unfortunate had befallen her, deserved or not.

"Fell overboard just out from Cape Town. Dead by the time the crew got her back on the ship; no one heard her cry for help. Can't help but wonder if she'd thought to—well, mustn't speak ill of the dead. Point is," he said sternly, "that while your father can't be faulted for a preference that nine out of ten men would've shared, that don't give him leave to force his attentions on a lady, especially when the constraints of a long sea voyage make it impossible for her to avoid him."

"It certainly does not," Pickett agreed, although he rather doubted if the three letters in his father's valise—perfumed, no less, and tied with a ribbon—were pleas from the lady to her unwanted suitor begging him to leave her alone. "Allow me to apologize for any distress my father's importunities may have caused Lady Stapleton. In any case, she need not fear being troubled by them any longer."

"I must say, that's prettily spoken of you." Sir Horace's voice held something akin to approval, although Pickett suspected the bureaucrat was mollified not so much by his apology for actions that were, after all, not his own, but by the knowledge that Jack Pickett was no longer alive to present a temptation to his lady wife.

In fact," Pickett said disingenuously, as one who has just had a brilliant idea, "if you will furnish me with her direction, I shall call on her and make my apologies for my father's behavior in person."

"I'm sure that won't be necessary," Sir Horace said hastily, as if he feared the younger Pickett might attempt to pick up where the elder had left off. In any case, Pickett decided, his conversation with Sir Horace had settled one question.

As soon as he returned to Curzon Street, he was going to read those letters.

* * *

With a sigh of resignation, Pickett finished reading the last of the three letters and handed it to Julia. It was almost half-past ten o'clock in the evening, and he had delayed his nightly exile to his camp bed in favor of sitting cross-legged on the bed facing his wife. It had been mutually decided (albeit not without considerable regret) that they should not read the letters until they could be certain that Kit was not only in bed, but also sound asleep, Pickett having strongly suspected their contents would prove inappropriate reading for an inquisitive ten-year-old.

He'd been right.

"It's pretty clear, isn't it? They may not have been lovers —I would imagine clandestine meetings would be hard to manage on a crowded ship—but it sounds as if they sailed as near to the wind as they could without actually doing the deed."

Julia held up her index finger for silence until she reached the end of the flowing script. Having reached the signature—which, in this last letter of the three, was not signed "Sarah S." as the first two had been, but "Yours, Pookie"—she allowed the letter to fall into her lap, then pressed her hand to her abdomen. "And I thought I was done with morning sickness! I know my own father was not without his own amorous intrigues, but whatever else his sins, I hope Papa never called any of his inamoratas 'Pookie'!"

"It is rather nauseating, isn't it?" Pickett agreed. "Still, it's plain as a pikestaff that Lady Stapleton was no persecuted female trying to fend off importunate advances. I don't know if her husband really believes that, or if he only hoped to convince me of it."

"If she wanted to hold your father at arm's length, she certainly had a strange way of going about it." Julia very pointedly picked up the letter again and inhaled deeply of the scent that still permeated it. "It would be interesting to hear her side of the story, wouldn't it?"

"It would," Pickett agreed. "Unfortunately, I have no

idea where she and her husband are staying, and no way of finding out without arousing undue suspicions. I suggested that perhaps I ought to go and offer the lady an apology for my father's supposedly unwanted attentions, but Sir Horace put paid to that idea."

"Perhaps he feared his lady wife would once more succumb to the notorious Pickett charm," Julia suggested coyly.

He gave her a reproachful look, but unfolded his long legs and slid off the bed, saying only, "I thought tomorrow morning I would go to Coutts and look into Da's safe deposit box."

"Literally, or figuratively?" Julia asked.

"Both," he told her. "I shouldn't be gone long."

Over the last few weeks, he had made a point of telling her exactly where he was going every time he left the house and when he expected to return, just in case she should go into labor and a footman must be dispatched to fetch him without loss of time. He had not realized that Julia had noticed this practice, until she smiled at him and said, "You need not rush on my account, John. Childbirth isn't as quick as all that."

"Maybe not." He readily conceded the point. "But when it's my wife doing the birthing, I'm taking no chances."

She saw nothing to dispute in this very satisfying sentiment, so he bent and kissed her, then repaired to the camp bed in the dressing room. She waited until he was settled, then snuffed the candle and spoke tenderly into the darkness.

"Good night, darling."

"Good night, Pookie."

She threw a pillow at him.

17

In Which John Pickett Receives an Offer He Can't Refuse

As it happened, Pickett's visit to Coutts was delayed by some minutes, for as he descended the stairs clad in what Julia called "town dress"—in this case, a double-breasted tailcoat of forest green merino over a cream-colored waistcoat with a subtle pattern of brown stripes—he was brought up short by Rogers, on the way up in search of him.

"Begging your pardon, sir," the butler said, drawing even with his master as he reached the half-landing, "but there is a caller below who is hopeful of a word with you."

Pickett cast an impatient glance at the long-case clock just visible in the foyer below. "Who is he? Did he say what he wanted?"

"No, sir. That is, his name is Mathers, but he did not state the purpose of his call." Rogers gave a discreet cough. "I thought perhaps he wished to procure your professional services."

Pickett sighed. "I suppose I must see him, then," he said without enthusiasm. It was true that he had no ongoing cases at present, except the one for which Kit had engaged him, but although his fledgling investigative concern needed a steady influx of business in order to survive, he had no desire to accept any commission, no matter how lucrative, that might take him away from Julia when she was so near to her confinement.

He descended the remaining stairs and entered the drawing room, where a portly man with mutton-chop whiskers stood warming his hands before the fire.

"Mr. Mathers? John Pickett. I'm pleased to meet you." He held out his hand, and when the visitor shook it, he found that the man's hands were cold. There was no help for it; he would have to offer the caller some form of hospitality. Making an effort to conceal his reluctance, he said, "Would you care for something hot to drink? Coffee, perhaps, or tea?" He gestured toward the sofa nearest the fire, an invitation the visitor did not hesitate to accept.

"Thank you, Mr. Pickett, but no, nothing to drink," said Mr. Mathers, disposing himself on the sofa as if he intended to spend the rest of the day there.

Not if I can help it, Pickett thought. Aloud, he merely said, "What can I do for you?"

"I wonder if I might interest you in a business proposal."

It appeared Rogers's assumption was correct. "And what is the nature of this business?"

"I understand you to have come into the possession of a tract of land in New South Wales. If you have no plans for the property, I wonder if you would consider selling it." In case his host failed to understand the proposal, he added, "To me."

Whatever Pickett had expected, it was not that.

"You want to buy my father's property." It was a statement, not a question.

"I want to buy *your* property," the visitor corrected him gently. "If you have no other plans for it, that is."

"To tell you the truth, sir, I never knew the property existed until yesterday. I haven't had time to consider what to do with it."

"I understand perfectly," Mr. Mathers assured him warmly. "The question of what to do with an inheritance is always difficult—and doubly so when the inheritance in question is more than ten thousand miles away, where one cannot easily inspect it oneself. I am, of course, prepared to offer you a good price."

Exactly what constituted a "good price" for property that was worthless scrub, according to the only man still living who had actually seen it, Pickett had no idea.

"Mr. Mathers," Pickett said, "how did you even know about this property? My father only returned to England a few days ago."

The visitor shrugged. "These things are a matter of public record."

"Yes, but aren't those records, as you say, more than ten thousand miles away?"

Mr. Mathers either did not hear the question, or chose not to answer it. "I am prepared to offer you the sum of twenty pounds for the property, sight unseen. You will be hard pressed to find a better offer," he added, when Pickett did not jump at the chance to rid himself of a white elephant which he could neither use nor dispose of.

As for Pickett himself, his feelings were conflicted. It would certainly be a relief to settle the matter of his unwanted legacy so easily, and twenty pounds would be enough to repay him for the money he'd sent his father over the years, with a considerable profit besides; Mr. Mathers had no doubt spoken the truth when he'd said Pickett would be unlikely to get a better offer. And yet he could still hear the words of his father's friend: *The land in the interior is worthless...* Clearly, Mr. Mathers did not think so. And yet it seemed wrong to take advantage of the man's ignorance, eager as he might be to display it.

"Forgive me, Mr. Mathers, but—why do you want it? What do you hope to use it for?"

His visitor chuckled indulgently, as if Pickett were a precocious child asking questions whose answers he could not possibly comprehend even if they were told to him. "Well, Mr. Pickett, that is what I do, you see. I speculate in land; that is, I buy up properties, and then sell them at a profit, often many years later. You are thinking, I daresay, that only a fool would want to own land where there is nothing but a penal colony. Ah, but what if you are wrong?" He wagged an admonitory finger. "Already New South Wales boasts a thriving trade in timber and flax, and the new governor plans to encourage colonization far beyond the requirements of the penal colony. What then? Eh, Mr. Pickett, what then? Those settlers will need land! Land for building houses on, land for establishing farms, perhaps our own government will need to enlarge its own holdings there. And *that*, sir, is where my investment, and my patience, will be rewarded."

"But what if you're wrong?" Pickett asked. "That is, what if all this new development you expect doesn't come to pass, at least not in your lifetime?"

The visitor shrugged. "Well, that's my lookout, isn't it? I'm out twenty pounds."

Take it, Pickett's brain urged him. *You'd be a fool to refuse.*

And yet, even as he acknowledged the wisdom of this sentiment, he found himself saying something else entirely.

"Forgive me, Mr. Mathers, but it's too soon for me to make any decision in the matter just yet. I'm still trying to put my father's affairs in order. In fact"—he glanced at the ormolu clock on the mantel—"there's somewhere I'm supposed to be—"

"Of course," his caller assured him, rising from the sofa and allowing Pickett to show him to the door. "There's no need to make a decision right away. Take all the time you need. But"—he stepped out onto the portico and turned back—"don't take *too* long."

And in spite of the man's *bonhomie*, it seemed to Pickett that there was something vaguely threatening in his parting words.

* * *

When he arrived at Coutts (the same banking establishment where he had once harbored hopes of obtaining a position as a clerk), Pickett was given the key to the strongbox so readily that he could only assume the solicitor had advised someone at the bank to expect him. A clerk was dispatched to escort him down the stairs to the basement, where he was left to cool his heels while the clerk, promising to return directly, disappeared into the depths of stygian gloom at the rear of the building, his progress marked by the bobbing of the light from the single candle he carried.

"Here we are," he declared a short time later, returning with a strongbox under his arm. "I'll just place it on this table, shall I, along with the candle? That should give you enough light to read by."

Pickett thought the clerk would do better to keep the candle for himself, so as not to be obliged to navigate the stairs in the dark. It soon transpired, however, that although he was more than willing to remove himself to a discreet corner, allowing Pickett to examine the contents of the box in privacy, he had no intention of returning to his post upstairs without Pickett in tow. Yielding to the inevitable, Pickett made no objection to the clerk's continued presence, but inserted the key into the lock, turned it, and raised the hinged lid.

There was more inside than he'd expected, although Pickett had no doubt the box itself was more valuable than all its contents combined, not least because these seemed to comprise nothing but papers. The one on top was a folded sheet of parchment which Pickett, having opened it, instantly recognized as the will.

This being the last will and testament, he read, *of John Pickett, also called Jack, native of London and late resident of Botany Bay in His Majesty's colony of New South Wales. I, the aforesaid John Pickett, being of sound mind and body, bequeath all the money, property, and other assets of which I die possessed to my son, he also being called John Pickett, native and resident of London.*

It was dated *2 December 1809* at the bottom, signed *Johnn Pickett* (spelling had obviously not be Da's strong suit), and witnessed by ship's master Josiah Tubbs, along with passengers Sullivan Bradley and the Reverend Edwin Marsh. The signature of Sir Horace Stapleton, which might have been thought desirable in order to lend weight to the document by virtue of that gentleman's position as undersecretary to the governor, was conspicuous by its absence.

And that was all. Two sentences and three signatures—four, counting the testator's own. But then, his father hadn't owned enough to have any need for a longer document. It was a wonder that he'd taken the trouble to make a will at all.

Pickett frowned thoughtfully. *All the property...of which I die possessed...*

Property. There was that word again. Clearly, his father had come into something—or at least *thought* he'd come into something—worth making some provision for, even posthumously. Pickett recalled that morning's unexpected visitor. Had he been a fool for not snapping up Mr. Mathers's offer before the man could think better of it? It wasn't as if he had anything else to do with the property, for he certainly didn't intend to emigrate.

Some slight noise from the clerk hovering in the background reminded Pickett that he was keeping the man from his work, so he folded the parchment and set it aside, then turned his attention to the next paper. Unlike the thick vellum on which the will was written, this was an ordinary sheet of cheap paper, yellowed with age and bearing in faded pencil the image of a curly-haired child shown in profile. It was unsigned, but at the bottom, in a rounded cursive he had once seen in a church registry, was written, *John, age 4.*

My mother's. He had no real memory of her, but he knew it as certainly as if she had signed her name in inch-high capitals. Had his father kept it all these years for the sake of its subject, or its creator? The son he would someday leave behind, or the wife he had lost?

He supposed Julia, no contemptible portraitist herself, would want to see it, all the more so now that they were soon to have a child of their own, but there would be time for that later. He laid the drawing on top of the will, took out the next document, and swallowed hard, feeling a sudden thickness at the back of his throat. These were his parents' marriage lines, dated 4 April 1783 and bearing the signatures of *John Pickett, servant,* and *Ly. Lydia Melrose,* the latter in a round schoolgirl hand. That *Ly.,* which he had first noticed when he'd looked up the record of their marriage in the church registry of St. Giles-in-the-Fields and taken for some error on his mother's part, he having at that time no reason to even suspect that he had descended from so exalted a bloodline.

If Lord Melrose had not cast the young couple off, he wondered, how differently might his own life have played out? He might never have contracted the illness that had ended his mother's life much too soon, and his father would not have been obliged to turn to thievery in order to procure medical treatment for her, the pair having exhausted their meager savings trying to save him. Both of his parents might still have been alive today.

As for him, he would have been sent to school at Eton and, later, to Oxford or Cambridge—an education he secretly longed to provide for his own sons someday, albeit without any help from his overbearing grandfather, thank you very much—but what then? He would certainly have participated in the London Season; Lord Melrose would have seen to that, eager to procure for his lowborn grandson a bride whose own pedigree might erase, at least to some degree, the stain of his mother's *mésalliance* upon the family honor.

And at some point, he would have been introduced to the beautiful and unhappily married Julia, Lady Fieldhurst. Would they still have fallen in love, or was it the obstacle presented by their widely divergent social classes—the lure of the forbidden, in fact—that had first attracted them to one another? It was a disconcerting thought. More disconcerting still was the thought that they might have settled for one of the discreet extramarital arrangements to which London society turned a blind eye—an arrangement, in fact, very similar to the one Julia had proposed to him in Scotland, before the thought of marrying someone so far beneath her had ever crossed her mind.

But then Lord Fieldhurst would have been murdered, and he, having never learned how to go about conducting a criminal investigation, would have been powerless to save her from the gallows. He might even have come under suspicion himself, since her husband's murder would have left her free to marry Lord Melrose's grandson—provided, of course, that neither of them were hanged first.

Suppressing a shudder at the thought, he put his parents' marriage lines on top of the sketch and withdrew the final document, a large sheet of thick vellum folded into fourths, from the strongbox. He unfolded it and began to read, his eyes growing wider with every line. Much of its language eluded him, larded as it was with surveyors' jargon describing the exact location of the property, but he deciphered enough to recognize that at the time of his death, his father had been the possessor of some six hundred acres just east of the Blue Mountains, near the western frontier of the Colony of New South Wales.

Well, I'm damned! Pickett thought. *Da really was a "man of property"!*

Worthless property, perhaps, but property nonetheless. Its remote location, along with the fact that the soil wasn't suitable for farming—or much of anything else—explained why his father had been able to buy so large a tract of land with the meager sums he himself had sent at regular intervals over a period of five years. He wondered if the fact that it was so large a property would prove to be a blessing or a curse, and told himself that he would be wise to accept Mr. Mathers's offer without delay, before the man had time to look more closely into the land he was proposing to buy.

And yet he could not quite convince himself that his father would have approved of this plan. There was, however, another course of action, a more immediate one of which his father would vehemently disapprove, and yet one which

Pickett fully intended to take, whatever his father's theoretical sentiments.

And so, after returning all the papers to the strongbox, at least for the nonce, he returned to Curzon Street, whence, the following morning, he set out for the Bow Street Public Office with the little glass vial in the inside pocket of his coat.

The awkwardness of his departure from that institution two months earlier had long since been forgotten (if it had ever existed in the first place, apart from Pickett's imagination), and he was warmly welcomed by the officers present, admitting to Dixon that no, he was not a father yet, although he lived in daily expectation of that honor, and assuring Maxwell that his young half-brother was doing very well, and would be starting to school next month, at the beginning of the Hilary term.

"Is Mr. Colquhoun in?" Pickett asked at last, jerking his thumb in the direction of the closed door to the magistrate's office.

The question was directed toward the two men equally, but it was no surprise that it was Dixon, rather than the much more reticent Maxwell, who answered.

"Aye, that he is. And I don't doubt he'll be right pleased to see you."

Pickett thanked him, then strode across the room and rapped on the door.

A voice called to him to "come in" in a pronounced Scots burr, so Pickett opened the door and entered the magistrate's office.

"It's good to see you, John." Now that he was no longer

employed at Bow Street, Mr. Colquhoun had no compunctions about addressing by his first name the former Runner whom he had known since he was a fourteen-year-old pickpocket. "What brings you here? Not that you have to have a reason, mind you."

"Thank you, sir. I've been trying to settle my father's affairs, and something has come up that—well, I should like to ask your advice."

The magistrate's bushy white eyebrows rose. "Oh? And what is that?"

"On the day before he died, Da called on me in Curzon Street. While he was there, he boasted about becoming a 'man of property.' "

"And so he might have done," Mr. Colquhoun pointed out. "Many of the transported felons choose to remain there, and some do surprisingly well for themselves."

"Yes, sir. A couple of days ago, I fetched his valise from the boardinghouse where he'd taken a room. I found this inside." Pickett withdrew the vial from his coat pocket and handed it over the desk. "Presumably, it was taken from the property in question—property Bradley says is worthless. Then yesterday morning, a man named Mathers turned up on my doorstep, ready to pay twenty pounds for it, sight unseen. He says he's a speculator in land, buying it up cheap and selling it later at a profit."

"And did you sell it to him?"

"No, sir. I haven't given him a final answer yet, but I"— Pickett shook his head"—I don't know, I'm not entirely sure he's not a rum 'un."

"Such men do exist," the magistrate assured him. "And land in the colonies is always ripe for this sort of investment. In that regard, at least, he's very likely telling the truth. Where is the land? Do you know?"

"It's on the western boundary of New South Wales. Just east of the Blue Mountains, if that means anything to you. It didn't to me, not until yesterday when I actually saw the will. Sir, it covers six hundred acres!"

Mr. Colquhoun pondered this information for a long time before he spoke. "Just because a property is worthless now doesn't mean it will always remain so," he said at last. "St. Giles was once nothing but marshland, fit only for lepers and others whom those within the City considered undesirable."

Pickett frowned over this claim. "Begging your pardon, sir, but it doesn't seem to have improved much in the interim."

"Not the best example, I'll admit," the magistrate conceded with a sigh, "nor are the marshes of Southwark much better. My point still holds, however. Cities don't remain static. Today's untamed wilderness may be tomorrow's crowded suburb."

"Then you think I should accept his offer."

"I think you should at least try to discover a bit more about the land before you decide one way or the other. If it's too rocky or simply not fertile enough for growing crops, then what other uses might it be put to? Sheep have a long history of thriving on land unsuited to arable farming, and I believe sheep stations were established in the colony almost as soon as the First Fleet had cast anchor. If the land is unable to sustain sheep, or if you've no taste for animal husbandry, there is always mining to consider. If the land sits over a seam of coal, for instance—" Mr. Colquhoun had been examining the vial of dirt as he spoke, turning it over in his hand in order to study it from all angles. Now he broke off, asking abruptly, "Look here, what are these particles that gleam? Have you noticed them?"

"Not until Julia pointed them out. They only show up when the light hits them." He hesitated for a moment, then asked diffidently, "I don't suppose they could be—that is, you don't think maybe—"

"Before you run away with that idea," the magistrate said sternly, "bear in mind that rumors have cropped up now and again for decades. Nothing has ever come of them, and in one case, a man admitted to making the claim as a hoax in order to avoid fifty lashes for absconding into the bush. When he was threatened with hanging if the claim should prove to be false, he confessed the whole, and received one hundred lashes for his pains. In any case, he ended up being hanged three months later on a different charge, so his fraudulent claim didn't profit him much."

Pickett sighed. "Yes, sir. To be honest, I thought it was too much to hope for. That's why I dared not breathe the word in front of Julia, much less Kit."

"A wise move on your part," the magistrate said, nodding sagely. "Still, if this Mr. Mathers wants to pay you twenty pounds in order to go chasing after mare's nests, who are you to say him nay?"

"Yes, but how am I going to go about learning anything about coal mining, or sheep farming, or anything else involving land usage? I don't even know where to start!"

"Nor do I," Mr. Colquhoun readily admitted, handing over the glass vial. "But I know of someone who might, someone who has the entrée into scientific circles. I suggest you give this to Dr. Gilroy and see if he knows anyone who might be able to analyze it."

Pickett did not look forward to the prospect of explaining again the vial of dirt and the dilemma it presented. Still, the physician-surgeon Dr. Gilroy had been of great help to him in the past, not only in his care for Julia over the past six or seven months, but also in treating the head injury he had suffered in the wake of the Drury Lane Theatre fire and, more recently, giving him insight into the uses and abuses of opium and its effects on those held in thrall to the narcotic's siren song. And so, after bidding farewell to his former magistrate and his erstwhile colleagues, he left Bow Street and called on the doctor at his residence.

"What you want," pronounced the physician, having listened to Pickett's explanation and subjected the vial and its contents to a close inspection, "is a metallurgist, or perhaps a chemist—someone with the knowledge and the equipment needed for a chemical analysis. Although I feel I should warn you that with so small a sample, it's quite possible that no firm conclusions may be drawn."

Pickett nodded in understanding. "Do you know of any such person?"

"I believe I may," the doctor said thoughtfully. "Friedrich Kellermann and I were at school together at Edinburgh for a time, until he left off the study of the human body in favor of natural philosophy. He is a professor of chemistry at Heidelberg University, but he's currently here in Town, delivering a series of lectures to the Royal Society. He's a busy man, of course, but if he hasn't the time to look into the matter himself, he may be able to suggest someone else who might."

"I wouldn't want to put anyone to any inconvenience," protested Pickett. "It isn't as important as all that."

"Maybe it isn't, or maybe it is," Dr. Gilroy said with a shrug. "That is what Dr. Kellermann, or perhaps a colleague, will decide."

18

Which Introduces a Mysterious Lady

S ince there was nothing to be done about his father's
property until Dr. Gilroy had made his inquiries, Pickett
could devote his full attention to investigating his father's
murder. His next move, he decided, must be to discover where
Sir Horace and his wife had taken up what was quite likely
temporary residence, and to pay a call on Lady Stapleton at an
hour when her husband was least likely to be at home. In fact,
he was undecided as to what his attitude should be in
approaching the lady. Ought he to be a former Bow Street
Runner determined to bring his father's killer to justice, or a
bereaved son trying to piece together the last few days in the
life of a parent from whom he had long been estranged?

When the following morning found him still undecided,
he presented his dilemma to Julia as he sat cross-legged at the
foot of the bed, idly grazing from the leftovers on the breakfast
tray that was, along with all her other meals, brought up to her

room every day so that she might partake of it in bed.

She did not disappoint him. Julia had no hesitation in plumping for the latter of the two alternatives. "You wish to express your gratitude to her for the friendship"—she gave the word the slightest of emphases—"that brought your father so much happiness in what were to prove his final days."

"You think so?" he said doubtfully.

"I know so. What a pity there is nothing amongst your father's effects which you might present to her as a remembrance! You could say you were sure he would have wanted her to have it, *et cetera*."

Pickett cast his mind back over his father's possessions, then offered, "I wonder what she would say to six hundred acres along the western border of New South Wales."

"The perfect gift, to be sure!" exclaimed Julia, entering into the spirit of the thing. "What a pity you've given it to Dr. Gilroy instead! I daresay she would have leapt at the chance to unburden herself to so sympathetic an audience." Her smile faded, and she added in a more serious vein, "If she was sincerely attached to your father, it cannot be very comfortable for her, being obliged to grieve in secrecy."

Pickett leaned forward to dip the remaining crust of Julia's toast into the small pot of honey on her tray. "What makes you so sure she *is* grieving him? For all we know, she may have been the one who killed him."

"My dear John, what makes you think she can't do both? A lady may love a man and yet still be quite capable of murdering him."

He paused with the toast halfway to his mouth. "That

ought to make me sleep better at night."

"As well it should!" she retorted, choking back a laugh. "If it hadn't been for Camille de la Rochefort, we would never have met, and you would be sleeping alone."

"I'm sleeping alone now," he pointed out, regarding the camp bed in the dressing room with disfavor.

"It is rather beastly, isn't it?" She bent a reproachful gaze upon her distended abdomen. "It seems to me that this child of ours has a great deal to answer for."

Pickett, his mouth full of toast, was spared the necessity of uttering what could only be inane assurances that it would not be much longer now—a fact of which she was quite as fully cognizant as he, and very likely more so. In any case, the conversation was interrupted by a light scratching at the door.

"Come in," Julia called.

The door was opened to reveal the butler framed in the doorway. "Pray forgive the interruption, madam, but there is a lady below who wishes to see the young master on a matter of some delicacy."

"Oh?" Julia's blue eyes shifted from Rogers to Pickett, who was even now unfolding his long legs and reaching for his boots. She had no fears at all concerning her husband's fidelity, but although *he* might be rather endearingly unaware of his own appeal, *she* was not—and there was no denying the fact that the advanced state of her pregnancy made her feel at a decided disadvantage where other females of the species were concerned.

"As the lady asked only for 'Mr. P,' I believe it is in response to Mr. Pickett's most recent advertisement in the

Times," Rogers offered, by way of either explanation or assurance; she was not quite sure which.

"Did she give her name?" Pickett asked.

"She did not, sir." After a brief but significant pause, Rogers added, "She is heavily veiled, which I took to mean that she did not wish for her identity to be known."

"Oh!" Julia said again.

"Tell her I'll be down directly, and offer her a glass of whatever it is that ladies drink at this hour," Pickett instructed the butler, then turned his attention back to Julia. "Is there anything I can do for you before I go? Plump the pillows, or move the tray, if you've finished with it?"

Julia agreed to both of these proposals for her comfort, well aware that her consent had more to do with asserting her prior claim than with any real need for the services he offered. Pickett removed the tray and set it on the floor beside the bed, then removed the two pillows supporting her back, punched them into shape, and replaced them.

"Better?" he asked.

"Much better," she assured him. "Now if you will only put Mrs. Edgeworth within reach, I shall do very well."

Pickett, happy to oblige, placed her book on the bedside table, well within her reach. "I'll be back shortly," he promised, and she resisted the urge to detain him still longer by lifting her face to be kissed.

He started down the stairs, but when he reached the half-landing, he paused before the gilt-framed looking-glass on the wall to straighten his cravat and brush what looked like a crumb of toast from the lapel of his coat. He wanted to present as professional appearance as possible to a potential client, but had no desire to give his wife the idea that he was preening himself for a tête-à-tête with another woman—even if it was, strictly speaking, true.

Upon his entrance into the drawing room, the lady rose from her seat on the sofa to dip a curtsy, and Pickett found that the butler had not exaggerated. His visitor was a tall, slender lady, although her height might have been exaggerated by the lady's costume, which was one of unrelieved black. Her pelisse was severely plain, with no ribbons, ruffles, buttons, or any other of the ornamentation that usually adorned ladies' apparel. Clearly, her determination to remain anonymous extended even to her clothing; anyone asked for a description would be hard-pressed to supply any detail of either the lady herself or her toilette. As for the veil Rogers had mentioned, it fell from the brim of her plain black bonnet to somewhere below her chin, and comprised so many layers of black netting that Pickett could only wonder how she had contrived to enter the house without running into the wall.

All these impressions flitted through his brain in less time than it took to cross the room and take her black-gloved hand.

"I'm sorry to have kept you waiting, Mrs.—er, Miss—?"

"I think we shall dispense with names, if you please, at least for the nonce."

Her voice was low and somewhat husky. If her face matched her voice, Pickett decided, she would be a very attractive woman, albeit one no longer in the first blush of youth, who had given her husband the requisite heir and so was now free to indulge in "matters of some delicacy"—one of which, seemingly, must have gone awry.

As if aware of this silent appraisal, she said, somewhat defensively, "Your advertisement said you would undertake discreet inquiries. You *are* 'Mr. P.,' are you not?"

Pickett nodded, then realized she could probably not see this gesture through the many layers of black netting. "I am, and it did. Am I to understand that you wish me to make such an inquiry on your behalf?"

"Perhaps."

Obviously, the lady would not be rushed into confidences. When the butler entered the room at that moment bearing a silver tray, Pickett all but fell upon his neck.

"Here is Rogers with some refreshment for you," he said, with more enthusiasm than was warranted by the appearance of a glass of sherry and a plate of cakes. In fact, he had no idea if it was customary for ladies to drink alcoholic beverages so early in the day—he had assumed Rogers would furnish the caller with a glass of the lemonade which Cook made daily for Kit's benefit—but if sherry would lower the lady's inhibitions and loosen her tongue, so much the better. "Won't you sit down? Perhaps we can determine how I might be able to help you."

The lady sank gracefully onto the sofa and accepted the glass, but any hopes Pickett might have entertained of her putting back her veil were doomed to disappointment. The glass, along with the black-gloved hand that held it, disappeared beneath the curtain of black netting, only to reappear a moment later with the level of liquid it contained slightly lowered. Still, the sherry had its effect, for after a few minutes of the most banal conversation he had ever endured, much less instigated, she was at last ready to talk.

"I confess, I had expected someone rather older," she began.

The usual irritation Pickett felt at the inevitable reference to his lack of years was on this occasion secondary to a feeling of surprise that she could see him well enough to make any judgments as to his age at all.

"But as they say, beggars can't be choosers," she continued, then paused to fortify herself with a long pull from her glass. "Here is the situation in a nutshell. My husband and I have just returned from—from a colonial posting abroad. The passage was quite long, you understand, with few amusements and only a handful of one's fellow passengers for companionship. After a couple of months at sea, we were all heartily sick of our own company."

A chord of recognition stirred in Pickett's brain. "Go on."

"Yes, well, one of these passengers was a man—not a gentleman, you understand, but he was good-looking, and amusing, and he and I—well, I suppose you could say we began a flirtation. Nothing so serious as an *affaire de coeur*, of course," she put in hastily, "just a way of beguiling the tedium of the journey."

"I see." In fact, Pickett suspected the lady would be surprised to know just how much he *did* see.

"At least, that was the plan," she said with a sigh. "But as we drew nearer to London, I thought how much I should dislike to drop the acquaintance. There is so little privacy on board a ship, and I had become quite curious about how our friendship might develop if only we were free of such artificial restraints."

What was it about Da, Pickett wondered, *that made otherwise sensible females completely lose their heads over him?* Aloud, he merely observed, "And so you hoped to continue the flirtation, perhaps even expand upon it, once you reached London."

She nodded, or rather, the folds of netting pooled about her neck as her black bonnet dipped, then straightened as the bonnet lifted. "In short, I wrote him letters—three, in all. You will say it was foolish, even reckless of me, and you would be right, of course."

At some point, Pickett knew, he would have to take pity on her and tell her that her shipboard suitor was none other than his own father, and that her incriminating letters were even now in his own possession. But not just yet. Not until he learned a bit more about the Stapletons' marriage. "Did your husband know about this, er, flirtation?"

"He could hardly have been unaware of it, given, as I said, the lack of privacy on board a ship. Still, he had no reason to suspect that it might develop into anything more than an amusement to pass the time at sea. And it is imperative that he should remain in ignorance," she added urgently. "As I said, we have only just returned to London. His position abroad was not a particularly illustrious one, but the limited society of the colony meant that we were received in all the best circles. He quite enjoyed the illusion of belonging to a higher rank than ever he would hold in London society, but not I. The long, tedious dinners at Government House, where one saw the very same people one had seen at the last long, tedious dinner at Government House, and the one before that, for five years on end—I can't bear it, not again! I crave the theatres—the concerts—the balls! But if my husband had cause to believe that I was pursuing what he would term—quite correctly, I suppose—an adulterous union, he would apply for a position in the remotest colony he could find! I have endured five years of exile; I can't bear the thought of being dragged off again to parts unknown! And who knows where or how long this time?"

"And the content of these letters would be enough to enlighten him? Is that it?"

"Yes, but I fear it is worse than that. Within twenty-four hours of disembarking, my—my friend's body was discovered in a back alley. He'd been stabbed to death, and now I have no idea what has become of my letters—into whose possession they may have fallen, or what that person may do with them once he realizes their potential. It is imperative that they be retrieved before they fall into the wrong hands."

"Exactly what is it that you fear, ma'am?" He knew, of course, but he dared not appear to know any more about the letters than a stranger would.

She made a sweeping gesture no doubt intended to suggest any number of possibilities. "Oh, any one of a dozen things! Someone might offer to sell them to my husband, or coerce me into paying him not to do so—I believe such a coercion is called 'blackmail,' is it not?—or, given the manner of my friend's death, the letters might even be taken as evidence that I myself might have killed him." She gave a shaky little laugh. "I fear I rather threw myself at his head. I had so little time to make my case, you see, until we made port and parted forever." Covered with chagrin at the memory of her own lack of discretion, she pressed a hand in the general direction of her forehead. For a brief moment, the layers of black veil molded themselves to the shape of a short, straight nose.

It was almost unfair, Pickett knew, to use her ignorance against her, but considering that he was about to refuse payment for a potentially quite lucrative case that he could have resolved with almost no effort at all, he thought he could be forgiven for taking full advantage of an opportunity that had fallen quite unexpectedly into his lap.

"Given your fondness for the fellow, why would your letters constitute evidence of murder? I should think they would be more likely to exonerate you." But even as he made this optimistic prediction, Pickett recalled Julia's words to the contrary. *A lady may love a man and yet still be quite capable of murdering him...*

His guest must have let out a long breath, for her shoulders rose and fell, while the curtain of netting covering her face fluttered ever so slightly. "They might have proven my innocence if I could produce any passionate letters that he had written to me in response. But I can't. In fact, there were no letters from him at all. His communications to me were always spoken, never committed to paper." She sighed. "I suppose he was wiser than I."

Or more experienced in duplicity, Pickett thought, but

did not say.

For the first time, it occurred to him that his surrender of the letters, along with the revelation of his true identity, might not be greeted with unadulterated joy. In fact, the lady might well be furious with him for stringing her along. It was her own fault, really, he reasoned. If she hadn't insisted in swathing herself in black veils, she would have recognized her lover's son at a glance. Emboldened by the thought, he continued his probing.

"Tell me, did your husband make a habit of collecting curiosities from any of his colonial postings?"

"Curiosities?" she echoed in bewilderment. "I'm afraid I don't follow you."

"I believe many of the men who hold such positions return to England with items crafted by persons indigenous to the regions where they served—carved figurines, or weapons, or musical instruments—"

She stiffened as the meaning behind this simple query became clear. "It is true that my—friend—was stabbed with a knife made by the natives of—of that particular colony. I don't know how you were aware of that, but surely you don't mean to suggest that I would steal such a weapon from my husband in order to murder the man with whom I had thought to cuckold him!"

"Not at all," Pickett assured her with perhaps more tact than truth. "In fact, I was thinking of your husband. You say he was aware of your flirtation with this man. Is it possible that he might have killed Da—er, this 'friend' of yours, in a fit of jealousy?"

"I should say no, of course not," she said with a marked lack of conviction. "It is true that my husband was absent from the house that night, but he had gone to his club. At least, he'd said that was his intention, but when my friend's body was discovered later that same night, I did wonder. I had hoped to meet with my friend, you see, perhaps for the last time—and yet the first truly private meeting we'd ever had. Indeed, when the time of death was fixed at so late an hour, I wondered if he had been on his way to my house when—when it happened."

As the narrow passage called Gin Alley would make a very odd route to the sort of neighborhood where Sir Horace and Lady Stapleton would no doubt have hired lodgings, Pickett rather doubted this, and said so.

"But," he continued, "you think your husband's temperament would not rule out his taking such a course of action?"

She spread her black-gloved hands in a gesture of helpless confusion. "As to that, who can say what another person might do, given the right circumstances? My husband is almost fifteen years my senior, and I believe it was not uncommon for the men of his generation to settle such matters with pistols at twenty paces. In fairness to him, however, I must admit that although ours has not been a passionate union for many years, I myself would not greet with equanimity the realization that some other lady was setting her cap for my husband. Does that make me a shocking hypocrite? I suppose it does."

"I should say, rather, that it makes you human," Pickett said, judging it time. "If you will excuse me, ma'am, I shall be back directly with something that I think will interest you very much." *Or something that will make you want to hurl that glass of sherry at my head,* he added mentally as he betook himself from the drawing room. *I'm not quite sure which.*

"Done so soon?" Julia asked, looking up from her book in pleasurable surprise as he entered the bedchamber and headed straight for the worn valise standing against the far wall.

"Not quite," he said, opening the valise and extracting the three perfumed letters, once again tied together with their ribbon, just as his father had left them. "Although I'm about to resolve a case in record speed. I shall tell you all about it directly."

He sealed this promise by dropping a light kiss onto the top of her head, then hurried down the stairs and back to the drawing room where his visitor waited.

"I believe this is what you're looking for," he said, and dropped the neatly tied bundle onto her lap.

He didn't have to see her relief on her face. It could be read in every line of her suddenly relaxed form. "You've had them all along? But how—why—?"

"At the beginning of this interview, you chose to dispense with names, so I didn't give you mine. But if you will lift your veil, I think your questions will answer themselves."

She hesitated only a moment before seizing the lower edge of the black netting and pulling it up. Wide blue eyes stared up at him. "Why, you—you must be—"

Pickett nodded, and supplied the answer she couldn't seem to form. "Jack Pickett's son—John Pickett the Younger, you might say."

"Although not quite so young as I originally thought," she said, subjecting him to a long, appraising look as she rose to her feet.

The observation contained an unspoken question. Following her lead and abandoning his place on the sofa, Pickett shrugged and said, "I suppose that depends on what you originally thought."

She tilted her head and regarded him through narrowed eyes. "Twenty-three, perhaps?"

"Twenty-five," he said, yielding to the inevitable.

"Goodness! Your father must have been very young when you were born."

"Yes, I believe he was."

"Very well then, John Pickett the Younger, age twenty-five, how much do I owe you?"

He shook his head. "Not a thing. I've been trying to settle my father's affairs, and I'm pleased that this, at least, was resolved so easily, and so satisfactorily."

She offered her black-gloved hand, and he took it.

"You do look very much like him, you know," she said wistfully. "I don't suppose you would be interested—? No," she conceded with some regret, seeing Pickett blush crimson. "I feared as much. Lightning rarely strikes twice in the same place. Still, nothing ventured, nothing gained."

And with this philosophical pronouncement, she took her leave.

19

In Which Two Unwelcome Visitors Descend upon Curzon Street

As it happened, Lady Stapleton was not the only visitor to Curzon Street that day. Nor, for that matter, was she the most interesting. The afternoon saw the return of Mr. Mathers, still intent on purchasing the property in New South Wales, for which, he said, he was now prepared to give twenty-five pounds.

"As I told you before," Pickett said with rather less courtesy than he had shown on that persistent gentleman's earlier visit, "I haven't had time to decide what to do with the property. I only became aware of its existence yesterday, and in addition to settling my father's affairs, I live in daily expectation of my wife's confinement with our first child. So as you can see, it isn't a good time—"

Far from being repelled by this revelation, Mr. Mathers, undaunted, greeted the news of Pickett's impending fatherhood with an enthusiasm bordering on delirium.

"Allow me to extend my heartiest congratulations!" he exclaimed, grabbing Pickett's hand and pumping it with enthusiasm. "But only think of what twenty-five pounds would mean to you and your growing family!"

In fact, this argument touched Pickett on the raw, for he knew quite well what twenty-five pounds would mean. Indeed, he sometimes lay awake at night on his uncomfortable bed, speculating as to how much it would cost to educate a boy in a manner worthy of that boy's mother, or to provide a girl with a dowry sufficient to make it possible for her to marry back into the class her mother had given up when she'd married him.

Mr. Mathers, taking Pickett's silence for encouragement, judged it time to increase his offer. "I can see you drive a hard bargain, Mr. Pickett," he said, wagging his head in the manner of one forced to surrender to the inevitable. "Thirty pounds, then."

"I told you, I'm not ready to—"

"Oh, very well. Forty pounds, and that's my final offer!"

Pickett made no answer. From where he stood in the drawing room (for he had quite deliberately *not* invited his unwanted guest to take a seat) he had glimpsed Rogers crossing the foyer, and cast the butler a look of such desperate entreaty that that excellent servant, sizing up the situation at a glance, stepped in and took control. Within minutes, and without knowing quite how it had happened Mr. Mathers was accepting his hat and gloves from the butler and stepping out onto the portico.

"Thank you," Pickett said with feeling, as soon as Rogers had closed the door behind the departing caller. "If that man shows his face here again, deny him the house!"

"Have no fear, sir," Rogers said, his usually impassive countenance betraying a gleam of anticipation, "I know just how to deal with such ill-bred persons as Mr. Mathers."

"I knew you would. I'm obliged to you, Rogers."

But even Rogers was unprepared for dealing with the next visitor to Curzon Street.

* * *

"*Hssst!*"

Roused from a deep sleep and a dream in which Julia was in the throes of childbirth while he was prevented from going to fetch the midwife by the relentless Mr. Mathers, who stood in the doorway making ever higher offers for the property and refusing to let him pass, Pickett became aware of someone shaking him by the shoulder. Wakening with an effort, he saw Rogers bending over him with a glowing candle in a tall brass candlestick, his black coat thrown over a nightshirt stuffed into the waist of his black breeches.

"Rogers?" Pickett mumbled sleepily. "What—"

"*Shhh!*" There was something of urgency in the way Rogers pressed his finger to his lips, enjoining silence. Whatever the butler's reason for his waking his master in the middle of the night, he clearly did not intend for his mistress's slumber to be disturbed by it.

"What is it, Rogers?" asked Pickett, lowering his voice to a near whisper.

"There is someone in the house, sir," Rogers answered in

kind.

Through the fog of sleep, Pickett was conscious of a feeling of annoyance. Of course there was someone in the house; Rogers need not wake him up for that. Besides himself and Julia and the butler, there was Kit, and Thomas the valet, and Julia's lady's maid Betsy, and Andrew the footman, and Cook, and—

Suddenly the fog lifted, and the butler's meaning became clear. Pickett sat bolt upright, almost overturning the camp bed and himself with it. "Someone in the house?" he hissed, casting a cautious glance at the bed where Julia lay sleeping. "Are you sure?" Even as he asked the question, he acknowledged that Rogers was unlikely to be mistaken about such a matter. "Never mind, you can tell me about it in a minute."

As he spoke the words, Pickett pulled on the breeches he had taken off only a few hours earlier and buttoned the fall front over the tails of his nightshirt, this latter garment, with which he usually dispensed, being a necessity, now that he was denied the warmth of Julia's body beside him. Eschewing cravat and waistcoat, he shrugged into his plum-colored tailcoat and wished his biscuit-colored breeches were not of so light a hue. There was nothing to be done about them, but he could at least cover his white shirtfront by buttoning his coat over it.

Having made these preparations, he crossed the dark room to the clothespress and opened its doors, then stooped to pull out the bottom drawer. From its depths he withdrew a pistol. With this in his hand, he stood and motioned for Rogers to follow him. Outside in the corridor, he closed the door on his slumbering bride and turned to the butler.

"What's happened?"

"I was awakened by a noise, and lay awake trying to identify it, or perhaps hear it again, when I saw a figure pass before my open door. He was dressed all in black, and carried a dark lantern with its shutter open just enough to light his passage."

From his own brief stint as a footman, Pickett knew that most servants slept in shared chambers in the attic, but the highest figures in the servants' hierarchy, primarily the butler and the housekeeper, had private rooms in the basement.

"So this person must have got in through the service entrance, or else the window that looks down on it," Pickett observed.

"Very likely, sir. I daresay that was the noise that woke me. I did not take the time to go and investigate. I thought it best to see where he was going, and then come to inform you as soon as I could do so without putting him on his guard. I lay in bed feigning sleep until he was well past my room, then rose from my bed, scrambled into my clothes, and followed him from a safe distance. He went down the corridor to the kitchen, then started up the servants' stair. At that point, I came to warn you."

"The servants' stair?" Pickett echoed in bewilderment, fixing on what was to him the most pertinent point in Rogers's account. "Where the devil was he going?"

Rogers shook his head. "I couldn't say, sir."

Pickett cast a speculative glance up toward the upper floors. From the servants' stair, the intruder could access any other floor in the house through the cleverly concealed jib doors that opened directly onto the family's rooms—including the one right behind him, where Julia lay sleeping. He wrestled with indecision. He couldn't go through that door in pursuit of the intruder, for he wouldn't know whether to go up the stairs or down. But nor could he go down to the kitchen and follow the intruder all the way all up the servants' stair from its base, leaving Julia alone, oblivious and unprotected. It would help, of course, if he knew the fellow's intentions, but failing that...

"I'm going downstairs," he told Rogers, his mind made up. "I want you to stay here and guard the jib door. If anyone opens it—anyone at all—don't hesitate." He jerked his head in the direction of the heavy brass candlestick in the butler's hand. "Crown him with that thing."

"You may count on me, sir," Rogers said with relish.

Not until Rogers was installed at his post did Pickett realize that the only light had been supplied by the butler's candle. Now that he was alone in the corridor the blackness was almost complete. He told himself it was better this way, since it would allow him to pursue the intruder without betraying his own presence. He had lived in the house for nine months—surely long enough for him to be able to find his way in the dark. Bolstered by this thought, he trod barefooted all the way down the stairs to the basement, from the carpeted treads of the upper floors through the green baize door and down the uncarpeted stairs that opened onto the kitchen, groping his way one cautious step at a time. Having reached the lowest level without encountering the intruder—or, indeed, anyone else—he began to climb, his ears straining to hear any sound from above that would betray his quarry's presence.

As he passed each floor, he grew more puzzled. It was not that he *wanted* the fellow to enter Julia's room by stealth; on the other hand, as he passed the door where Rogers waited on the other side with candlestick in hand, with still no sign of the man whose footsteps he fancied he could sometimes hear some distance ahead of him on the stairs, he had to wonder what the deuce the fellow was after. The silver was below stairs in the butler's pantry, and the ready money needed for running the household or paying the servants' wages was locked in a desk in the ground floor study, while his wife's jewelry—and her far more valuable person—was in the room whose jib door he had just passed.

He paused and peered ahead as far as he could see in the darkness, considering the remaining floors. The schoolroom could hold nothing to interest a grown man—unless it was Kit, sought by someone of the criminal classes, someone like the men who had used the boy to squeeze through the windows that were too tight for an adult…

But no, he decided this scenario was highly unlikely. Anyone who moved in the same circles as the recently executed Rogers and Jud would have heard by now that Kit had a well-connected guardian in the form of his elder half-brother, who in addition to having been a Bow Street Runner, was on the friendliest of terms with the Bow Street magistrate, Patrick Colquhoun.

Besides, he thought on a purely practical level, *any ten-*

year-old boy being unwillingly spirited away in the middle of the night would howl like the very devil.

Still, it was with a sense of relief mixed with bewilderment that he passed the door opening onto Kit's bedroom—relief because it appeared that whatever the intruder was after, Kit was not it, and bewilderment because there remained only the attic floor comprising the servants' bedrooms and a small box-room used for storage—the same room, in fact, where the despised camp bed had been unearthed. Pickett thought it a great pity that the intruder had not come a month earlier, when he might have had it and welcome.

Still, the box-room seemed so unlikely an objective that he was still puzzling over it when he turned the half-landing and almost walked right into his quarry in the dark. He took a cautious step backwards, intending to make a silent retreat to the next floor down; he would much prefer to discover what the intruder was about and catch him in the act than to confront him on a staircase, and from the lower and more vulnerable position at that.

Alas, the uncarpeted board creaked beneath his weight. The intruder whirled about, dropping his shuttered lantern and in the same swift motion planting his foot in Pickett's chest and giving a hard shove.

Pickett contrived to regain his footing before he had fallen more than three or four steps, but his abrupt and ungainly descent, swift as it was, gave his adversary the few seconds he needed. Ignoring the pain in his chest, Pickett scrambled to the top of the steps and paused there to listen for some sign of his quarry.

"You there!" he shouted, leveling his pistol in the direction of the footsteps pounding down the corridor. "Halt, in the name of—"

In the name of the King. He broke off, annoyed with himself for resorting to the familiar cry of all those charged with enforcing the law, from the elderly Charlies in their boxes to the principal officers of Bow Street, among whose number he could no longer be counted. He might no longer be a Bow Street Runner, Pickett resolved, following at a run the footsteps that gave no indication of slowing, but he was something more dangerous still: a man defending his family after his home has been breached.

"Stop...stop or I'll shoot!" His ribs burned like fire—he wondered if one was cracked—and he hated the breathlessness in his voice.

The only response was the groan of stiff hinges and, a moment later, a dull *thud* as the trapdoor opening onto the roof was thrown back. Pickett aimed and fired. A muffled curse, choked with pain, seemed to indicate that he had found his mark.

Unfortunately, this led to an entirely new set of problems. A feminine scream pierced the darkness, and every door on the attic corridor flew open.

"Mr. Pickett, sir? Is that you?" Pickett recognized the voice of his valet, Thomas.

Andrew, the footman, was more direct. "What the devil was *that?*"

"We're going to be murdered in our beds!" moaned Julia's maid, Betsy.

"*Shhh!*" Pickett instinctively held up his hand for silence, although no one could see it in the dark. "Listen!"

Surprisingly, they did. A shuffling sound at the end of the corridor accompanied by the faint creak of weight-bearing wood suggested that whatever injuries Pickett's gunshot might have inflicted, it was not so serious as to prevent the intruder from climbing the ladder through the trapdoor to the roof. Pickett was slightly relieved that he would not be called upon to explain to the nearest constable just how the man had met his death at the hands of a former Bow Street Runner, but he was not so relieved that he intended to let the fellow escape.

"Housebreaker," he said curtly in answer to the servants' questions, then hurried toward the trapdoor as quickly as his aching ribs would allow.

Thomas fell into step behind him. "I'll come with you, sir," he declared, although whether this was due to loyalty toward his master or a young man's love of adventure was perhaps a question best not examined too closely.

"Wait!" cried Andrew, nothing loth. "I'm coming, too!"

Pickett hadn't the breath to argue with them. Alas, it soon transpired that he hadn't the breath to climb the ladder, either. By the time he reached the third rung, he was gasping with the effort to draw air into his bruised lungs, and when he couldn't summon the strength to hoist himself up to the fourth, he was forced to yield his place on the ladder to the two young men in his employ.

After urging Betsy to go back to bed (albeit without any noticeable degree of success), he waited at the foot of the ladder awaiting his servants' return. They were not long in coming, but the dejected looks on the two faces, seen by the light of Betsy's candle, told their own tale.

"I'm afraid we lost him, sir," Thomas said, painfully aware of having disappointed the master who had raised him from the ranks of footmen to the rarified heights of gentleman's gentlemen.

"There's not much of a moon tonight, and he was all dressed in black," Andrew said, apparently feeling some justification of their failure was called for.

"Never mind," Pickett told them. "You did your best."

"Yes, but—sir, who was he?" asked Thomas, fearful that he was overstepping, but too curious to resist. "What was he doing here?"

"I'm afraid your guess is as good as mine," Pickett said. "According to Rogers, he entered the house through the basement, then started up the servants' stair. I followed him all the way up, and he never made the slightest attempt to steal anything, or even enter any of the rooms at all. In any case, it looks like the excitement is over, so we all might as well go back to bed and get what sleep we can."

And that, he thought, is going to prove a lot easier said than done.

20

Which Concerns Itself with the Aftermath

It was not to be expected that Pickett would suffer no ill
effects from his nocturnal adventures. He spent a very
uncomfortable night on his temporary bed, and when he arose
the following morning, he had to make a conscious effort not
to let out a groan that echoed the protests of his sorely abused
muscles. Alas, he lowered his guard too soon, for although he
remembered to turn his back to his wife before pulling his
nightshirt over his head, he reckoned without the mirror above
her dressing table.

"John!" cried Julia, regarding his reflection with dismay.
"What happened to you?"

He looked down the long length of his person, then,
seeing where her gaze was fixed, looked up at his reflection
in the mirror and saw the reason for her reaction. He had
known, of course, that turning over on the camp bed had hurt
like the very devil, but he had not expected the source of this

pain to be so very large.

Or so very colorful. Near the center of his bare chest bloomed a hideous flower mottled with shades of red, blue, and purple. A further examination of his person disclosed a constellation of smaller contusions—souvenirs, no doubt, of his tumble down the narrow, uncarpeted stair.

Knowing that Julia would not be satisfied until she had an answer, Pickett equivocated. "How much do you know about last night?"

"I know Rogers heard a noise last night and came to fetch you, thinking—quite rightly—that you would want to investigate."

Pickett cleared his throat. "Yes, well—"

"And I might as well tell you up front that I know there was someone in the house. You need not blame Rogers," she added quickly but firmly. "He had to tell me *something*, when I woke up to discover him standing guard over the servants' door with a large brass candlestick, and you nowhere in sight!"

"Yes, we had a housebreaker," he conceded with a sigh, oddly grateful to the butler for sparing him the necessity of deciding whether or not to tell her—or, rather, how much to tell her, given that his last attempt to shield her had led to her being abducted—about the events of the previous night. "I followed him up the stairs as far as the attic, when I came upon him suddenly. I'm not sure which one of us was the more startled—no, on second thought, I think that would be me. He at least had the presence of mind to kick me down the stairs."

Ignoring the end of this speech, Julia fixed on the same

point that had so baffled him. "Why the attic?"

Pickett shook his head. "I have no idea. While I was picking myself up off the stairs, he climbed the ladder up to the roof. Thomas and Andrew went after him"—he made no mention of his own futile attempt at pursuit—"but they lost him in the dark."

Julia frowned thoughtfully. "And nothing was taken?"

"Nothing at all," he assured her. "So you see, there was no harm done."

"I don't know about that," she said, eyeing his bruises with disfavor. "I rather liked your chest the way it was."

There was only one way to respond to this claim, so he tossed his neglected shirt over the back of a chair, crossed the room, and sat on the edge of the bed, flinching only slightly when she flung herself into his arms.

"Oh, John, when I heard that gunshot—I thought it was you!" She buried her face in his shoulder, blinking back the tears that filled her eyes all too frequently these days.

"It was," he said, stroking her hair soothingly. "Only I was the one behind the gun, not in front of it. I hit him, too, although I don't know where he was shot, or how badly— obviously not very, since he was still able to climb the ladder and make his escape. Which reminds me, I need to go up on the roof and look about for traces of blood, or anything else he might have left behind."

Still resting her head on his shoulder, she dabbed at her eyes with a corner of the counterpane. "And so you shall," she agreed, "right after you've seen the doctor."

* * *

"The good news is, nothing is broken."

As Dr. Gilroy had delivered this diagnosis only after a thorough examination which had consisted mostly of the physician-surgeon's poking and prodding at his patient's aching ribs, Pickett was led to wonder aloud whether the treatment was worse than the injury.

"Ach, I don't doubt you're sore, for you've bruised yourself up good and proper. What did you do this time? Were you kicked by a mule?"

"Something like that," Pickett said cryptically, wincing as the doctor poked a particularly sensitive spot.

"I can bind your ribs if you like. It won't make you heal any faster, but it might make you a bit more comfortable."

Pickett declined this offer, explaining, "I don't want to upset Julia by making more of the incident than it deserves. It won't do to have her see me going about swathed in bandages."

Dr. Gilroy shook his head. "Aye, this sort of thing can't be good for her."

Pickett paused in the act of pulling his shirt back on and regarded the doctor in some indignation. "It wasn't much good for me, either!"

"Very likely not. Still, I can't say I'm sorry you had cause to summon me, for I was on the point of writing a note to send 'round. I had dinner with Friedrich Kellermann last night, and he was intrigued by this little puzzle of yours. I gave him the sample, and he promises to run a complete analysis on it as soon as may be."

Which meant, Pickett supposed, that he could expect to

hear nothing until the chemist's lecture series was over and he had returned to the university where he taught—and where, presumably, he would have ready access to a laboratory.

"Thank you, doctor. I'm obliged to you."

Inwardly, however, Pickett sighed. He'd hoped to have his father's affairs settled before Julia's confinement—which meant within days, rather than weeks or even months. He reminded himself that it was only dirt; there was no reason why he couldn't dump it into the garden and toss the empty vial and have done with the whole business. Still, his father had clearly thought it worth bringing back to England—and, given what Mr. Colquhoun had said about the rumors that occasionally swept through the colony, Pickett could now form a very good idea of why. Da had been convinced he'd come into a fortune; it had stuck out all over him. Perhaps it was a good thing he hadn't lived long enough to see his supposed riches turn, quite literally, to dust.

* * *

Pickett sat back on his haunches, regarding with satisfaction the last of the dark brown spots that formed a trail stretching from the trapdoor of his own roof across the rooftops of the house adjacent to it, and the house adjacent to that one. The drops of dried blood came to an abrupt end behind the chimney of the fourth house in the terrace row. Pickett was under no illusion that a grown man had somehow made his escape down a chimney so narrow that a careless climbing boy might find himself stuck in it; still less did he believe the man had disappeared into thin air. It was far more likely that, having put some distance between himself and his pursuers, he had hidden behind the chimney while he did what he could to stanch the flow of blood that he must know would mark his trail once the sun rose. Whatever the intruder's purpose had been, Pickett hoped he'd been given such a fright that he would think twice before making a second attempt. In the meantime, he had his own plans for the day: He intended to pay another call on Sullivan Bradley and see what the former clerk thought of Mr. Mathers and his continued—and increasingly expensive—attempts to buy a property that, according to Sully, was worthless.

Descending the ladder was not quite as excruciating a procedure as climbing it had been, and so it wasn't long that, after stopping by Julia's bedside to give her a farewell kiss, he gingerly made his way down the front stairs to the foyer just in time to hear Rogers addressing an unseen caller with excruciating courtesy.

"If, ma'am, the young master is indeed on your roof as you say, then you may be sure he has good reason to be."

"I would give much to know what it is, then," retorted an irate female voice which Pickett readily identified as their neighbor from two doors down—upon whose roof he had indeed been walking less than fifteen minutes earlier. "This was a quiet, respectable street, until Lady Fieldhurst brought *that man* here!"

Having reached the bottom of the stairs, Pickett gritted his teeth against the pain in his ribs and strode across the foyer, a devil of mischief lurking in his brown eyes. "Good morning, Mrs. Pitney-Hughes," he said cheerfully. "Did you see me up on your roof? I'm sorry if I gave you a fright."

"Fright?" she echoed in frigid tones. "It's my opinion that you must be mad!"

"Not at all," he assured her. "We had an uninvited 'guest' last night who made his escape through the hatch to the roof, and across the roofs of the neighboring houses, if the trail of blood he left behind is anything to judge by. I hope the gunshot didn't disturb you."

The ostrich plumes adorning her stylish hat fairly quivered in indignation, but the angry face beneath it paled visibly. "*Blood? Gunshot?* I should like to know just what has been going on here!"

Pickett heaved a sigh of regret. "I'm afraid I shot him, ma'am. I confess, I may have acted too precipitously, for he didn't take anything, so far as I can tell. Now that I think of it, he couldn't have been a burglar, for what could a poor Bow Street Runner have that would be worth stealing?" While the lady pondered this rhetorical question, Pickett delivered his *coup de grâce*. "Unless, of course, he mistook our house for another on this same street."

"You don't frighten me, sir!" she retorted, although her voice lacked conviction.

"Frighten you? I should hope not! Now," Pickett said, in the tone of one who considers the subject closed, "were you coming to call on my wife, or may I give you my arm back to your own house?" Suiting the word to the deed, he offered his arm.

"I thank you sir," she said, although her voice contained nothing indicative of gratitude, "but I shall see myself home."

And with these words, she turned on her heel (drawing

the skirts of her wool pelisse close as if fearful of contamination) and marched back down the street to the next house but one. Pickett waited only long enough to hear the firm *click* of the latch as her door closed before turning to address the butler.

"I'm going to be gone for a bit, Rogers. If anything happens"—a quick glance toward the ceiling, and the bed-chamber above it, made it clear just what sort of happening he anticipated—"I'll be in Limehouse, at the boarding-house in Narrow Street where Mr. Sullivan Bradley is staying."

"Very good, sir," Rogers said, then added, "Begging your pardon, sir, but surely you don't intend to walk all that way!"

"Walk? Oh, no. I'm only walking as far as Piccadilly. It should be easier to hail a hackney from there. Although"—he made an anticipatory grimace—"I might find it easier to walk than to hoist myself into a carriage."

To Pickett's misfortune, this prediction proved to be all too accurate. Once the climb into the hackney was achieved, however, he was free to collapse against the squabs and recruit his strength not only for the climb down from the vehicle, but also for the much longer climb up the narrow staircase to Sully's second-floor room. By the time this latter was accomplished, Pickett's knees were weak and he was gasping for breath, clinging to the banister with one hand while he pressed the other to his aching ribs. He knocked on Sully's door, then quickly pulled the handkerchief from the pocket of his coat and wiped off the perspiration that dotted his brow in great drops. He stuffed the handkerchief back into his coat pocket, and by the time a voice on the other side of the door called for him to "Come in!", no one who saw Pickett stroll into the room would have imagined that the previous night could have held anything for him but complete repose.

"Well, if it isn't Jack's b-boy!" Sully, seated at the small table with paper, quill, and ink spread out before him, made no move to rise, but his greeting held as warm a welcome as anyone might wish. "This is a p-pleasant surprise, 'pon my w-word it is! Come in, won't you?"

Pickett obeyed this behest, striding across the small room to shake hands with his host across the width of the table.

"I'm glad I found you at home," he began, only to be cut off by another invitation.

"Sit d-down, sit down!" Sully urged, waving Pickett not toward the worn horsehair sofa where he'd sat on his earlier visit, but to a rickety straight chair adjacent to his own. "Doesn't look like much, b-but it's sturdy enough. But what b-brings you to Limehouse? No t-trouble regarding Jack's affairs, I hope."

"Well, yes and no," Pickett confessed, pulling out the chair and very cautiously easing himself onto it. "No trouble, exactly, but a curious thing has happened, and I thought you might be the best man to advise me."

Sully shook his head in ready sympathy. "It's a sad b-business, and you with no b-brothers or sisters to share the b-burden. Well, anything I can do to help Jack's boy, you can be sure I'll do it."

"I'm obliged to you," Pickett said, accepting this offer with real gratitude. "It's about this property Da left."

"What about it?"

"I know you said it's worthless, but there's this fellow named Mathers who's called twice at my house to—what?" Pickett broke off, puzzled by the former clerk's rather knowing smile.

"So Mathers c-called at your house, d-did he?" Sully's smile broadened into a grin.

"Yes," said Pickett, unamused. "You find that funny? I should like to know why."

Now it was Sully's turn to be puzzled. "You m-mean your employer's house, d-don't you?" Reading the answer in Pickett's face, he said in some confusion, "I b-beg your pardon, John, but I thought you were j-just j-joking. At the in-=quest, when you g-gave your residence as C-Curzon Street, I thought you must be a f-footman, like your father had b-been many years ago, long b-before I knew him. I m-meant no d-disrespect."

"It's an honest mistake," Pickett said, although in fact he was more than a bit nettled by the man's assumption. "The house came to me when I married." He kept to himself the fact that the house had belonged to Julia until she had married him, at which point it, along with all the rest of her earthly possessions, became his in the eyes of the law.

Sully nodded in understanding. "Now that we've g-got that sorted, t-tell me about this Mathers fellow. You say he's c-called on you t-twice? Why? What d-does he want?"

"He wants to buy Da's property."

His host seemed to see no difficulties with Pickett's dilemma; in fact, he was quite enthusiastic. "How much d-did he offer?"

"Twenty pounds, sight unseen. He calls himself a land speculator—a man who buys land and sells it later at a profit."

Sully's eyes grew round, and his stammer became so pronounced that he could hardly speak at all. "T-T-Take it! W-What are you w-w-waiting for?"

Pickett sighed. "Believe me, I asked myself the same question after he'd gone. I suppose that, since it constitutes the whole of my inheritance, I didn't want to dispose of it without giving it a bit more thought."

"F-Fair enough." Sully acknowledged the wisdom of this decision—or, rather, *in*decision—with a nod. "But you said he c-called t-twice?"

"On his second visit, he increased his offer to twenty-five pounds, then thirty, and then forty pounds."

As Sully's only response to this was a long, low whistle, Pickett continued. "He said forty was his final offer, but I can't help thinking I haven't seen the last of him."

"Play him as you w-would a f-fish on a line," recommended Sully. "See if you can g-get him up to f-fifty, that's my advice."

"Yes, but that's beside the point," Pickett said impatiently. "Why is he willing to pay so much for land you say is worthless?"

Sully shrugged. "M-Maybe I'm wrong; this Mathers f-fellow obviously thinks so. Or maybe *he's* wrong, and you need t-to snap up his offer b-before he d-discovers his mistake. You know what they say about a f-fool and his m-money."

Pickett was still not entirely convinced, but he recognized the futility of discussing the matter further, and so made no objection when the other man changed the subject. Upon discovering that his host had been engaged in writing letters to potential employers, he told Sully that he himself had spent almost a month working as a clerk for the very same shipping company that had provided transportation back to England for Sully as well as his own father.

"I pity the man who has to spend his entire career there," he said, shuddering to think how close he himself had come to that fate. "Still, it might suffice until you can find something better."

For the next quarter hour, the two men exchanged anecdotes from their respective careers as brethren of the quill, until Sully suddenly remembered his duties as host.

"Here I've b-been prosing on when I p-promised you a c-cup of t-tea! Or would you rather have c-coffee?" Without waiting for an answer, he strode across the room to the fireplace, where he snatched up the poker and stirred the coals back to life.

"No, no, you need not trouble yourself on my account," Pickett protested. "I need to be getting back home in any case. I don't like leaving my wife for long, not with her confinement so near at hand."

"As you w-wish, then," Sully conceded, setting the poker aside. "Some other d-day, perhaps."

Pickett agreed to this, but as he rose from the rickety chair, Sully's eyes widened in distress. "I s-say, you're rather young to b-be m-moving so stiffly. Have you s-suffered an injury since I last saw you?"

"Only my own carelessness," Pickett said with a shrug. "In fact, we had a housebreaker last night. I tried to catch the fellow, lost my footing, and tumbled down a few steps in the dark."

"Oh, b-bad luck!"

"*Very* bad luck," Pickett concurred, wincing at the memory.

"I t-trust nothing was s-stolen?" The slight lift on the last word gave Pickett to understand that this was a question, and not merely an observation.

"No, nothing so far as I can tell. In fact, I think the fellow must have got into our house by mistake. These terrace houses all look alike, at least from the outside, and, well, what do I have that would be worth stealing?"

Sully chuckled, but offered no answer to this purely rhetorical question. "I d-daresay you've scared the f-fellow off, anyway."

"Very likely," Pickett agreed somewhat sheepishly, "for I made enough noise to wake the dead."

After saying all that was proper, he thanked Sully for his advice (agreeing to his host's request that he be told how much Pickett was finally able to wring out of that Mathers fellow), and took his leave.

Once the door had closed behind him, however, he lingered in the corridor with a thoughtful frown creasing his brow. Was it only coincidence that as Sully had crossed the room to the fireplace, his gait had betrayed a slight but unmistakable limp?

21

In Which a Stranger Brings Surprising News

*N*o, Pickett thought as he cautiously navigated the steep, narrow staircase down to the ground floor of the house and thence into the street. *It's not possible.*

Julia echoed this opinion some time later, adding, as a seeming *non sequitur*, "John, you're getting water in my eyes."

"Sorry, love," he said, pausing in his account long enough to dab at her eyes with a towel. "Better?"

"Mmm, much better." She closed her eyes in ecstasy. "You may have acquired a permanent position. I'm afraid poor Betsy can never compete."

Upon his return from Sullivan Bradley's boardinghouse, he'd gone upstairs to share his theories with Julia only to find her out of bed and standing before the washstand, struggling to bend her head over the basin while Betsy washed her hair— no easy task, now that Baby Pickett took up entirely too much room to permit of her bending at her nonexistent waist. He had promptly dismissed the lady's maid, then scooped up his wife, dripping hair and all.

"John, you're going to hurt your ribs!" she'd protested, half laughing.

In fact, there was no "going to" about it; his mistreated midsection had vehemently protested the added weight it was suddenly expected to support, but, having committed himself to this course of action, he'd been determined to see it through. He'd deposited her on the camp bed, then placed the basin on the floor at one end of the hard, lumpy mattress. As she lay down and squirmed to find a more comfortable position (a lost cause, as he could have told her), he'd stripped off his coat and waistcoat and rolled his shirtsleeves up to his elbows.

"*This* is what you've had to sleep on every night for the past two weeks? Poor darling!"

At any other time, he might have taken advantage of this expression of sympathy and tried to coax his way back into the big four-poster, but at the moment he had more pressing concerns even than this. And so he'd knelt on the floor beside the camp bed and picked up where Betsy had left off, working into her scalp the preparation of violets she favored and rinsing it out with hot water.

"Getting back to the subject at hand," he said with mock severity, "why do you say it isn't possible?" Unlike Julia, he'd had the advantage of half an hour in a hackney during which to consider the matter. Now he was curious to know if her reasoning matched his own.

"Because it makes no sense!" she insisted, opening her eyes and, consequently, putting them once more at risk. "Setting aside the fact that Mr. Bradley was your father's closest friend—although Lady Stapleton might dispute that—why should he break into our house only to follow the servants' stair from basement to attic without making the slightest attempt to even enter any of the family's rooms, much less steal anything from them?"

"Because he was looking in the wrong place. He thought I was a servant, so he was on his way to the servants' quarters when I surprised him on the landing. Close your eyes," he added, and poured more water over her hair.

Having successfully defended her eyes against this fresh assault, she relaxed once more in blissful anticipation of his long, slender fingers on her scalp. "It's true that your father came to the service entrance. I daresay he must have said something to give Mr. Bradley the same idea, and didn't live long enough to correct the false assumption. But that still doesn't explain why Mr. Bradley broke into the house! Even if he *did* think you were a member of the household staff, he could have called at the service entrance and asked for you."

"Perhaps. But I don't believe it was me he was looking for. It was something I had, something he'd hoped to find in my room. Hmm," Pickett said as a new thought occurred to him, "I wonder what he would have done if I'd woken up while he was searching."

"Don't," protested Julia, shuddering. "He sounded rather meek, the way you first described him, but if your ribs are any indication, he can be dangerous when cornered. Tell me, what do you think he'd hoped to find? I suppose the deed to the property is the obvious answer, although why he should want it, when he says it's worthless, quite escapes me—unless, of course, he knows more about it than he's telling."

"Very likely," agreed Pickett. "What I don't understand is why he should take such a risk when the property might have been his for the asking."

"Oh?"

"When I went to fetch Da's valise, I told Bradley he could keep any of Da's things that he wanted," he explained. "He took a few pieces of clothing, but he never mentioned the land at all, until I brought it up. Why didn't he just ask me if he could have it, or else offer to buy it for a pittance? He must have known I would have no interest in owning land in that part of the world, now that my father was back in England."

His fingers grew still as he considered the odd behavior of Sullivan Bradley, his left hand cupping the crown of Julia's wet head as if he held something precious. Although she found this sensation far from unpleasant, the water in the pitcher was beginning to cool. She reached up to nudge his bare forearm.

"You are neglecting your work," she chided him. "The water will soon be cold."

"What? Oh. Sorry." Recalled to his duty, he picked up where he had left off. All the while, however, his mind continued to turn over that conversation with Bradley. "On second thought," he said at last, "that's not entirely true."

"You're *not* neglecting your work?" she challenged in mock indignation. "I beg to differ!"

His lips twitched, but he refused to take the bait. "I said he never mentioned it, but I was wrong. Sully never asked if he could have the property, but he did offer to find a buyer for it."

"John!" Julia opened her eyes wide, then thought better of it and closed them again. "Do you suppose he already had a prospective buyer in mind? Perhaps he'd intended to sell it to Mr. Mathers all along. *He* certainly doesn't seem to consider it worthless."

"True. Perhaps he wants to pocket that twenty-five, or thirty, or forty pounds before Mathers discovers he's been had. Or," he added with growing conviction, "it might have been the other way 'round. Mathers might have been acting as a third party, buying—or trying to buy—the property on Sully's behalf, allowing him to gain possession without ever seeming to appear in the business at all. Except that I'm not inclined to sell, so he tries the next best thing: stealing it."

Whatever Julia might have said to this proposition was interrupted by a light rap on the door. The Picketts, both man and wife, called "Come in," and a moment later Rogers entered the room. If the butler was at all surprised to discover his master performing a task usually delegated to the mistress's lady's maid, he was too well-trained to show it. Then, too, this was far from the most shocking behavior he had ever witnessed from his current employers; more than once, he had entered a room only to discover master and mistress locked in a passionate embrace, with madam's hair tumbling down and the carpet at their feet littered with hairpins. On those occasions, he had silently withdrawn from the room without their knowing he had ever entered it at all. In this particular instance, however, a discreet exit was not an option, for he had a message to deliver.

"Begging your pardon, sir, but there are two men below who wish to have a word with you."

Pickett blew out a long breath, then picked up the towel and wrapped it around Julia's wet hair. "If it's that Mathers fellow again, this time with reinforcements—"

The butler was quick to reassure him. "No sir, not at all. One is the physician, Dr. Gilroy. His companion"—Rogers glanced down at the card in his hand—"appears to be a native of one of the German states. His name is Kellermann."

Recognizing the name, Pickett sat back on his haunches and began to roll down his sleeves. "Thank you, Rogers. You may tell them I will be down directly."

"Very good, sir," the butler said, and withdrew, closing the door behind him.

Once they were alone, Julia swung her feet off the camp bed and pushed herself up to a sitting position while Pickett buttoned his sleeves at the wrist. He interrupted this task in order to take her hands and pull her to her feet. God knew it was difficult enough to climb out of that accursed bed every morning; he couldn't imagine how she would accomplish this feat unassisted.

"Why is it," he complained, reaching for his waistcoat, "that suddenly everyone wants to see me when I'm undressed?"

Julia smiled slyly at him from the corner of her eye. "Oh, but you do so much of your best work that way."

"Someday, after this baby is born," he promised, "I'm going to remind you you said that."

* * *

Pickett reached the drawing room moments later and saw at a glance that Rogers had gone one better than delivering his message, for both men were seated on the sofa, and on the small table at the doctor's elbow stood a silver tray containing three small crystal glasses and a decanter half-filled with some amber-colored liquid. Pickett wasn't quite certain what it was, but he had the lowering conviction that it should have been he, and not the butler, who had thought to offer it. If Rogers were so inclined, Pickett reflected, he could tell such tales to his cronies as would make it impossible for his master to hold his head up in public.

"I'm sorry to keep you waiting," he told his visitors, who both rose as he entered the room.

"Not at all." Dr. Gilroy shook him warmly by the hand. "I trust Mrs. Pickett is doing well?"

"She's ready to be done with the whole business, but other than that, quite well," Pickett said.

The doctor chuckled. "A perfectly normal sentiment at this stage, I assure you. Mr. Pickett is about to become a father," he explained to his companion, "for his wife is due to be confined any day now. Mr. Pickett, allow me to present Herr Friedrich Kellermann—an old friend and a fellow man of science, albeit in a different field from my own."

Pickett turned and offered his hand to a tall, broad-shouldered man with fair hair and a square jaw. "Thank you for taking the trouble to look into this, Herr Kellermann. I suppose Dr. Gilroy has explained the situation. Let's sit down, shall we?"

"A wise precaution," Dr. Gilroy murmured cryptically, as he and his colleague resumed their places on the sofa.

Pickett sat on the identical sofa set at right angles to its counterpart. "I'm very much obliged to you," he told the German. "I'd hoped to have my father's affairs in order by the time you returned to the university, but I realize it may be some time before you—what?" he asked, breaking off at the curious expressions on the faces of his visitors.

"The tests have already been done," Kellerman said. "The doctor has brought me here to share the results."

"Oh," Pickett said, taken aback by this revelation. "Forgive me, but I thought—that is, don't such tests require a laboratory?"

"On the contrary, many tests may be conducted anywhere, with things that may be found in any well-stocked kitchen," the German said. "Still, in a case where one wishes to be absolutely certain, a laboratory is needed. I am grateful to our mutual friend, Dr. Gilroy, for, what do you say, pulling some strings and obtaining permission for me to use the laboratory at the Royal Society."

"Oh," Pickett said again. In fact, he had never thought of the Royal Society as being equipped with a laboratory. His impression, when he thought about it at all—which was admittedly not often—was of a room full of well-educated men discoursing on various learned topics incomprehensible to such lesser mortals as himself.

"In this case," continued Herr Kellermann, "the results

of the simple tests were such that I felt they should be—should be—"

"Confirmed?" Pickett suggested, seeing the German searching his excellent English for the right word.

"Corroborated," Dr. Gilroy offered at the same time.

Kellermann nodded. "*Danke*, either of these words will do. In science," he added for Pickett's benefit, "it is important that one repeats his experiments, perhaps many times, to be sure his results are the same each time."

"And were they?" Pickett asked.

"They were." He withdrew the vial of dirt from the inside pocket of his coat and studied it, turning it over in his hands. "Our friend the doctor says you have six hundred acres of land from which this sample was taken. Is this correct?"

"The deed says six hundred acres. As for whether it's all just like this"—he gave a brief nod in the direction of the vial in Kellermann's hands—"I couldn't say. I've never actually seen the property." Recalling the silver tray with its three glasses, Pickett rose from his seat on the adjacent sofa and topped off his guests' glasses, then poured a measure into his own.

The German raised his broad shoulders in a shrug. "It makes no difference. As it happens, there is a man in the Royal Society who has explored the region as far as the Blue Mountains. I have put the question to him, and he seems to think it very probable that this sample is representative of the entire tract—probable enough, in any case, that I need not hesitate to say that you, Herr Pickett, are in all likelihood an extremely wealthy young man."

22

In Which John Pickett Hosts a Most Unusual Party

*Y*ou are now an extremely wealthy young man...an extremely wealthy young man... extremely wealthy... The German kept talking—Pickett could hear his excellent though heavily-accented English—but his voice seemed to come from very far away, and his words, which took some effort to understand even under far more tranquil conditions than those under which Pickett now labored, seemed to have no meaning. It took nothing less than the crash of shattering glass to rouse Pickett from his stunned stupor, and he found himself staring down at his empty hand, his fingers curled as if he still held the glass that lay in shards at his feet, the liquid it had contained now spreading in a widening pool of amber.

"I beg—I'm—I didn't—Rogers!" Stammering incoherent apologies for his own clumsiness, Pickett greeted the appearance of the butler with patent relief.

"Begging your pardon, sir, but I heard the crash and

thought you might be in need of some assistance. If you will excuse me, I will return directly to clean it up. In the meantime, may I suggest that you and your guests might be more comfortable in the dining room?"

"What—oh—yes—yes, of course." Pulling himself together with an effort, Pickett turned to the two men still seated on the sofa, both of them trying to pretend they were not watching the expanding puddle with wary eyes lest their shoes suffer collateral damage. "If you will come with me?"

Neither man took him up on this invitation, both citing instead their need to go about their respective businesses now that they had accomplished their purpose for having called in Curzon Street, that of reporting to Pickett the results of Herr Kellermann's analysis. Now, the physician said, they would be on their way so that he could impart the good news to his wife in privacy.

The chemist gave Pickett his card, then recollected that this was printed in German—a language in which Pickett was very likely untutored—and assured that rather dazed young man that if he had any further questions regarding the chemical composition of his inheritance, Pickett might contact him through the Royal Society, as he was fixed in London for the next fortnight.

Pickett walked with them as far as the front door and said all that was proper. At least, he hoped he did; he could never afterwards remember. He thanked Herr Kellermann again for his services and accepted the return of the glass vial, then, as soon as his visitors had gone, closed the door behind them and sagged against it as if for support.

He had no idea how long he remained there, but eventually he found himself climbing the stairs and entering the bedchamber. Julia, sitting up in bed with her damp hair tied back in a single braid, looked up from the book she was reading and tried without success to interpret the expression on his face.

"John? What's the matter?" Receiving no answer, she scooted toward the center of the mattress, making room for him to sit on the edge of the bed. "John, has something happened?"

He gave an odd little laugh. "You might say so."

This answer didn't tell her much, for his tone of voice was as uncommunicative as his facial expression. She took his hand and pulled him down to sit beside her.

"Tell me."

And so he told her, haltingly at first, then in a great rush of words to which she listened in growing astonishment, her blue eyes growing ever wider.

"You don't seem very happy about it," she said when he at last fell silent.

"I'm stunned," he said, and looked it. "It's a lot to take in."

She regarded him shrewdly. "But not entirely unexpected, I think. If *I* noticed those little flecks that gleamed in the light, I'm sure *you* did. I wondered at the time, but I didn't want to say anything in front of Kit." She also hadn't wanted to say anything that might raise false hopes in her husband's breast, but she would keep this observation to herself.

"Oh, I noticed them. I even pointed them out to Mr.

Colquhoun. He said there have been rumors for decades, but they've all turned out to be false."

"All but this one, it seems." She laced her fingers through his, adding in a much lighter tone, "So, Mr. Pickett, now that you're a wealthy man, what do you intend to do?"

He replied without hesitation. "Tell Lord Melrose to go to the devil."

"I thought you'd already done that."

"Yes, but this time, he won't be able to convince himself that it's only a matter of time before I come to him with hat in hand. Now, where was I? Oh, yes: Next, I'm going to go to Rundell and Bridge's and buy you something extravagant— something blue, maybe, to match your eyes. What would you like?"

"Sapphires," she said promptly. "It cost me *such* a pang, surrendering the Fieldhurst sapphires to George—Lord Fieldhurst, I should say—to give to his wife. I take some comfort in the knowledge that at least Caroline is not the one wearing them."

"Sapphires, then," he agreed. "Or should I make Cousin George an offer for the Fieldhurst set?"

"Don't you dare!" she exclaimed, choking back her laughter. "Poor George would go off in an apoplexy!"

But Pickett did not join in her merriment. "You realize, don't you, that this is it?" he asked, suddenly serious. "This is what our intruder was after, what my father was killed for."

"Oh, certainly." She sounded almost dismissive. "But John, what about your father's will?"

He gave her a blank look. "What about it?"

"What good would the deed do him, when the will says explicitly that it belongs to you?"

"That's just it: The will *doesn't* say it explicitly. It says only 'money, property, and other assets.' If someone else has the deed in his possession, who's to say it ever belonged to my father at all?"

"But surely there must be records," Julia insisted.

"Perhaps," conceded Pickett, although he sounded doubtful. "But in a place where most of the land is unsettled, and many of the residents are illiterate"—he shrugged—"who knows?"

Julia looked rather daunted. "So where does that leave us?"

He liked that "us," with its casual assumption that whatever concerned him must of necessity concern her, too. At the same time, he wished he could keep her well out of it.

"He's going to try again, you know. Now that we know exactly what's at stake, it's plain as a pikestaff that he won't give up that easily. He went to the wrong part of the house before, but now that he knows his mistake, he'll try again. I let him think I considered the whole thing an error on the intruder's part, that he must have chosen the wrong house by mistake. Unless I overplayed my hand, he'll think we won't be expecting a second attempt. He'll probably search the study first—that would be the logical place to keep important papers, besides being easier to access from the street than the bedroom would be—but it's just possible that he'll expect me to keep all Da's effects closer at hand until I decide what to do with them."

He glanced toward the corner of the room where the paper-wrapped package and the valise awaited his decision on their eventual fate. If he hadn't been so taken aback by the revelations of his father's papers that he'd dumped them all back into the strongbox and left the lot in Coutts's basement, it was very likely that they would be here, too, with all the rest.

"So, if he doesn't find what he's looking for in the study," Julia deduced, "then he'll come here. To this room, I mean."

He sighed, uncertain whether to be relieved at having been spared the necessity of pointing out this disturbing possibility, or regretful that his wife was sometimes much too perceptive for his peace of mind.

"Oh, he'll find it in the study," he promised. "Make no mistake about that. Still, I won't leave you alone. I'll be waiting for him in the study—I still think it's his most likely course of action—but I'll have Rogers stay with you, or Thomas or Andrew, if you would feel safer with a younger man. If Dr. Gilroy hadn't ordered you to stay in bed, I would send you to Lady Dunnington for the night, but as matters stand—"

"Oh, yes!" exclaimed Julia, although her tone was more suggestive of accusation than agreement. "I could have gone off to Emily Dunnington's, and we could have placed wagers on whether or not my husband would still be alive come morning. It is too bad of Dr. Gilroy to deny me such a treat!" In a very different tone, she added, "Really, John, how can such a clever man be so obtuse? I won't beg to keep you company, for I am sure I would be very much in the way, especially in my present condition, but as for the idea that I should leave you to your fate while I go merrily off to Park Lane—no, John. Just—no. Pray don't ask it of me. Not now, not ever."

He raised their joined hands to his lips and kissed the fingers that were intertwined with his. Finding this expression of marital affection unsatisfactory, he kissed her on the lips instead—an exercise so protracted that not until Julia's book slid off the bed and landed quite noisily on the floor did both participants return to their senses.

"And then there's Kit," Pickett said, returning the book to his wife and the conversation to the subject at hand. "Should we have a pallet made up for him in our room, or, since I'll be downstairs, should we let him sleep in the camp bed for the night? I shouldn't think he would want to be left alone, in any case."

"He most certainly will not," said Julia, readily conceding the point. "But if you think for one minute that he is going to be content to sleep—on a pallet or a camp bed or anywhere else—while all this excitement is going on, I can only say that your assessment of his character is very different from mine."

He acknowledged this home truth with a grin. "I suppose I'll have to think of something for him to do that will keep him out of harm's way. Perhaps the schoolroom needs guarding," he suggested blandly. "I wouldn't wonder at it if all sorts of important papers were hidden amongst the copybooks."

"Yes, indeed! Someone must certainly stand guard."

"Armed," Pickett continued, "with a cricket bat."

Julia choked back a gurgle of laughter. "Poor Kit! You shouldn't tease him."

"I'm perfectly serious! And what's more, he'll have a fine time on guard duty; you just see if he doesn't."

"I'm sure he will—at least until he begins to suspect there's no real threat to the schoolroom after all."

"Oh, the threat is real enough," Pickett said dryly. "Because this time, our intruder is going to be armed."

* * *

Pickett left the house a short time later, but in spite of his previously stated intentions, his peregrinations took him neither eastward to the Ludgate Hill showroom of Rundell and Bridge nor westward to the Park Lane residence of the Marquess of Melrose. Instead, he went first to Coutts in the Strand, where he closed his father's safe deposit box and took possession of its contents, after which he paid a certain call and issued an invitation, of sorts, to a select group whose presence was requested in Curzon Street that very night.

It was an odd way of celebrating an inheritance, even for a house of mourning. The guests did not arrive in Curzon Street until eleven o'clock, and although they were dressed in the deepest black, this circumstance seemed to be unrelated to the fact that their host had suffered a recent bereavement; indeed, only one of the visitors had been in any way acquainted with the deceased.

In any case, this uniformity of dress appeared to be the only point of similarity between them, for in every other particular, they appeared to be an ill-assorted lot. There were four in all, ranging in age from a white-haired, bushy-browed man in his sixties to a slender youth whose smooth cheeks had almost certainly never known a razor. The other two fell somewhere between these extremes, one being an incredibly handsome man in his late twenties with fair hair that glinted like burnished gold in the candlelight, while the other, fully a decade older, was a tight-lipped man whose erect posture suggested a military career presumably cut short by the same injury that had left him with a slight limp.

Nor was the entertainment of a sort that most visitors would find amusing; certainly it was unworthy of anyone claiming to be a wealthy man. There were no cards, nor was there any dancing or, for that matter, any music at all. As for refreshments, Pickett offered his guests no other sustenance but a meager repast of cold meat, bread, and cheese, eaten in a dark dining room with no more illumination than that afforded by five tin lanterns, each one with adjustable shutters that could be opened or closed. Even with all the shutters open, the light they afforded somehow seemed to emphasize the shadows more than it banished them.

None of Pickett's guests seemed to object to these peculiar arrangements, however, or indeed to find anything amiss with them at all. For these were no ordinary guests, but his former colleagues at Bow Street: the magistrate, Patrick Colquhoun; Mr. Maxwell, the soldier who had come to Bow Street after an injury at Corunna had put paid to his military career; Mr. Carson, previously of the Horse Patrol, who had been promoted to Principal Officer and now occupied the place Pickett had held before turning in his resignation; and young Mr. Yates, who had recently been assigned to Carson as a partner and assistant.

"But what if he doesn't come?" The slightly tremulous voice betrayed Yates's youth, containing as it did eager anticipation mixed with nervousness and perhaps just a hint of fear.

It was the magistrate who answered. "Then we try again tomorrow night, and the night after that, and the night after that. But I don't think we'll have long to wait. He'll want to get his hands on that deed before Mr. Pickett discovers exactly what it represents."

He's a bit late for that. Pickett thought the words, but did not say them. He'd been obliged to disclose the whole to Mr. Colquhoun when he'd asked for Bow Street's assistance, but as for how much the magistrate had told the others, he wasn't quite sure. He thought it unlikely that they knew the whole, for Harry Carson would never have wasted an opportunity to roast him on his newfound wealth.

"Mr. Pickett, can you furnish Mr. Yates with paper and pencil?"

Pickett nodded. "Yes, sir. I shall do so as soon as we remove to the study."

"Good man." The magistrate turned his attention back to the youth. "Mr. Yates, once we assume our positions, I want you to take down every word said in that room, whether by our quarry or amongst ourselves. I want a record that will stand up as evidence in court, no matter how much the defense counsel may try to discredit it."

"Yes, sir. But won't I need light to see the page?"

"You will. And that's why you will go with me through the service door. But while I will be just inside the door ready to intervene if necessary, you will set up shop on a step low enough that the light from your lantern can't be seen."

"Yes, sir."

The youth's face fell, and despite the strain of the moment, Pickett had to smile a little at Yates's obvious disappointment at being relegated to the rôle of clerk. He suspected Kit would enter wholeheartedly into Yates's sentiments. He thought of Kit standing guard upstairs with his cricket bat, and hoped some obliging mouse in the wainscoting would create enough of a stir to give the boy some sport.

"Mr. Maxwell," Mr. Colquhoun said, turning to the soldier, "I want you to go outside and take up a position that gives you a view up and down the street for some distance. If you see anyone coming, anyone at all, you sound the alarm. I seem to recall that you can imitate certain bird calls; can you do a nightjar?"

Maxwell frowned, the light from his lantern casting his features into sharp relief. "Yes, sir, but—forgive me, but a nightjar in December?"

"Bear in mind that our man is accustomed to the seasons of the Southern Hemisphere. It's midsummer in New South Wales." Maxwell nodded thoughtfully, although his expression still appeared doubtful, and Mr. Colquhoun addressed the group as a whole. "Once Maxwell sounds the alarm, hold yourself in readiness and listen for a repeat. If he makes a second call—the 'all clear,' you might say—it will mean the man he saw, or thought he saw, proved to be a false alarm."

Uneasy glances sought each other in the dark room, until at last Carson spoke for the group. "Sir, what if we hear what we think is Maxwell sounding the all clear, when really he's just spotted a second person coming up the street? One of those people could be our man, and we'd never know it."

"Your point is well taken, Mr. Carson," the magistrate conceded with a sigh. "It's an imperfect plan, I'll admit, but if any of you can think of a better one, I am open to suggestion. If not, we'll just have to trust to there being few people about in a quiet residential street at such an hour."

"Begging your pardon, sir," the usually taciturn Maxwell spoke up, "but what if, instead of a second signal as an all clear, I give the second signal to confirm that the person I saw is our quarry?"

Mr. Colquhoun shook his head. "I'm afraid it won't do, Mr. Maxwell. You yourself noted the unlikelihood of a nightjar in December. While a single call may go unremarked, if we're lucky, I'm afraid a second such call—one at close range, at that—would only make our man get the wind up." A related thought occurred to him, and he added, "While we're on the subject, I should caution you against taking up your sentry post on the service stair. If he chooses to enter the house the same way he did before, we don't want him stumbling over you in the dark."

Although a member of the Bow Street force for only a month, Yates recognized in these instructions a missed opportunity. "But—forgive me, sir, but Maxwell might be able to restrain the man before he could enter the house at all."

Far from being offended at having his word questioned by a mere stripling, Mr. Colquhoun regarded Yates as he might a small child who had not perfectly ciphered a difficult sum, but had come very close. "Just so, Mr. Yates. But when we make an arrest, it will be for murder, or perhaps attempted murder, not housebreaking."

Yates's smooth brow puckered in confusion. "Attempted—?"

"He means me," Pickett told the youth. "Mr. Colquhoun thinks our man will try to kill me."

Yates's eyes grew wide with alarm. "Oh!"

"You need have no fear for Mr. Pickett's safety, Mr. Yates, for he was clearly born to be hanged. Now," the magistrate added briskly, as the long-case clock in the foyer chimed the half-hour, "are there any more questions?"

Silence and a few head shakes in the negative were his only answer.

"Well, then, since it's half past eleven, I suggest we take up our posts. Let me remind you all that I want *no* shooting in the dark! You're not to go letting off firearms unless you know exactly who you're shooting at. Remember, too, that if you must shoot, you're shooting only to wound, not to kill. We're not after vigilante justice here; we want this man to answer for his crimes in a court of law."

The group left the dining room and made their way to the study. Maxwell parted from the others as they reached the foyer, wishing them all luck before he opened the door and slipped silently out into the night.

The others repaired to a small but well-proportioned room at the front of the house with a single window that overlooked the street. Upon Pickett's successful completion of his first case as an independent investigator, Julia had dubbed this chamber his study, and had taken great pains to furnish it accordingly. Now it boasted an elegant mahogany desk with scrolled legs, half a dozen pigeonholes, and four drawers in which Pickett might keep the records (assuming he eventually had some) pertaining to his fledgling investigative business. In addition to the straight chair behind the desk, there were two button-backed wing chairs facing it, which would, according to Julia, allow him to interview potential clients in comfort as well as privacy, without his having to banish his wife and half-brother to some other part of the house. Finally, the window had been hung with new curtains, which were now tightly closed.

Pickett went at once to the desk, then pulled open one of the drawers and withdrew a pencil and three sheets of paper. "Will this be enough?" he asked, handing them to Yates.

"It should be." It was Mr. Colquhoun who answered. His gaze rested briefly on the desk before flicking back up to Pickett's face, barely visible in the feeble light penetrating through the half-closed shutters of his lantern.

"You've planted it there, I suppose?"

"Yes, sir, in the bottom drawer on the left." His smile held a hint of mischief. "Not too well-hidden, just enough that it'll take two hands to search for it."

Mr. Colquhoun nodded. What Pickett had not said, what

the magistrate had not had to ask, was that the intruder would have to put down anything he might be holding—a lantern, for instance. Or a gun.

The narrow jib door that gave the servants access to the room was difficult to see even in daylight, so Pickett felt for the catch and opened it, sparing the magistrate a possibly lengthy search. Mr. Colquhoun gave a gallant little wave of his hand for Yates to precede him, and once the youth was settled in relative comfort on the fourth step down, with paper and pencil laid out on the third step as if it were a desk, the magistrate stepped through the jib door and pulled it as nearly completely shut as possible, leaving a gap wide enough to give him a view of the desk while still concealing the light from Yates's lantern.

Carson, meanwhile, had positioned himself behind the door through which they had just come, pulling it as wide open as possible so that he would not be visible from anyone entering the room either through the door itself or through the window in the opposite wall.

Pickett pushed the drawer closed, then left the desk and pressed himself against the exterior wall as near as possible to the window, putting him out of the range of vision of anyone attempting a clandestine entry by that route. If the intruder should enter through the front door, however, and access the study by the same door through which they had all come, and behind which Harry Carson was now hidden...

Pickett tried not to think about that. If the intruder was bold enough to enter by the front door, the four people hidden within the room must surely hear some sign of his entry, in which case he would...what? He wouldn't have time to dart behind the door with Harry, and there were surely enough people on the servants' stair already to preclude his diving through the jib door; he would surely stumble right into Mr. Colquhoun and Yates, and he'd had his fill of tumbling down stairs of late. He supposed he could hide under the desk if needs must, but every feeling revolted at the thought of being discovered cowering on the floor like the merest craven.

It was, as Mr. Colquhoun had said, an imperfect plan. Still, it was his best chance to see his father's killer brought to justice, and in any case, it was too late to back down now.

Thrusting his misgivings to the back of his mind, he withdrew the pistol from the waistband of his breeches, feeling the weapon solid and heavy in his hand. He took a deep breath, then thumbed the safety catch off and settled himself to wait.

23

In Which an Intruder Returns

And so they waited.

And waited.

And waited.

Some few minutes after midnight came the *crick-crick-crick* of Maxwell's nightjar, and when the second call followed moments later, Pickett felt rather than heard the release of tension in the room as he and his colleagues recognized the signal for a false alarm.

It's too early, he thought, as if he could convey the message to his fellow watchers through sheer force of will. *He'll wait until he reckons everyone in the house is asleep, thinking the time for any danger has passed.*

Still, he had never found the Whittington chimes of the foyer clock so nerve-racking as he did now, listening as it marked half-past midnight, then one o'clock, then half-past one, then two...

Shortly after two o'clock, Maxwell signaled the approach of another suspicious person, although in this case his second signal was unnecessary, accompanied as it was by the decidedly blue lyrics of "Seventeen Come Sunday" rendered in a discordant baritone.

Then again, Pickett thought, what better way to avert suspicion than to present the appearance of a man returning home from his club decidedly the worse for drink? He had resorted to a similar charade on one occasion himself—only to be trapped in the unflattering rôle when he'd unexpectedly crossed paths with Lord Rupert Latham, the most likely claimant to the recently widowed Lady Fieldhurst's affections.

In the present instance, such a disguise would carry its own risks, primarily that of wakening the very people the intruder would most wish to be asleep.

In any case, Pickett thought as a door some distance down the street opened and then closed, swallowing up both singer and song, poor little Yates must have got an earful.

By the time the clock struck three, Pickett's legs were growing numb, and the sound of heavy breathing from the opposite side of the room suggested that Harry Carson was more than half asleep. Then the call of the nightjar beyond the window jerked Pickett to attention, and Carson's noisy breathing cut off abruptly with a snort. The room itself seemed to hold its breath as the watchers waited for the second call of the nightjar.

It did not come. Instead, the sound that met their ears was a sharp grating noise like metal scraping against glass. To

Pickett, with his back pressed against the wall just inside the window, the sound seemed to be only inches from his ear. Every instinct urged him to twitch back the edge of the curtain a fraction of an inch, just enough to catch a glimpse of whatever was happening on the other side of the glass. He resisted the temptation, although it took every ounce of self-restraint he possessed.

At length the sound stopped, only to be followed by a faint *click*. A moment later, something landed softly on the carpet at his feet. Then the curtain stirred, and Pickett realized that one of the panes of glass had been removed from the window frame. A moment later, the susurration of well-oiled wood against wood gave him to understand that the lower sash was being pushed up. In the next instant, the curtain was pushed aside by a black-gloved hand, and suddenly the intruder was in the house, thrusting aside the heavy folds of curtain that clung to him.

Pickett held his breath, but he need not have feared discovery; all the intruder's attention was focused on the desk.

As he approached it, however, some slight noise must have warned him of imminent danger, or perhaps, having almost been apprehended in his earlier attempt, he was suffering from overwrought nerves. Whatever the reason, he froze where he stood. Slowly, one hand raised the lantern while the other withdrew something from beneath the breast of his black coat. As he slowly moved the lantern in a wide semi-circle, its yellow light glinted off the barrel of a pistol.

Pickett took no satisfaction in the realization that he'd been right in thinking the intruder would be armed. He wished he might edge a bit to his right, to better avail himself of the shadow afforded by the disarranged curtain, but he dared not move lest the intruder hear some whisper of sound, or glimpse the movement in his peripheral vision. Pickett feared that if he were caught out this time, he would suffer a good deal worse than a tumble down the stairs.

But the intruder was apparently satisfied, for he set his lantern down on the desk and pulled open the top drawer. Having accomplished this, however, he was obliged to place his pistol beside the lantern, leaving both hands free to sift through the contents of the drawer. Clearly, he found nothing here to interest him, for he cautiously eased the drawer closed and turned his attention to the one below it.

And so it went. The intruder rifled through each drawer in turn until at last, with a faint cry of triumph, he withdrew a folded sheet of heavy vellum and spread it open on the desk, holding the lantern over his prize and adjusting its shutters to better illuminate the close lines written on the document.

Judging it time to make his presence known, Pickett leveled his weapon at the intruder. "Find what you were looking for, Sully?"

The light from the man's lantern bobbed drunkenly as the clerk whirled to face him, crumpling the document as he snatched ineffectually at the pistol with a hand that was not free to hold it.

"I wouldn't, if I were you," Pickett advised. "My body shot dead here, in my own house, might be a bit harder to explain than Da's in Gin Alley with a hole in his back."

On his earlier visit, Pickett thought, there had been

something inexplicably terrifying about the dark figure moving silently up the stairs, more sensed than seen, his destination unknown, his intention impossible to guess. Now, stripped of his anonymity, he cut an almost ludicrous figure, quaking in fear with the light from the lantern reflecting off the lenses of his spectacles and giving his pink nose a ruddy glow. Pickett realized with some surprise that he himself was now the sinister one. To the clerk, he must look a bit like his father's unquiet spirit, the facial features with which Sullivan Bradley would have long have been familiar now eerie and strange, cast into sharp relief by the lantern's yellow glow.

Bradley, at least, must have found the sight of him disconcerting, for his hand fell away from the gun, and he pressed the document to his chest, running his hand down it in long, quick strokes in a feeble attempt to smooth the creases from the vellum.

"It-It-It's that M-Mathers fellow," he stammered with a shaky and slightly hysterical little laugh. "Won't t-take 'no' for an answer; you said as m-much yourself. I knew you were c-conflicted as to what you ought to d-do with it—worthless land, but—still, J-Jack's legacy and all—I reckoned you'd be easier in your m-mind once the thing was d-done, especially once you had fifty p-pounds in your p-pocket—"

"Fifty pounds?" Pickett echoed with mock incredulity.

Bradley, quite mistaking his tone, was emboldened to continue. "Yes, yes!" His head bobbed up and down as if it were mounted on a spring. "I feel certain I can p-persuade him to g-go to fifty p-pounds, and then you'd be spared the p-painful decision—"

"Setting aside the fact that it isn't yours to sell, you'd never let a gold mine go for so paltry a sum as fifty pounds!"

"Well, now, we d-don't—we don't *know* there's g-gold," Bradley protested feebly. "J-Just a rumor, m-most likely. B-Better to sell it to M-Mathers now, b-before the t-truth comes out—"

"It's out now," Pickett interrupted tersely. "A German chemist has tested the sample and confirmed that it's gold."

The clerk's sloping shoulders lifted and fell in a shrug. "Well, b-but *foreigners*, you know—"

"Let's have done fencing," Pickett said. "My father knew he'd got his hands on a fortune, and however he came by that information, you were convinced enough that once your ship returned to port, you either lured or followed him into Gin Alley and stabbed him in the back."

"*Me?* Why would I d-do such a thing?" Bradley's incredulity was so compelling that for one brief moment, Pickett almost had to wonder if he'd got it wrong.

Almost, but not quite.

"Envy, I should think," he said, then added, "It would be a very rare man who would not envy a friend who stumbled onto a gold mine—especially, as I suspect, when that friend boasted of his good fortune every chance he could."

Pickett had spoken kindly, almost gently, but Bradley would have none of it.

"Much *you* know!"

Before Pickett's eyes, the slightly ridiculous clerk with his sunburned nose and thick-lensed spectacles seemed to change as suddenly as if he'd stripped off a mask. For the first time, Pickett saw Bradley Sullivan as he really was: an embittered man with a countenance prematurely aged not only by a hard life in a wild and rugged land, but also, and perhaps even more so, by jealousy and greed.

"You, with your fine house!" Even Bradley's nervous stammer was gone, driven out by a resentment bordering on hatred. "But you're a fraud, aren't you? Aye, well may you stare! I know what you were as a boy, for Jack told me. What is it about you—both of you—that lets you land on your feet like a cat? Money, women—you don't know what it's like, loving a woman who can never be yours!"

"Well, actually—"

"I loved her, do you hear?" Bradley's voice broke on a sob. "I knew she was married—knew she would never look at me, even if she was free—but I loved her all the same."

I don't think we're talking about gold mines anymore, Pickett thought, hoping Yates was able to keep up with the conversation.

"Loved who?" he asked softly, but Bradley appeared to take no notice.

"When that—that harpy said such things about her—'no better than she should be,' all but calling her an adulteress— it was blasphemy, I tell you—"

"She isn't a saint," Pickett objected. Whoever the object of Bradley's adoration—and he had his ideas about that—he felt this was a safe assumption.

"She *was,*" Bradley insisted, with another hiccuping sob, "at least, she was until—but I wasn't going to let *her* say those things, not when she wasn't worthy to touch the hem of her gown—so she had to go."

"Who had to go, Sully?" Pickett asked, lost in a welter of feminine pronouns.

"She had to go," Bradley said again, with satisfaction. "And so she went—right over the taffrail."

"Who?" *Fell overboard just out from Cape Town... Dead by the time the crew got her back on the ship... No one heard her cry for help...* Even as he repeated the question, he heard again the words of Sir Horace Stapleton. He hadn't given Mrs. Marsh's death much thought at the time, as his mind was wholly occupied with his father's, but now he recollected hearing somewhere that drowning was usually a very quiet death, its victims too desperately gasping for breath to call out for help. "Are you talking about Harriet Marsh?"

Bradley's lip curled scornfully. "Aye, Harriet the Harridan. She got what she deserved. And then"—his voice cracked—"and then I saw a letter she'd written to Jack. He'd debauched her, the bastard! Why shouldn't I steal his land, after what he'd stolen from me? Tell me that!"

"It seems to me," Pickett said with some asperity, "that if Da 'debauched' Lady Stapleton, as you claim, then he did it with the lady's full cooperation." He kept to himself the knowledge that he himself had been offered the opportunity to debauch the lady, and had declined; in his present state of mind, Bradley might interpret his refusal as an affront to his goddess and decide that he, too, "had to go." "You said yourself that the lady didn't belong to you, and never would. So if Da stole her from anyone, I should say it was Sir Horace."

But Bradley had no thought to spare for the wronged

husband. "Jack stole every dream of love and beauty that I'd ever had," he insisted, his voice rising on a note of hysteria.

Pickett recalled his impressions of Lady Stapleton as a woman who fancied herself as a dramatic heroine, and for a moment, he could almost find it in his heart to pity Bradley. The woman he loved was unworthy of the pedestal on which he'd placed her.

"So why shouldn't I steal *his* dreams?" the rant continued. "Mean, contemptible things they were, ambitions of gold and money and wealth—nothing so noble as a man's love for a woman."

"No, not that," Pickett said thoughtfully, "but perhaps something like a father's love for his son."

"Meaning you, I suppose," the clerk said contemptuously. "And what do *you* care about land in New South Wales? *I'm* the one who spent seven years of my life there, transported for a crime I didn't commit! *I'm* the one who walked over every inch of that ground, taking samples and making notes and acting as drudge to a man who was in very truth the man I'd been accused of being—a criminal not only unrepentant, but proud, even boastful of his crimes. He might have taken me on as a partner, at the very least!"

He wanted to take me *on as a partner*, Pickett thought. *And every time he tried to bring it up, I cut him off, thinking it was idle boasting. Well, and so it was, but that's not to say even idle boasting might not contain a good deal of truth.*

"And yet, for all his sins, Da never murdered anyone," he said aloud. "It must have been a bad moment for you, killing him only to discover that the deed wasn't there, either on his person or in his valise. Even ransacking the solicitor's office failed to turn it up."

Bradley made no attempt to deny the charge. "A temporary inconvenience. I knew you would lead me to it eventually, and here we are."

"Yes, here we are. And we seem to be at something of an impasse," Pickett observed coolly, judging that the magistrate ought to have enough evidence by now to hang Sullivan Bradley several times over. He wondered whether Lady Stapleton would read an account of the trial in the *Times*—or, if she read it, whether she would care. "Of course, I could shoot you in the time it would take you to reach for your pistol, but the fact that you would present a moving target would make it difficult to aim for any particular spot with any degree of accuracy—"

He got no further, for at that moment a small fury burst into the room like some avenging angel, his white nightshirt flapping about his knees and the cricket bat he clutched in both hands describing menacing arcs through the air.

"You killed my da, you—you—!"

"Kit, *no!*" cried Pickett, as Bradley snatched up his pistol.

Suddenly the room was swarming with people. Pickett flung himself on his adversary, bearing the man's gun arm down as he pinned him to the desk.

Carson stepped out from his position behind the door and halted Kit's charge by the simple expedient of grabbing the boy from behind and lifting him off his feet.

"Lemme go! Lemme *go!*" Kit wailed, his legs kicking

and his cricket bat flailing ineffectually.

Mr. Colquhoun emerged through the jib door in the paneling and stepped to the window, stooping to the hole left by the absent pane and through it summoning Maxwell to join the others inside the house, in case Mssrs. Pickett, Carson, and Yates should need his assistance in subduing the miscreant.

Yates, clutching two sheets of paper inscribed front and back with crossed lines, entered the room in the magistrate's wake, then strode up to the desk where Pickett held the clerk spreadeagled, and said calmly, "By the authority of His Majesty, King George III, I am placing you under arrest for the murders of..."

And it was into this chaos that Julia walked, clutching her pink wrapper closed over her night rail and calling breathlessly, "John? John, I think—I think it's time."

24

In Which What Began with a Death Ends with a Birth

Is it supposed to take this long?"

Raking his fingers through hair that was long past the point of being merely disheveled, Pickett turned to make yet another circuit of the drawing room. Morning had come, and then afternoon. Now it was evening, and while Maxwell, Carson, and Yates had taken the culprit back to Bow Street in irons, Julia had labored to bring her child into the world, and Pickett—unwashed and unshaven, and still clad in the black garments he'd worn the night before—paced a hole in the drawing room carpet, leaving untouched the various dishes brought up from the kitchen to tempt him.

Mr. Colquhoun looked up from his seat on the sofa and turned the page of the newspaper that had just been delivered. "Babies come into the world when they're good and ready, so there's no sense in thinking you can rush them by worrying— and first babies, especially, are notorious for taking their time."

Pickett made no response, having frozen in his tracks when his ears caught some faint disturbance from the floor above. No further sounds followed, however, nor did anyone come down the stairs to inform him of any new developments. He resumed his pacing.

The magistrate, seeing his duty clear, folded the newspaper and laid it aside, then set about the task of giving his young protégé's thoughts some other direction. "Tell me, what do you intend to do with this fortune of yours? Have you decided?"

Pickett sighed. "No. I haven't had time—truth to tell, it's all been a bit much."

"I don't doubt it!" Mr. Colquhoun said, chuckling. "It's not every day a man inherits a gold mine."

"It may be years, perhaps even decades, before it begins to pay out," Pickett said. "As I understand it, there aren't even any roads into the interior yet."

"Aye, you'll want to line up investors who'll foot the bill for putting the necessary improvements in place in exchange for a percentage of the profits. I can put you in touch with a few good men, if you like."

"Thank you, sir. But—well, if they're going to be given a portion of the profits in exchange for their investments, what happens if it turns out that it's all a hum, and there *aren't* any profits?"

"That is a chance they're willing to take. In the meantime, you turn around and invest the money they give you in other enterprises. That way if, as you say, it turns out to be a hum, you're still a wealthy man, because you've got money coming in from other sources."

A smile tugged at Pickett's lips. "Oh."

"You've thought of something," observed the magistrate, regarding him keenly from beneath bushy white eyebrows.

"I was just thinking of a fellow I met about this time last year. He's a weaver—that is, he's the foster son of a man who owns a cotton mill. He has a few ideas of his own that his foster father won't even consider, him being an old-fashioned sort. I think I should like to put some money into the business, once he comes into full ownership."

"You'll want to do as you think best, of course," Mr. Colquhoun conceded with a nod. "I won't deny, I consider British textiles a sounder investment than these fellows who think they can make a carriage that runs by itself on a track, without so much as a pony to pull it."

In fact, Pickett found the idea of such a vehicle intriguing, and might have said so, had not a flurry of sounds from overhead recalled his attention to the matter at hand. He strode across the drawing room to the foyer, pausing at the foot of the stairs with his hand gripping the newel post.

"Don't go up there, John," cautioned the magistrate, who had not moved from his position on the sofa. "They'll come for you when they need you. In the meantime, you'd only be very much in the way."

After a moment's severe struggle with himself, Pickett released the newel post and returned to the drawing room with a sigh. He had his reward a few minutes later, when Lady Dunnington came slowly down the stairs with a blanket-wrapped bundle in her arms.

"Julia?" he croaked, finding his tongue at last. "Is she—?"

"Julia is rather tired, which is only natural, but other than that, she is quite well," she assured him. "You may go up and see her directly. In the meantime, come and meet your son."

"Son?" he echoed sharply. "It's a boy?"

"Most sons are," she said with mock solemnity.

Curiously, after pacing the floor for hours on end, his feet now seemed to be rooted to the spot where he stood. Only with a great effort did he cross the drawing room to the foyer, where he met Lady Dunnington at the foot of the stairs and looked down at the infant in her arms.

He wasn't quite sure what he'd expected, but he was fairly certain this wasn't it. The baby's face was red, and though its eyes were closed, it wore a rather fierce scowl, as if annoyed at having been ejected from a dark, warm place where it had been quite content to remain. Its hair was dark, and was plastered to its pink scalp in damp curls.

Pickett had no time to register more, for Lady Dunnington was shifting the baby, blanket and all, from her arms to his. All his attention from that point was concentrated on the necessity of not dropping the child that Julia had worked so hard to deliver.

"All right, then, let's see what you've got here." Mr. Colquhoun joined them in the foyer, then looked down at the baby in Pickett's arms. He subjected the infant to a thorough inspection, then pronounced, in a voice Pickett had never heard him use before, "Well, now, aren't you a braw, strapping laddie?"

Pickett found the magistrate's attempt at infant communication not unamusing, but as the words Mr. Colquhoun spoke (or rather, cooed) penetrated Pickett's dazed brain, he had to wonder if his mentor had lost his mind. Mr. Colquhoun might talk all he wanted of braw, strapping laddies, but to Pickett, the baby in his arms was terrifyingly small.

Meanwhile, Mr. Colquhoun, no stranger to the nursery, tickled the baby's chin with his index finger, an imposition to which it responded by wrapping its tiny fingers around his much larger one. "What are you going to name him? Have you decided?"

"Yes, sir. We thought—that is, unless you have some objection, we had thought to call him John-Patrick."

The magistrate bent upon him a scowl every bit as fierce as the baby's, save for the fact that he blinked very quickly, several times. "You'd give a Gaelic name to an English child?"

"This particular English child," said Pickett, regarding it with a singularly fatuous smile, "has a mother who was a viscountess and a father who was a pickpocket." He looked up at the magistrate. "What's a bit more confusion?"

* * *

Summoned a short time later to his wife's bedside, Pickett took the stairs two at a time. Once inside the bedroom, however, he stopped just inside the door and stood there looking at her, his heart too full for speech.

She smiled at him as he entered, a rather self-satisfied smile reminiscent of the cat that ate the canary.

And well she might, he thought.

She was sitting up against the pillows, wearing a blue bed jacket of quilted satin over a clean night rail, and her hair had been brushed and neatly braided, but the short tendrils at her brow were damp with perspiration, a silent proof of the ordeal she'd endured.

"Oh, Julia," he breathed, "I don't know what to say."

Julia, at least, had no doubts at all on that head. "You can come here and tell me what you think of your son," she said, patting the edge of the bed. "Is he not beautiful?"

"Beautiful," he agreed, seating himself on the spot she'd indicated. "Like his mother."

She gave a weary little laugh. "How can you say such a thing, when he looks just like you?"

"His eyes are blue," Pickett objected. In fact, the baby was now awake, and regarded its father with bright, shoe-button eyes. He bent and nuzzled the soft little cheek, and as he drew back, one tiny arm rose jerkily and batted at his nose.

"Yes, but so dark a shade that Emily predicts they will soon turn brown," Julia said. "And since she has three brown-eyed children of her own, she ought to know."

Pickett had no thought to spare for Lady Dunnington's children, for he was far too caught up in his own.

This, then, was the end result of the chain of events that had begun on that spring night almost two years earlier, when Lord Fieldhurst had been discovered murdered in his wife's bedchamber, throwing together the viscount's widow and the Bow Street Runner who had been sent to investigate. And now this—this *person* existed, who had not before, the fruit of a deep and unexpected love between two people who should never have crossed one another's path.

And yet, it was not quite the end. There might be other children, and their children, and their children's children. His sons would be educated as gentlemen and his daughters would have dowries that would allow them to look as high as they wished for a husband—or as low, should they happen to meet any promising young Bow Street Runners. Tomorrow, he decided, while Julia rested, he would go out and buy her those sapphires. Just because he could.

With that thought, he tore his gaze from his son and looked up at his wife. "Are you all right?" he asked, studying her radiant but weary face for any signs of lasting damage. "Is there anything I can do for you? Anything you need?"

Please don't say you want the camp bed to be a permanent fixture, he silently begged. *Even if you never want me to touch you again, please, not that…*

"Just you." She put up a hand to stroke his bristly jaw. "All I need is you."

* * *

Much later, however, after Master John-Patrick Pickett had been borne away by his nurse and Julia had rolled over to blissfully sleep on her stomach for the first time in six months, she awoke in the middle of the night, having bethought herself of one bit of unfinished business.

"John?" She gave his shoulder a shake. "John, wake up."

"Wha—?"

"John, I've just thought of something."

"What"—he yawned widely—"what is it?"

"Tomorrow will you have Andrew return that camp bed to the box room? Better yet," she added as a new thought occurred to her, "have him break it up and burn it!"

"First thing in the morning," promised Pickett, and fell instantly into dreamless sleep.

About the Author

At the age of sixteen, Sheri Cobb South discovered Georgette Heyer, and came to the startling realization that she had been born into the wrong century. Although she probably would have been a chambermaid had she actually lived in Regency England, that didn't stop her from fantasizing about waltzing the night away in the arms of a handsome, wealthy, and titled gentleman.

Since Georgette Heyer died in 1974 and could not write any more Regencies, Ms. South came to the conclusion she would have to do it herself. In addition to the bestselling John Pickett mystery series (now an award-winning audiobook series!), she has also written several Regency romances, including the critically acclaimed *The Weaver Takes a Wife*.

A native and long-time resident of Alabama, Ms. South now lives in Loveland, Colorado.

She loves to hear from readers, and invites them to visit her website at www.shericobbsouth.com; follow her on social media through Facebook, Goodreads, Pinterest, Instagram, or Twitter; or email her at Cobbsouth@aol.com.